Adirondack Mysteries

And Other Mountain Tales

Adirondack Mysteries

And Other Mountain Tales

Compiled and Edited by Dennis Webster

John H. Briant • Tico Brown • Cheryl Ann Costa
S.W. Hubbard • Paul Nandzik • David J. Pitkin • W.K. Pomeroy
Gigi Vernon • Dennis Webster • Angela Zeman

North Country Books, Inc.
Utica, New York

Adirondack Mysteries
And Other Mountain Tales

Design by Zach Steffen & Rob Igoe, Jr.
Cover photograph by Carl Heilman II

ISBN-10 1-59531-032-0
ISBN-13 978-1-59531-032-3

Library of Congress Cataloging-in-Publication Data

Adirondack mysteries, and other mountain tales / compiled and edited by Dennis Webster.
p. cm.
ISBN 978-1-59531-032-3 (alk. paper)
1. Detective and mystery stories, American--New York (State)--Adirondack Mountains Region. 2. American fiction--New York (State)--Adirondack Mountains Region. 3. Adirondack Mountains Region (N.Y.)--Fiction. I. Webster, Dennis, 1966-
PS648.D4A28 2009
813'.0872083587475--dc22

2009034547

North Country Books, Inc.
220 Lafayette Street
Utica, New York 13502
www.northcountrybooks.com

This collection is dedicated to all those
who love and are committed to the preservation
of the Adirondack Mountains.

Contents

Acknowledgements

There are many people who provided friendship, feedback, and editorial advice in the creation of this book. Thank you to Larry Clever, Ph.D., Amy Dickenson, Don O'Hagan, Linda Miller Poore, and Evelyn Webster. A tremendous thank you to Rob Igoe, Jr., Zach Steffen, and the entire staff at North Country Books. Finally, thank you to all the wonderful authors who contributed their stories to this collection.

– Dennis Webster

Losers Weepers

by S.W. Hubbard

When Trout Run Municipal Park Spring Clean-Up Day rolled around, Ardyth Munger knew better than to arrive late.

Last year she had stopped at Malone's Diner for breakfast—never a quick affair—and by the time she got to the park the only assignment left was cleaning behind the rest rooms, a part of the park that saw all its activity after the sun went down. This year, when police chief Frank Bennett arrived at eight forty-five to coordinate the day's activities, Ardyth was already sitting in the parking lot, work gloves in hand, ready for her assignment.

"How about cleaning the toddler playground?" Frank suggested. Still lean and spry at seventy-two, Ardyth strongly resisted efforts to shunt her off to little old lady activities. But Frank knew she'd rather collect chewed up old pacifiers than empty beer bottles, Skoal tins, and butts that even Ardyth knew didn't contain tobacco.

"If that's where you need me," she said, and marched off.

Although the weather had been uncommonly balmy for an Adirondack May, only a fool or a tourist would believe spring was here to stay. With snow showers predicted later in the week, Frank was anxious to get all the park improvement projects finished. Engrossed in unclogging the water fountain, he didn't notice Ardyth's return.

"Look at what I found, Frank." She dangled something shiny in her hand. "A gold locket."

He reached for a wrench. "Finders keepers. Lucky you."

"No, Frank—I can't keep it. This is valuable."

She pushed the necklace under his nose. The clasp on the delicate gold chain had caught on something and snapped.

"Feel how heavy and satiny the locket is; I'm sure this is 18-carat gold." Ardyth examined the intricate filigree design of the case. "This is an heirloom. We have to find the person who lost it."

Frank sat back on his heels and stared at her.

"Oh, relax. I didn't mean you had to launch an investigation. Just keep it at the police department and I'll put a lost and found ad in the *Mountain Echo*."

"Take that up with Doris." The town secretary maintained a huge lost and found box behind her desk into which a stream of single mittens, reading glasses, umbrellas, and sneakers thrown out the school bus window made their way. So far as Frank knew, no one had ever claimed anything, although occasionally people trapped by a sudden Adirondack rainstorm came in and borrowed one of the umbrellas.

"No, it can't go in that box with all the junk. It would be safest with you."

Frank sighed and held out his hand. As Ardyth dropped the locket in his palm he noticed the tiny hinge. "Why don't you open it? If there's a picture inside maybe we can figure out who it belongs to."

"Of course—how silly of me." Ardyth popped the locket open.

Inside was a black-and-white photo, maybe an inch and a quarter long. A young man, cocky and grinning, stood with his arm around the shoulders of a slender woman. He wore a military uniform, she a dress with a cinched waist and a wide, white collar.

Ardyth tilted the locket into the sunlight. "From the hairstyles and the clothes, I'd say this was taken in the fifties. His face is clearer than hers. She must've moved right when the camera snapped. There's something about them…but, no, I can't tell who they are. Can you?"

Frank squinted for a better look, although if a lifelong Trout Runner like Ardyth didn't recognize the couple, he surely wouldn't. The picture was tiny and faded, but one thing was clear. They were in love.

Frank pulled the patrol car into the town office parking lot and dragged himself out of the vehicle. Keeping the men with chainsaws apart from the middle schoolers with rakes was more exhausting than digging a ten-foot trench. Next year, he'd put Earl in charge of cleanup day.

As if on cue, Earl came charging out the office door, drawing up short at the sight of his boss. "Wow, what timing! I thought I was going to have to go on this call alone."

Frank detected a note of disappointment. There was a time when he wouldn't have let his civilian assistant handle a stray-dog call on his own, but the kid had come a long way in two years. Earl was studying at the police academy now, and by next year he'd be sworn in as an officer. As long as this call wasn't dangerous, Frank was happy to let Earl take it.

"Roy Corvin's been shot!" Earl practically bounced with excitement. He still hadn't mastered a cop's unflappable detachment.

"Hunting accident?" Frank asked.

Earl pulled a face. "Roy Corvin's no hunter. More likely he pissed someone off."

Frank got back in the patrol car, waiting for Earl to buckle in before flipping on the siren and peeling out of the lot. "Which way?"

"Roy rents that little house behind Bill McKenna's machine shop out on Ridge Road." Earl was a human MapQuest for Trout Run, able to provide not only addresses and directions for every home in town, but also complete background information on every resident.

"Roy Corvin was way ahead of me in school," he continued. "But he never graduated. Dropped out and couldn't hold a job. Finally he joined the Army, but he was back home in four months. Claimed he had bad hearing in one ear, but I bet he got thrown out."

"The Army needs every warm body they can get these days. They're willing to overlook quite a few problems."

"Army didn't even want him to defuse roadside bombs. That says a lot."

Frank took his eyes off the road for a moment to look at his assistant. It wasn't like Earl to be so negative. This must be personal.

"What'd Roy Corvin ever do to you?"

Earl turned his head toward the window. Gazing at Whiteface, shrouded in clouds, or Stony Brook, winding through a stand of white birch, could be irresistible, even to a native, but at this particular moment they were passing Al's Sunoco.

"Earl?"

"My cousin Ruthann dated him for a while. Got taken in by his looks. Let's just say it wasn't a happy time for anyone in the family."

"Abusive?"

"First Ruthann stopped coming to family parties. Then my Uncle Dave spotted her at the supermarket with a black eye. A couple of us paid Roy a little visit. Now Ruthann is engaged to a schoolteacher from Saranac Lake."

Frank slapped the edge of the steering wheel. "Earl, I'm warning you, when you become a sworn law enforcement officer you can't take part in these family vengeance operations. 'Protect and serve' is our motto, not 'judge and punish.' Roy is the victim here," Frank said as he pulled up beside an ambulance parked in front of Corvin's house. "Keep an open mind."

Two members of the rescue squad carried a stretcher toward them. A young man, his face starkly pale against his dark hair and red-soaked shirt, lay limp as the third member of the team labored over him. "Looks like the bullet collapsed his right lung," the paramedic said to Frank. "He's lost a lot of blood. We have to get on the road."

The ambulance took off as Frank and Earl turned toward the house. Bill from the machine shop waited for them on the porch. He didn't need questions to get him talking.

"I was working on a lawnmower engine when I thought I head a shot. Then I heard a car tearing out. By the time I got outside, the car was over the crest of the hill. Roy didn't answer the door, so I went in." He paused for a breath. "Roy was layin' on the kitchen floor, a hole in his chest. I called you guys and did what I could to help him." He looked down at his hands, black with grease and red with blood.

"Did he say who did it?" Frank asked.

"His lips moved a little, then he passed out." Bill shook his head. "I don't know 'bout Roy. For a while he was working regular over at the lumberyard, but lately he's been home all day and out all night. Two months behind in his rent. Now this."

Frank thanked Bill and sent him on his way before he and Earl entered the house. Passing through the beer can-strewn living room, they stopped at the door to the kitchen. Blood had pooled in a low spot on the cracked linoleum floor. A chair lay on its side, drawers and cabinets hung open, papers and food wrappers covered every level surface. It was hard to know if the place had been ransacked or if this was the usual state of Roy's housekeeping. Frank picked his way carefully through the mess, his eye drawn by a spot of orange plastic on the table.

A prescription pill bottle, empty. He used the tip of a pencil to roll it over and read the label aloud. "OxyContin."

"That's a powerful narcotic," Earl volunteered, having recently aced an exam on abuse of drugs.

"It was prescribed for a Marcus Philhower," Frank said.

"We prayed for him in church last week. He's got liver cancer."

Frank sighed. "Nice. Roy stole a dying man's painkillers, then someone popped him to get them."

Earl did not say "I told you so." Didn't even smirk. More and more these days, Frank thought the kid had the makings of a damn good cop.

Earl hung up the phone and spun around on his desk chair as Frank returned from canvassing Corvin's neighbors. "Mrs. Philhower didn't even notice the OxyContin was gone. Her husband's on morphine now."

"Interesting," Frank said. "I wonder if Roy knew the drugs wouldn't be missed?"

"Mrs. Philhower says she doesn't know Roy. She was a little freaked out thinking that he came right into her husband's room to steal the stuff."

"I suppose she leaves her doors unlocked like everyone else in Trout Run." Frank stuck his hands in his pockets and jingled his change, pacing the office as he thought aloud. "Roy could have taken the drugs himself, but maybe he had an accomplice. I don't suppose you know which unlucky lady took your cousin's place in Roy's affections?"

"No, but I can ask the bartenders at the Mountainside. Roy's a regular."

"Good. The hospital will call us when Roy's able to talk. No one on

Ridge Road saw or heard anything. What about Roy's parents?"

"His dad was killed in a motorcycle accident when he was a baby, then his mom ran off with another guy and left him with his grandparents, Deke and Connie Steuben."

Frank looked up a number, reached for the phone, and dialed. After a moment he announced, "No answer. They're probably over at the hospital with Roy."

Frank's brow wrinkled as his fingers touched something unfamiliar in his pocket. He pulled out the locket. "Here's another mystery for you, Earl. Do you recognize these people?"

Earl studied the picture. "Don't know the guy. There's something kinda familiar about the woman, but her face is blurry. Where'd you get it?"

Frank explained Ardyth's discovery. "She wants me to keep it here while she runs a lost and found ad in the *Echo*. I'd better tell Doris, in case someone really does call."

Frank took the locket to the secretary's desk in the outer office. Doris immediately put aside her filing for this far more interesting project.

"Hmm. I don't recognize them, but the guy's awful handsome." She ran her rough fingers over the gold wistfully. "This sure is beautiful. Expensive, too. Ardyth is right—I can't just throw it in the lost and found box."

Frank peered into the overflowing bin behind her desk. "Why don't you get rid of some of that stuff, Doris? Face it—tourists who left their gloves here during the '80 Winter Olympics aren't coming back for them."

"None of it's that old, Frank. Why, I didn't even start the lost and found until '86…or was it '88?"

"Doris," Frank warned.

"All right, I guess I could give some of the stuff on the bottom to the church clothing bank."

"Great idea." Frank returned to his office and left her to her new assignment. Half an hour later, Doris appeared in front of him, a loaded shopping bag in one hand and a little, yellow rain slicker printed with green frogs in the other.

"I'm going to take this bag over to the church now," Doris said. "But

I was wondering about this rain coat. It's Hanna Anderson…"

"So if you know it belongs to Hanna, call her mom to come get it." Why Doris needed him to authorize the simplest phone call was beyond Frank.

"No, no—Hanna Anderson is the designer who makes it. Her stuff is so cute, but it's awful expensive." She stopped and looked at the coat longingly.

Frank took a deep breath. "What are you getting at, Doris?"

"I was just wondering…well…" She spit the rest out in a rush, "if you thought it would be okay for me to give this coat to my granddaughter, Julie."

"Sure. Go ahead."

"Really? Because I don't want to do anything dishonest. Maybe I should wait another year."

Do not yell. Do not yell. She can't help herself. "Give it to her now, Doris. She's not going to want it when she goes off to college."

"Oh, Frank! You're such a card. You make me laugh all the time."

Frank massaged his temples. "Yeah, same here."

"I hope we have better luck finding the owner of that locket." Doris pointed to the puddle of gold on Frank's desk blotter. "You'd better not leave it lying around."

He pulled his keys from his pocket and looked at Earl and Doris. "Remember, if someone actually comes to claim the necklace, they have to describe it to get it. So don't go telling everyone in town what it looks like. I'm locking it up in my top desk drawer, right in the petty cash box."

"Roy Corvin's taken a turn for the worse," Frank reported as Earl came into the office the next morning. "He picked up an infection in his good lung. He's on a respirator, under heavy sedation."

"That's one way to get your drugs." Earl handed Frank a cup of coffee, a sweet roll, a quarter, and a dime. "They were out of jelly donuts at the store so I had to get you a Danish. That's why your change is only thirty-five cents."

"Good choice. Did you get to the Mountainside last night?"

"Yeah, I took Molly over there for a drink and—"

"Molly? Molly Lynch?" Frank whistled. Molly was a cute little college girl who wouldn't have given Earl a second glance a few months ago. "Man, you're a regular babe magnet since you enrolled in the police academy. Just wait'll you get your badge and gun."

Earl's grin was something between shy and smug. "So anyway, the bartender says Roy was hooked up with Tiffany Kass. Guess what she does for a living?"

"Cleaning lady? Home health aide?"

Earl shot a rubber band at his boss. "Bingo. I stopped in at the Philhowers this morning. Tiffany's been working there three days a week for the past month. Mrs. P. says she wasn't crazy about her, but she needed the help."

"Outstanding, Earl." Frank downed the last sugary bite of his breakfast. There was a time when Earl wouldn't have shown the initiative to substitute a Danish for a donut. Now he was following up on leads and asking all the right questions. "Let's go pay a call on this little angel of mercy. If Roy dies, we've got a murder investigation on our hands."

Tiffany Kass lived with her mother and sister and a passel of kids of various ages. The house slumped like one good Adirondack snowstorm would flatten it, but since it was still standing in May, Frank figured it was good for another six months. Tiffany herself was not bad looking, if you could get past the dark roots and unicorn tattoo. She sat at her sticky kitchen table, radiating resentment.

"I don't know nuthin' about it."

"Let me refresh your memory," Frank said. "You were working as a home health aide for the Philhowers. You took a prescription bottle of OxyContin from the nightstand in Mr. Philhower's bedroom and gave it to your boyfriend, Roy Corvin. That's a felony."

Tiffany picked at a crusty clot of dried breakfast cereal. "You can't prove that."

Frank leaned across the table, forcing eye contact. "You know what, Tiffany? I don't have to prove it. All I have to do is tell your probation officer you've been associating with a known drug user." Frank shot a look at a T-shirt clad toddler waddling by with a sodden diaper drooping nearly to her knees. "And the child welfare department might be interested in hearing about it, too."

Tiffany tapped into a hidden reserve of energy. "You leave that bitch social worker out of this! I'm not losing my kids 'cause of Roy Corvin."

"Then talk. I know you were in Elizabethtown meeting with your probation officer at the time Roy was shot. Who else knew he had those drugs?"

Tiffany shrugged. "There was only a few left in the bottle. Roy wasn't about to share them."

"How about selling them? Does he have regular customers?"

Tiffany shook her head. "Roy's not into dealing. You gotta be able to collect enough from everyone to pay your supplier. Roy got messed up with that once. He don't do it no more."

"So who had a beef with Roy? Who could have shot him?

"Roy's had fights with half the guys at the Mountainside. And he's screwed half the girls. Go talk to them about it."

Tiffany rose and took a sudden interest in cleaning the kitchen. Frank thought the clatter of dishes flung into the sink very effectively masked her sniffling. "Was there another woman, Tiffany?" he asked gently.

"Some chick I don't know. He'd sit around waiting for her to call." Tiffany snorted. "Not that he could have been doing much with her, loaded up on painkillers like he was. I shoulda stolen him some Viagra."

The toddler reappeared and wrapped her arms around her mother's leg. Tiffany scooped her up. "I really don't care who shot him. I'm done with Roy Corvin."

"What do you think?" Frank asked Earl when they were back in the patrol car. "Does Roy really not have enough ambition to sell pills?"

"I think Tiffany's right—you have to be able to manage accounts to have regular customers. But that doesn't mean Roy wouldn't sell a pill or two to another druggie."

"I think I'll pay a visit to the Mountainside tonight," Frank said. "In the meantime, let's call on the grandparents."

The Steuben's house wasn't any bigger than Tiffany's, but it was light years apart in atmosphere. Cheerful clumps of daffodils lined the walk, a U.S. flag snapped smartly in the breeze, and a "Welcome Friends" plaque hung over a woodpecker-shaped doorknocker. Before Frank could bang the beak, the door opened.

"Saw you coming." Deke Steuben, still powerfully built although well into retirement, ushered them into the immaculate living room. "Have a seat." He pointed Frank and Earl toward the floral sofa draped in a zigzag afghan. "I suppose this is about Roy."

"Yes." Frank glanced around. "Is your wife home, too?"

"Nah, Connie's still at the hospital." Deke ran a big paw over his silver crew cut. "I couldn't take it anymore. I had to come home."

"I'm sorry for your trouble, Deke. We're working hard to find who did this."

Deke looked away, his eyes blinking hard. "What difference does it make? Roy's always mixed up with the wrong kind of people. You lock this one up, someone else'll come along to take his place."

Frank exchanged a glance with Earl. You might expect that kind of despair from a resident of a housing project in the Bronx, but it wasn't typical in Trout Run. "We're hoping you can tell us about Roy's friends, men and women. Especially if there are any you know are drug users."

Deke snorted. "I imagine all of them are. I don't want to know his so-called friends, or the sluts he sleeps with. Last winter we sent Roy to one of those clinics where they get you off the drugs. It cost a fortune. But it seemed like money well spent, because he came back here and got a job and everything was great. Didn't last, though. By March it all started again—the late night calls begging Connie for money, the lumberyard calling here when Roy didn't show up for work."

Deke nodded toward a cabinet in the corner. "He even stole one of my guns. That was the last straw. I changed the locks on the doors and now I keep this place bolted up like we live in goddam Detroit. I told Connie we're not giving him one more penny, I don't care if he's starving."

They sat in silence for a moment. But Deke wasn't done. He seemed relieved to abandon his North Country stoicism. Frank and Earl already knew the worst, so why not share everything? "You see that picture?" Deke pointed to a wall covered with framed photos interspersed with mounted deer antlers. Near the center was a picture of a little boy in a bow tie holding a trumpet. "That's Roy in fifth grade when he had a solo with the school band and won a prize. I swear that's the last time he ever did anything we could be proud of."

Deke shook his head. "Right after that was when our daughter Theresa, Roy's mother, disappeared for good. She left Roy with us and she never came back."

"Did you try to track her down?" Frank asked.

"Oh, yeah—for years. But it was too hard on Connie and Roy. Finally I said we just had to put it behind us. That's why Connie's always been soft on Roy, making excuses for him. She feels like she failed with Theresa. But none of the others turned out bad." He gestured back to the wall, where young women in graduation gowns and wedding gowns beamed. "We have two other daughters, Nancy and Karen. They're great girls, married nice fellas, had kids who all went to college and got good jobs. Only Roy. Only Roy has these terrible problems."

Deke leaned back in his recliner, his eyes still focused on the wall of photos, his mind somewhere far in the past. Frank could see he would be of no further use to them. He rose to go, nudging Earl, who also sat staring at the wall.

"You take care, Deke. We'll keep you posted on what we find."

Deke struggled to get up from his chair, and Frank noticed his hands were trembling. "Whatever it is, it won't be good."

"You're awfully quiet," Frank said, after they'd driven halfway back to the office without Earl saying a word.

"I'm thinking maybe I've been a little hard on Roy. Imagine your mom dropping you off for a weekend with your grandparents, then never coming back. And having aunts like Nancy and Karen who are nice, normal moms and yours doesn't give a damn. No wonder Roy's screwed up."

"Seems like his grandfather's given up on him," Frank said.

"But not his grandma. Maybe if Roy recovers from this gunshot, he'll finally be able to turn himself around."

"Possibly," Frank said. Earl's eternal optimism was one of his most endearing qualities, and Frank had to remind himself not to shoot it down. Maybe this was the rock bottom Roy had to hit in order to bounce back. Or maybe it was one more stop on a long, downward spiral.

"Why were you so interested in Deke's family photos?" Frank asked, to change the subject. "Do you know all those kids?"

"Not really," Earl said. "I've never been to the Steuben's house, but I had a feeling I'd seen some of the photos before. Weird, like whattyacallit?"

"Déjà vu."

Frank spent two hours that night in the Mountainside tavern, talking to Roy Corvin's known associates, but all he got for his trouble was a raw throat from breathing in secondhand smoke and a pounding headache from trying to hear over the blare of the jukebox. Roy's cronies, reluctant to speak ill of the almost-dead, had to be prodded to talk, but the general consensus was that since Roy had fallen off the rehab wagon, he was irritable and unstable, and everyone had been avoiding him.

Not that Frank expected anyone to own up to visiting Roy on the afternoon in question. But by getting each man propped at the bar to identify someone else as being a better friend of Roy's, he'd managed to compose a list of people whose whereabouts at the time of the shooting would have to be checked. But no one knew anything about another girlfriend.

Frank stopped back at the office to write up his interview notes while they were fresh in his mind. The fluorescent tube above his computer flickered maddeningly. He stood on his desk and jiggled it. The bulb settled into a steady glow. He sat back down and continued typing. Immediately, the light pulsed dim and bright and commenced a high-pitched hum. He typed a few more lines and decided to call it quits.

Hopping back up onto the desk, Frank yanked out the tube. Might as well stop by the hardware store on the way in tomorrow, he thought. And better take ten bucks from petty cash now, otherwise he'd forget to reimburse himself.

Frank unlocked the top desk drawer. Inside the olive green, metal, petty cash box was twenty-three dollars and seventy-four cents. He took a ten and shut the drawer.

Then he opened it again. Twenty-three dollars and seventy-four cents. That's all.

No gold locket.

After a restless night puzzling over the missing locket, Frank went directly to the Trout Run Presbyterian Church for a consultation with his friend, Pastor Bob Rush. He paced around the minister's book-crammed office, laying out the details of the problem as much for his own benefit as for Bob's.

"And the only people who know where I put the locket are Earl, Doris, and Ardyth," Frank concluded.

"But if it was locked in your drawer—?"

"Earl and Doris know where the spare key is, in case they ever have to use the petty cash when I'm out. And Ardyth is the town treasurer. She uses that key when she comes in to replenish the cash and collect the receipts."

"Well, it can't be Ardyth," Bob said. "No one does God's work more faithfully than she does."

Frank might have rolled his eyes if he heard anyone else described so piously, but in Ardyth's case, Bob was absolutely right. Ardyth was a good person. Not holier than thou, just good and kind, through and through. And not a Pollyanna either. Frank wouldn't have been able to tolerate that. No, Ardyth saw people's flaws clearly enough, but she helped them anyway. She would no sooner sneak into the town office and take that locket than she would rob a bank.

"I know," Frank said. "She made a big deal about turning it in when she found it, so why steal it back?"

Bob shook his head. "Definitely not Ardyth. So that leaves Doris and Earl."

Frank dropped his head in his hands. "It can't be Doris. She's just too, too…"

"Dumb?" Bob said helpfully.

"Yeah, but lots of crooks are dumb. Doris is transparent. She's like a cartoon character—I can practically see her thoughts floating in a bubble over her head. If she stole it, she'd give herself away."

The two men sat in silence.

"Earl?" Bob said finally.

Frank squirmed as if spiders were crawling over him. "I can't accept that. His work has improved dramatically. He's doing great at the Academy." Frank shut his eyes. "He's really coming along."

"Yet you have doubts," Bob said.

"Something he mentioned the other day. Apparently he's dating Molly Lynch."

"The dentist's daughter?"

"That's the one. What if he felt the need to impress her? You know—support her in the manner to which she's accustomed."

"A young woman like Molly wouldn't want some quaint old locket," Bob said. "Besides, Earl would be smart enough to know his girlfriend couldn't be seen wearing stolen goods."

Frank sighed. "He'd also be smart enough to know how to fence it. Trade it for something flashier, or to get cash for a night out in Lake Placid."

"Is he that crazy about her?" Bob asked.

"I don't know. Or maybe he needed money for some family emergency. Earl's passionately loyal to his family. But I can't believe he'd jeopardize his career as a police officer for something so stupid. Not after he worked so hard to get into the Academy."

Frank stood up and crossed to the window. He looked out at the town green, where the crocuses planted by the garden club were bowed down under the weight of the promised spring snow. "I don't give a damn about that stupid necklace. I just hate that three people I like and trust are the only ones who could have taken it."

"Morning, all," Doris chirped.

Frank jumped as she came up behind him, twitchy as a cat at the vet.

"Did I mention I ran into Ardyth the night before last, taking a casserole to Mrs. Philhower? I told her you had the necklace locked up safe and sound."

Frank watched Doris's every gesture, completely keyed in to her patter for the first time in their working lives together. He felt like a spy in his own office, a narc for internal affairs. No wonder everyone despised those guys. Was she testing him? Trying to determine if he'd discovered the loss?

"The ad will be in today's paper. Maybe someone will call." Doris chatted on, as excited and optimistic as a child with a raffle ticket.

"I almost described it to my husband last night, but then I caught myself. I remembered what you said about not spreading around what the locket looks like." She turned an imaginary key in front of her mouth. "Loose lips sink ships!"

Frank could barely stand to watch her. No way Doris knew the necklace was gone. No way she had taken it. He glanced over at Earl.

The kid's fingers flew over the keyboard, his eyes locked on the terminal screen. Was Earl pretending not to hear Doris, or did he have her tuned out, as they both usually did? Doris returned to her desk while Frank tapped a pencil on a pile of papers and listened to the rapid click of the keys. He realized how much he'd come to rely on Earl as a sounding board, tossing out ideas, thinking aloud. Keeping this secret felt ridiculously like infidelity.

The locket nonsense was distracting him from the real work of finding out who shot Roy Corvin. He wanted to shove the matter aside and forget about it, but sooner or later Doris would open that drawer and...

Frank's tapping became so agitated that the pencil bounced out of his hand and sailed across the room.

Earl looked up. "What's bugging you?"

"Nothing," Frank replied too quickly. "Here, I made a list of Roy Corvin's friends. You follow up on the first four. See where they were when he was shot."

"No problem." Earl took the list, giving Frank a puzzled look as he went out the door.

Frank sat and stared at the remaining names on the list. Two of them had had some trouble—drunk driving, a domestic disturbance—but that had been a couple of years back. They were good guys, working men—a little rough but basically decent. He would check them out, but he doubted it would lead to anything. Frank reached for the phone. Maybe Bill McKenna would remember something else, now that the shock of discovering Roy's bleeding body had subsided.

Bill tried his best to be helpful, but he had little new to offer. He hadn't noticed any car other than Tiffany's at Roy's house in the days before the shooting. He hadn't heard the sound of arguing—his shop was too noisy. Roy had never confided his problems.

"I suspected he must've lost his job, but I didn't like to ask," Bill said. "I figured I'd give him one more month on the rent before I made him leave. 'Course the phone company wasn't that generous. They had already cut off his service."

"How do you know?" Frank asked.

"When I found him I tried to call for help from his house, but the line was dead, so I had to run back to my shop. But I gotta give our rescue squad credit. They got there awful fast."

Frank's grip on the phone tightened. "Yeah…they sure did."

"Doris!" Frank bellowed for the secretary before the receiver was back in the cradle. "Check the log. What time did Bill McKenna's call reporting Roy's shooting come in?"

"At 4:47."

"And what exactly did you do next?"

"I told Earl, and he headed right out."

Frank nodded. He remembered glancing at the clock as he and Earl had pulled out of the parking lot that afternoon. It had been 4:49. They had arrived at Roy's at 5:02—yet the volunteer rescue squad, which was also coming from the center of Trout Run, was already there working on Roy when he and Earl showed up.

"Then I called it in to Roger from the rescue squad," Doris continued. "But the funny thing is, Roger's wife told me he was already on the way. Someone else must've called him directly."

"Yeah, someone. The shooter."

Roger Einhorn confirmed that the call reporting Roy's injury had come not from Bill McKenna or Doris, but from a woman—"screaming hysterically so I could barely understand her."

Frank smiled. The solution to Roy Corvin's shooting required nothing more than a request to the phone company to see whose phone had made the call. In less than half an hour he had the answer.

"Esther Neugeberger?" Frank repeated. "Are you sure?"

"Yes sir, that's who the cellular number is registered to."

Esther, an elderly lady hobbled by arthritis, certainly hadn't made a quick escape from Roy Corvin's house. Ten minutes of rambling, confused conversation with her revealed two salient facts: she hadn't used her cell phone since April, when her car stalled at the supermarket, and she now had some help with her housework. Tiffany Kass.

Frank leaned back in his chair and closed his eyes. He might have known finding Roy's shooter couldn't be that easy. But at least he knew the shooter was a woman. A woman who was upset about what she'd done to Roy and didn't want him to die. A woman who grabbed a stolen cell phone at Roy's house and used it to call for help. Frank reached for the phone again. He should call Earl back in—he was on a wild goose chase following up on Roy's male friends. Frank let his fingers slip off the phone. Easier to have Earl away and occupied than to be with him, pretending neither of them knew about the missing locket and what its theft meant to Earl's future in law enforcement.

Tiffany's suspicion that there was another woman in Roy's life seemed increasingly probable, so Frank set out to talk to the one person he hadn't yet asked about Roy's love life—his grandmother. Talking to Connie Steuben entailed a long drive to the hospital in Plattsburgh, where she was keeping a vigil at her grandson's bedside.

Frank felt his lunch curdle in his stomach at the first whiff of hospital air. He could cope with the stink of an autopsy better than this aroma of impending death. The intensive care unit bore uncanny similarities to a maximum security cell block: bright lights, constant noise, relentless scrutiny. Wires and tubes shackled the patients as effectively as chains.

Frank finally spotted a familiar, careworn face: it was Connie Steuben, sitting beside an inert form.

"Hello, Connie. How's it going?"

The question was purely rhetorical. Connie's sunken eyes and stringy hair told the tale of too many nights spent dozing in the hospital's hard, leatherette chair.

"Why are you here?" Her face was too haggard to register any further worry.

Frank told her about the hysterical woman's call to the rescue squad. "I think she might be the shooter. Do you have any idea what women he was seeing other than Tiffany?"

Connie shook her head and stroked her grandson's face. Even with the beard grown during his hospitalization and the tube forcing air into his lungs, Roy retained his handsome profile. "He always had girls chasing him, even in kindergarten. But he never stuck with any of them, not even the nice ones. I stopped keeping track. He was always searching, searching for something more. More love to fill up the hole in his heart."

"What about your daughters, would they know anything?"

Connie fussed with the bedcovers. "The girls don't bother with Roy anymore. Not since the drugs and the stealing. They side with their father."

Frank thought of the family pictures on the Steuben's wall. Karen and Nancy looked like Deke—broad, solid, placid. He imagined them forming an unyielding barrier against their nephew's restless, urgent needs. Or a united front to protect their parents.

Frank placed his hand on the old woman's plump shoulder. "Why don't you let me drive you back to Trout Run? You need a good night's sleep."

Connie shrugged out of his grasp. "No. I can't leave Roy. I'm all he's got."

"What's going on?"

Frank returned to the office to find Earl and Doris huddled over the drawer containing the petty cash box.

Doris jumped, so used to being scolded by Frank that she assumed she must have done something wrong.

Earl glanced up from fitting the key in the desk drawer lock. "I think I may have found the woman whose picture's in the locket," he said. "I need to see it again to be sure."

Frank watched the scene unfold with the sense of helpless inevitability he felt when a deer sprang in front of his car. The locket wouldn't be there. The three of them would confront one another. The crash would come.

Frank heard the cash box click open.

A moment later, the gold locket hung glimmering from Earl's fingers.

Frank felt words ready to surge out, but he choked them back. Relief at an impossible reprieve washed through him. All this worry for nothing. But at the same time, in a deeper part of his brain, confusion throbbed. Was he getting senile? How could he have overlooked the locket? But no—he'd dumped out the box and searched the entire drawer. Two days ago that locket hadn't been there.

Now Earl was trying to pry the delicate thing open, without success. Doris took it from him and sprung it with her fingernail. Her brow furrowed, her jaw dropped, her eyes saucered—a dead ringer for Olive Oyl.

"It's empty! The picture's gone."

At least this time, Frank didn't have to bother concealing his shock. He wasn't crazy—the locket had been gone, and now it was back. But he was wrong—wrong about why it had been stolen. Wrong, all wrong, to have suspected Earl. He felt a hot rush of shame race up his neck into his cheeks. He turned his head away, sure that Earl could read every despicable thought it had ever contained.

Doris hadn't stopped babbling. "Who took it? Did you, Frank? Why would someone take just the picture? Who could've got into that drawer? I swear I didn't tell a soul, not a soul."

"Okay, Doris—don't worry about it. A little mix-up. I think I hear someone in the outer office." Frank nudged her out toward her desk, then shut the door and faced Earl.

"What?"

"Remember when we were at the Steuben's and I said I felt like I'd seen those photos on the wall before?" Earl began. "Well, today, I was tracking down Roy's friend Butch Farley, the plumber, and I found him working on a job. And the house where he was working had a whole wall of photos, just like the Steubens, except arranged better, like a timeline. And I saw one of the same photos there as the Steubens have hanging in their house."

"Where? Whose house were you in today?"

"Ardyth Munger's. See, that's why I had the déjà vu. Because I've been to Ardyth's house lots of times, and whenever I'm there I like to look at the old pictures on her wall. The town green with horses and buggies going through it…Ardyth's dad on wooden skis. But this picture is from later—right before the photos switch over from black-and-white to color."

"So you're telling me the photo from the locket is also hanging on Ardyth's wall and the Steuben's wall?"

Earl shook his head. "No, I don't think so. That's why I wanted to look at the locket picture again. I think I recognize the woman from the locket, or really, the dress from the locket, because you can't see her face that clearly. The two photos at Ardyth's and Deke's have a woman in that dress standing next to a man in uniform."

Earl held the necklace up to eye-level. "But it's not the man in the locket. It's a different soldier—I'm sure of that."

Frank sneezed. "Have you found it yet?"

"Hold your flashlight steady," Pastor Bob said. The two men were combing through the archives of the Presbyterian Church, hampered by clouds of dust and the dim glow of a 40-watt bulb in the file room ceiling. "I think I'm in the right year. Yes, here it is: July 12, 1952, Constance Fortier married to Deke Steuben."

"Right toward the end of the Korean War," Frank said. "Now, look for Theresa Steuben's baptismal record."

"She was baptized in May of 1953. But she was born in early February."

"Less than nine months from the wedding." Frank moved the beam of his flashlight back to the marriage certificate file. "Hey, does the certificate say who the witnesses were?"

"Yes." Bob rechecked the file. "Witnesses: Ardyth Sampson and George Munger."

Bob tugged at his clerical collar, leaving a distinct black fingerprint on the pristine white. "Is it really necessary to confront Ardyth with this, Frank? She must've been trying to spare her friend more heartache by taking the picture out of the locket before anyone recognized that Connie had saved a memento of her youthful indiscretion."

"She didn't have to sneak in and steal it to do that," Frank said. "She could have come directly to me and I would've given it to her, no questions asked, no reporting to Doris or Earl. Ardyth knows me well enough to be sure of that. No, there's something more going on here."

Bob closed the file drawers and sneezed. "You're too suspicious, Frank. The poor woman took the photo out and put the locket back because she must've realized you'd suspect Doris and Earl. Where's the harm?"

"I told you before, Bob—I don't give a damn about that necklace. But I do care who put Roy Corvin into a coma that he may never come out of. And that broken locket's got something to do with it."

Despite serving Frank tea and gingersnaps in her parlor, Ardyth Munger sat looking at her guest as if she fully expected he would knock her around to get her to talk.

Frank clasped his mug and leaned forward. Ardyth shrank into the chintz. "Ardyth, I'm not mad at you for taking the locket and destroying the picture. But I think there's something you're not telling me. Something to do with Roy's shooting."

"Don't be silly. The locket has nothing to do with that."

Frank reached for another cookie. This might take a while. "Okay, start at the beginning and tell me how you realized the locket was Connie's."

"I can't believe I didn't make the connection to the dress when I opened the locket." She waved at her living room wall where Connie and Deke's wedding picture still hung. "These have been here so long I guess I don't see them anymore. If only I had…."

Ardyth twisted a loose thread on her sleeve. "Anyway, last week after

Roy was shot, I drove up to the hospital. I made Connie come with me to the coffee shop for a snack. To distract her from her troubles, I told her about finding the locket. Well, I thought the poor woman was having a stroke! When she finally got hold of herself, she told me some things I never knew.

"You see, Connie and Deke got engaged before Deke shipped out to Korea," Ardyth continued. "She was only seventeen—a beautiful girl, full of fun. A group of us used to go up to this dance hall in Plattsburgh, near the Air Force base. Connie couldn't stand to sit home, so she'd come along and dance with the airmen. That's where she met the other fellow."

Ardyth brushed some cookie crumbs into her napkin. "She and Deke got married when he came home on leave—a small wedding." She looked up. "Connie loved Deke, Frank, she did. I don't think she even knew she was, was—"

"Already pregnant with the other guy's baby."

Ardyth choked on her tea but kept talking. "So Theresa was born a little premature and Deke came home and everything was fine. Then Nancy and Karen came along. And people always commented how different Theresa was from the other girls. Slender and dark and quick as a whippet. And wild. She always had a bunch of boyfriends, and she fought with Deke about them nonstop. Connie thought she'd settle down when she married Roy's father and had the baby, but Theresa wasn't made for small town life. When her husband was killed, she left Roy with her parents and she never came back."

"And Connie kept the locket all those years?" Frank asked.

"Yes, it was all she had of Theresa's father. She thought if she ever found Theresa again, she might tell her the truth. You know, to explain why she was so different from her sisters, and why she never really got on with Deke."

"But then Connie lost it."

Ardyth examined her African violets. "Yes, Connie didn't like to say, but I suspect Roy must have found it and taken it to sell for drug money. He stole other things from them, you know."

"Uh-huh. So how did it wind up in the park?"

"I'm sure you're aware that people congregate there for illegal purposes," Ardyth sniffed. "I found all sorts of terrible things on park cleanup day last year."

"Over behind the rest rooms, not out in the open on the playground," Frank said.

Ardyth sat up straight with her hands folded tightly in her lap. "He's a drug addict, Frank. Who can predict what he's likely to do?"

Frank looked her in the eye. "Why was the clasp broken?"

"What?"

Frank pulled the locket out of his pocket. "See here? The loop that the hook fits into is completely ripped open. You know how I think that happened?"

Ardyth twisted her hands, her lips pressed shut.

"I think this locket was snatched off the neck of the woman wearing it. And Connie certainly never wore it anymore, did she?"

Ardyth flinched, as if he really had hit her. Frank pressed on.

"Roy took the locket, but he didn't steal it from his grandmother. He got into an argument in the park, an argument with his mother. He pulled this locket off Theresa's neck."

Ardyth's ramrod posture dissolved. "Out of the blue, Theresa contacted Connie last year. She was in AA and trying to make amends with people she'd hurt. Connie told her the truth about her father and sent her the locket, hoping it would help Theresa's recovery. But then Theresa wanted to come home and tell Deke and Roy the whole story. By that time, Roy was in the rehab place and Deke was footing the bill. Connie told her to wait—she was afraid of Deke's reaction, and she didn't want to jeopardize Roy's recovery. So Connie and Theresa argued again."

Frank rose and looked down at Ardyth. "When you told Connie about finding the locket, she realized it could only mean one thing. Theresa's back."

Ardyth stood and banged the cups and plates onto a tray. "Connie's had a hard life, Frank. If it turns out Theresa hurt Roy—" She pulled the mug from Frank's hand. "How much more suffering can a woman take? I had to help my friend. I'd do it again."

"I can't believe this town." Frank plopped their donuts on his desk and poured two cups of Doris's sludge. "The temperature in the store dropped about twenty degrees when I walked in."

"Guess they all heard you arrested Theresa Corvin," Earl said, examining his choice of sweets.

"I'm sorry I couldn't oblige them by collaring some anonymous drug addict for shooting Roy. I must have missed the line in my contract that said, 'Only go after New York City scum bags passing through the Adirondacks on their way to Montreal.'"

"Everyone was hoping for a happy ending now that Roy's off the ventilator and out of ICU," Earl said. "It is hard to believe he was shot by his own mother."

"She's a volatile alcoholic. He's an angry drug addict. There's a gun in the mix. I'd say it was a toss-up who would be the victim and who the perp." Frank dunked his cruller in his coffee. "She might have gotten away with it if she hadn't used Mrs. Nuegeberger's cell phone a second time. That made it easy to track her down in Syracuse."

"Couldn't resist calling the hospital to check on Roy. Ironic that Theresa would be tripped up by motherly love."

Frank crumpled the donut bag. "Honestly, I think she wanted to get caught. The cops who brought her in said she started confessing before they even had her in the patrol car." He believed that, so why didn't he feel the usual satisfaction in solving a difficult case?

"Maybe it's all for the best," Earl said. "Maybe the whole family can make a clean start now that the truth is out. Keeping secrets wears you down."

Frank tipped the dregs of his coffee into the terminally ill philodendron on the windowsill. "Earl, there's something I have to tell you."

"You wanted the jelly, not the cruller. Sorry."

"No, about the locket. I discovered it was missing right after Ardyth took it." Frank tossed the words out like he was bailing water from a boat. "I didn't say anything to you. Or Doris. When it reappeared in the drawer, minus the photo, I realized—"

"Oh."

The coffee pot sputtered. The florescent light hummed.

"I guess there are cases where the evidence is hard to accept," Earl said. "Because even people you know really well can surprise you."

Frank turned to face him. "I'm sorry."

"Like I said, people can surprise you."

Adirondack Antiques:

Another Jason Black Adventure

by John H. Briant

As I sat on the dock of my new home in Lake Placid, I reflected back to my active days as a member of the New York State Troopers. It was late spring; I looked across the lake and could see a flock of Canada geese landing near the shoreline. They appeared graceful; they had probably traveled hundreds of miles, undoubtedly swooping down on many a pond or lake on their long journey back to the north from their winter habitat.

How like their own journey was the one that had led me to purchase my home in the Adirondacks, the realization of my longtime dream. Preceding my retirement from the troopers, I had taken a vacation in the Long Lake area, with no intention of leaving the job that I revered. However, certain events had made circumstances so uncomfortable for me that I felt my situation was affecting my health and well-being. My visit made me realize life in the mountains was conducive to a more relaxing existence. With clear insight, I made my decision to give up my twenty-year career, the job I had loved so well, and began my search for a suitable dwelling.

Looking for a home in the Long Lake area brought disappointment: the real estate being offered in the region was way beyond my means. All my off-duty days, pass days, and annual vacations in Long Lake, meeting many of the local people, even joining the Long Lake Sportsman Club, were for naught, I felt.

During the summer and autumn months, I had kept my boat and canoe, along with my small camping trailer, at the Skip-Jack's Campsite, located just across the bridge on Route 30. It was an excellent camping area, and the owner had wood and ice available for guest campers. When fishing was good, I'd bring my catch back to camp to clean for supper. I would fry the fish in an iron skillet over an outdoor wood fire. As any real camper knows, there's nothing like freshly-fried fish.

It was such a relaxing environment, so different from the high-pressure job of an investigator with a heavy case load, constantly pursuing leads with one thought in mind: to close the case by an arrest or investigation. And that's to say nothing of the volumes of written reports required, often typed on my days off.

During my stint as a member of the Bureau of Criminal Investigation at Troop S, I was assigned a variety of cases, which included homicides, felonious assaults, robberies, burglaries, and numerous others. But there was one case that I'd always remember.

It was the mid-seventies. Assigned to the headquarters BCI unit, I was a couple of days from completing my first year in the famed Black Horse Troop. I received the telephone call on a Friday afternoon in late autumn. Fannie Mullens' voice sounded nervous over the phone. I had met Fannie prior to my assignment to S Troop. She owned and operated the well-known Moose Hotel located in Santa Clara, New York, a short distance from Saint Regis Falls. A group of my friends and I used to stay at Fannie's hotel for a week every winter. We were avid snowmobile enthusiasts, running the trails, always enjoying the area's pristine beauty.

"Jason Black, this is Fannie Mullens. Would you stop by the hotel?" asked a familiar voice. "I would like to talk with you in person."

"Is there something wrong?" I inquired with concern.

"I don't know, Jason. I…I want to tell you something in private," she said. Her voice sounded strained.

Immediately, I understood she needed my help. "I'll stop by in about an hour. Is that alright?" I asked.

"See you then, Jason."

I couldn't help but wonder about Fannie's situation as I hung up the phone. It had to be serious for her to call, because Fannie, such a gracious lady, had always seemed to me to be a private person. A smart businesswoman, she drove a 1960 Cadillac that was in mint condition. Her husband, Joe, had passed on at least ten years ago. Since his death, Fannie had run the hotel, preparing and cooking the most delicious meals, tending the bar, cleaning all twenty-nine rooms, with the help of her son and his wife.

Putting thoughts of Fannie's plea aside, I finished the report I was working on. Before I left the barracks, I spoke with my supervisor, Mel Nemer, and signed out on BCI patrol to Santa Clara. The receptionist, Donna, looked up as I passed and asked curiously, "Jason, where are you headed this afternoon in such a hurry?"

"I'm going to Santa Clara to interview someone," I replied.

"Have a good trip," she said with a comforting smile.

"See you later, Donna. If you need me for anything, you can reach me on the air," I called back to her as I headed out the door.

I left the headquarters building and proceeded to my assigned car, a maroon Plymouth with lots of miles on the odometer. I couldn't help but feel that driving across the Troop S territory was like driving across Texas: it was a long distance between some of the towns and villages. The district took in a big share of the Adirondack Park, sometimes referred to as being "Inside the Blue Line." I got into the car and started the engine, checking the fuel gauge and seeing that it registered full. I had to stop before entering Route 11 for oncoming traffic.

I took Route 30 south to Lake Meachum and turned right onto the Santa Clara–St. Regis Falls road. The foliage on both sides of the roadway was in full color, displaying blended red, brown, and yellow. It was a perfect autumn day. I recalled how my love for the Adirondacks had begun at an early age: my father, a logger and pulper at the time of my birth, had taken me along with him to all regions of these beautiful, aged mountains when I was just a young boy. I remembered peering out the side window of Dad's log truck and seeing deer, foxes, bears, bobcats, and many other wild inhabitants of the great forest, sometimes darting out in front of us as we drove.

I checked my watch: only thirty-five minutes to make the trip. Working in the Troop S district was much different than working in metropolitan areas. Busy constantly, we still had enough time to talk with the general population, and usually our members in uniform, as well as our investigators, were familiar with the citizens of their assigned districts.

As I pulled into its parking lot, I could see the stately looking Moose Hotel standing tall and proud. I parked and turned my engine off. Near the garage in the rear of the building, I observed the wide back end of Fannie's sleek, black Cadillac. It looked like a new car. Instead of going in the front door, I opted for the side entrance, which led into the rustic barroom just off the spacious dining room. There were over twenty-five deer heads, each displaying eight to thirteen points, mounted high up on the four walls of the massive room. As I stood there, the only sound was the loud ticking of a grandfather clock situated at the end of the bar. I knew that Fannie would be coming soon, as she had a bell hooked up to the door which alerted her of the arrival of a customer.

I heard the squeak of the door opening from the kitchen.

"Jason, is that you?" she called out.

"Yes, Fannie. It's me," I replied.

Fannie, a small, slender lady with gray hair who wore steel-rimmed eyeglasses, was approaching eighty years of age, but she still maintained her brisk walk. Anyone could tell by her demeanor that she was in charge.

"Have you seen any of your snowmobile friends, Jason?" she asked.

"The only one I've talked with lately was on the telephone. You remember Charles Tayson, don't you?"

"I certainly do. How is he?"

"He's good. Still working hard at the Cullen estate in Bridgeport," I replied.

"You have a great group of friends, Jason, all with a great sense of humor. And when they're here, they take good care of the rooms. It's too bad you couldn't get them together for a summer retreat here at the hotel."

"You've got a point there, Fannie. It's a great idea, but they're all busy in the summer season. Come winter, they just can't wait to come north to your hotel for a getaway."

"Well, you know you are all dear to me. You're like my extended family. Say, Jason, would you like to stay for dinner? I'm cooking for myself tonight and it happens to be your favorites: fried salt pork, boiled potatoes, spinach, and more. Oh, and with the milk gravy you enjoy so much."

"I'd like that, Fannie. Are you certain it won't be too much bother?"

"Bother! You know darn well it won't be a bit of bother."

It was time for me to find out why I was there. "What did you want to tell me, Fannie? Is something wrong?"

Immediately, her face revealed her concern. "No, not with me, but last night, just after I closed down the bar, one of my regular customers—I'd rather not mention his name—was the last to leave, and on his way out the door he told me that he had overheard two strangers talking oddly at the far end of the bar. We had a few more customers than usual last night; I even had to call my son Jim to come in and assist me."

"What was so strange about it, Fannie? You know how bar talk goes."

"Yeah, I know, but it's what he told me that's bothering me, and I feel so strongly about it I thought I'd better share it with you."

"Well, go ahead and tell me, Fannie. I'm a good listener."

"He said the two men, who were from Maine, were talking in suspiciously low tones. Well, anyways, my customer said he overheard some of their conversation—not everything that they said, but enough for him to worry."

"Go on, tell me more," I said.

"They were talking about antiques that they were carrying in their truck and the fact that they were going to Warrensburg to attend a large antique sale," Fannie went on.

"What's the matter with that, Fannie? That's not against the law," I countered.

"I know, but it is when the antiques are stolen, isn't it, Jason?"

"Now that's a different story! If it can be proven that they were actually stolen, yes, then of course it's a crime to be in possession of them. What made your customer think they were stolen?"

"Well, according to him, the two men were concerned about police patrols in the area and the fact that they wouldn't want to be stopped by the law. My customer, kind of an amateur detective, heard enough to make him leave the bar and pretend to walk toward the restroom, but instead he went outside to where the truck was parked and took down their plate number."

"He did, huh?" I was impressed by this customer's sharp thinking.

"Yes, he did, and here it is. I thought you would know best what to do with it." She handed me a slip of paper with a Maine registration number on it; it was a commercial plate number 340-211.

"Fannie, that was a good move on the part of your customer. I appreciate you calling me on this; it sounds like it could lead to something. I'll follow up on it and see what happens. Did he happen to mention what the make of the truck was?"

"Come to think of it, he did—a white, two-ton, enclosed Chevy."

"Did he actually see any antiques in the back of the truck?"

"He didn't say. And I think he doesn't want to be involved anymore. I hope this little bit of information will be helpful to you."

"It certainly is. I saw in the paper that Warrensburg is having the antique sale this weekend."

"Glad I called you, Jason. And there is something else I want to tell you which may be related. I cannot locate my expensive pitcher and bowl set, and I've searched everywhere for it. I have had that set for over sixty years. It came from England from a distant aunt, and to me it's priceless. The pitcher is blue with small roses near the top, and the bowl is blue with flowers on the outside and a white interior. As I recall, the bottom of the pitcher was inscribed with "Made in England H&K Tunstall."

"Do you think these two men had access to it?" I was perplexed that she hadn't mentioned it sooner. "When did you notice it was missing?"

"It was just last night when I was closing up the bar. I've been keeping it on top of the piano in the next room. I guess it could have disappeared any time in the past week," she said, shaking her head.

Fannie and I walked into the room and over to the piano. We both could see where the pitcher and bowl set had rested, in a circular area where no dust had accumulated.

"Do you suppose those two men could have taken it while I was out in the kitchen last night?"

"It's a possibility."

"I didn't have much conversation with them except for their drink orders. When I think about it now, though, they both seemed nervous and neither would look me in the eye. When someone doesn't look at me directly, I get a little suspicious. You know me, Jason. I've been in business a long time and I can smell a polecat a mile away."

"I know, Fannie. I know how you are," I replied with a small smile, while reaching inside my jacket for my notebook. I jotted down the information about the missing china.

"Jason, are you hungry?"

"Come to think of it, I am."

"Well, follow me out to the kitchen and we'll have some good vittles. No use worrying about something that's missing," she said, shrugging her shoulders.

While Fannie prepared dinner, I made further notations in my notebook about the two men from Maine and their truckload of allegedly stolen antiques. I knew many people gathered at the huge Warrensburg sale each autumn to sell antiques and other collectibles, and I planned to check it out over the weekend. It was possible that the two fellows from Maine had removed the bowl set from the piano and might try to get rid of it at the sale.

Kitchen aromas were teasing my taste buds. The fried salt pork was ready to be served as soon as Fannie finished seasoning the milk gravy. The big table in the dining room, covered with a white linen cloth, was set up with large china plates and silverware. Tall glasses of water stood just to the right of the plates.

After washing my hands, I sat down at the table, just as Fannie brought in the platter of salt pork. After setting it down, she returned to the kitchen for the boiled potatoes, spinach, and milk gravy, then made one last trip for homemade wheat bread cut into thick slices.

"There now, Jason, I guess we're ready for your favorite Moose Hotel special," she said with a chuckle, looking over her wire-rimmed glasses.

"Sure looks good, Fannie." My taste buds were now fully engaged.

After filling our plates, Fannie said grace, thanking God for the gifts we were about to receive.

We were quiet during dinner. Fannie's salt pork was a success, and both of us had seconds of everything. More memories arose in my mind of the numerous times our snowmobile group had benefited from the artistry of Fannie Mullen's cuisine, dining in this large room as we enjoyed each other's company and carried on lengthy conversations. The experience was always a wonderful treat.

After dinner I helped Fannie clear the table, then thanked her and told her that I would follow up on the information she had shared with me. Fannie accompanied me to the door and we said our goodbyes. I walked over to the car and climbed in, tooting the horn as I left the parking lot.

The road to St. Regis Falls and home was quiet and traffic-free. I called out-of-service with headquarters when I pulled into my narrow driveway.

The next morning at work, I briefed my supervisor, Mel Nemer, concerning the information I had received. Mel told me to follow up on the tip and, if anything materialized, to take a case on it. I advised Mel that I would keep him posted on further developments.

For my first step, I decided to check out the Maine license plate number. The headquarters dispatcher ran the data for me. To my surprise, it came back as "no such number on file," although I supposed there was a possibility that the plate had been newly issued and hadn't yet been entered into their computer system. I advised Mel of the results of my inquiry, and then signed out to the Warrensburg area on an investigation.

The highway traffic was light as I went south on Route 30, heading toward Route 87, commonly referred to as the Northway. When I reached Exit 23, I left the highway and drove into Warrensburg. The traffic in town was heavy, and the main street was lined with booths, some still in the process of being readied for the anticipated busy weekend.

Many of the people displaying their antiques had been coming to the Warrensburg sale for years. Word-of-mouth advertising and notices in small-town papers brought people from all over to the area. I located a parking space for my unmarked troop car. Removing my suit jacket, I draped it on a coat hanger and replaced it with a light jacket in preparation for my walk through the area where the dealers were set up. I glanced at my watch. It was 11:20, and I noticed that some of the dealers were starting up small cooking grills as lunch time approached.

I was impressed by the quality of the antiques on display. There were china cabinets, buffets, tables, and chairs, along with assorted dishes, pottery, and other items too numerous to mention. I thought back to Fannie Mullens' hotel with so many antiques of this vintage, and I wondered if the two alleged crooks had known about her collection before stopping there.

A cool breeze was sweeping through Warrenburg. I pulled up my collar and buttoned the top of my jacket. As I neared the end of the long line of antique dealers, I observed a white, enclosed, two-ton truck. It was pulled straight in, with the rear of the vehicle facing the street. I couldn't view the inside, as the sliding gate was pulled down to just about a foot above the bed of the vehicle. One Caucasian male about forty years of age was standing near the front of the truck. He had wavy brown hair and appeared to be approximately six-feet tall. Wearing a blue denim shirt with matching slacks, he was deeply engrossed in conversation with two customers. I walked on for a short way before turning back toward the truck. Although the license plate was caked with dried mud and barely readable, I made out the numbers: Maine 340-211. Yes, this was the vehicle that had been at Fannie's hotel yesterday.

When the potential customers had ended their conversation and were walking away, I spied a pitcher and bowl set matching Fannie's description sitting on a table. They had been standing in front of it, obstructing my view. I decided to walk over and speak to the man. He looked up as I approached.

"Can I help you, mister?" he asked with a broad smile.

"Oh! I'm mostly just looking today. Boy! What a crowd. This is my first time here. I'm just passing through town," I said.

"So you're looking for antiques. We've got some nice pieces, priced right."

"What are you asking for the settee? It looks old, but it appears to be in good condition," I remarked.

"Well, now, that's a good one, mister," he said. "It goes for six-hundred dollars."

"Say, where are you from? I thought I detected a New England accent," I asked casually.

Oh! I'm from Bar Harbor. I used to be a fisherman, but it was a losing proposition. So my buddy and I decided to go into the antique business. Don't have to worry about whether the fish will go into the net anymore," he said, shifting his weight against an oak table.

"I heard that some of the fishing folks in Maine are having it rough these days."

"Yep, mister, that's why I don't fish anymore," he replied with a touch of sarcasm.

"By the way, what's your name?" I asked.

"Just call me Josh. My full name is Josh Hammond."

"My name is Jason. Well, it's a pleasure to meet you, Josh. Oh, what about that pitcher and bowl?" I asked, pointing to the set sitting atop the oak table he had been leaning on. "My wife has been bugging me to get her one of those."

"You're in luck, my man. This was made in England, probably over a hundred years ago."

"It's beautiful, Josh. How much are you asking for the set? My wife would love it," I said.

Now I remembered seeing Fannie's pitcher and bowl set several times, sitting on top of her piano and in other places she had it displayed in the hotel. I looked at the bottom of the pitcher to confirm my suspicion: "Made in England H&K Tunstall."

"I've been asking five hundred dollars, but for you, Jason, I'll sell it for four hundred."

"Whew! That's a lot of money, Josh. Is that your firm price?"

"Yes, it is," he replied adamantly.

"Are you going to be here tomorrow?" I asked.

"Yes, I sure am," he replied. "I've got a lot of antiques to sell."

"What do you need to hold the pitcher and bowl set? I know that my wife would love it," I inquired.

"If you could put fifty dollars down, I'll hold it for you," he answered eagerly.

"Fair enough." I opened my wallet, took out the money, and handed it to him.

"I'll make out a receipt for you," Josh said as he put the fifty in his pocket.

"Yes, sir, my wife will love that set," I added.

"Here you go," Josh said, handing me the receipt.

"I'm going to look around at the rest of your antiques."

"You go right ahead. You may find something else you'd like."

A young couple appeared, and Josh turned from me to greet them. I pretended to examine the dry sinks, a couple of antique lamps, and two cherry tables. I wasn't an expert on antiques, but I realized the pieces displayed were not the usual run of old furniture.

As casually as possible, I jotted down the description of the furniture in my notebook. Fortunately, Josh was busy with his two potential customers, giving them his full attention. As I walked past the front of the truck, the passenger side door opened and a tall man about the same age as Josh got out. He looked sleepy and his hair was disheveled. When he asked if he could help me, I told him that I had been waited on and that I was just looking at more of the antiques. I'd been wondering where Josh's partner was.

"My name's Jason. What's yours?" I inquired.

"What? Oh, I'm Charles, a buddy of Josh," he replied, still a bit disoriented.

I told Charles of my dealing with Josh and that I would return the next day to pick up my purchase. I decided not to go into a lot of detail with him. My sixth sense told me that these two men were involved in much more than the theft of a pitcher and bowl set. I didn't want them to become suspicious of me, so I shook hands with Charles and, as matter-of-factly as possible, told him I'd see them tomorrow. As I left I thanked Josh, and then walked back toward my car.

As I walked, I went over the facts. Further investigation had to be initiated, because for now the only definite crime I could act on was their possession of the stolen pitcher and bowl set. But that sixth sense never failed me before, and I knew I'd find more.

Good weather made a perfect day for the event, the crowd was growing larger. People were easily able to browse from one dealer to the next, since they lined both sides of the street for what appeared to be a full mile.

When I finally reached my car, I decided that I would go back to the Moose Hotel and secure a formal statement from Fannie Mullens.

I arrived at the Moose Hotel in mid-afternoon after battling bumper-to-bumper traffic all the way. I could tell from the pleasant aroma of prime rib wafting from the kitchen that Fannie was preparing dinner.

"Jason, you're back! What's going on?" she called out anxiously.

"Fannie, I have to take a statement from you. I believe I have some good news about your pitcher and bowl set." I was glad to be able to tell her so.

"You what? You did? Oh, Jason, I'm so happy to hear this!" she exclaimed as tears formed in her eyes.

"That's the reason I need a statement from you, Fannie. Can I use your typewriter for a few minutes?"

"You certainly can, Jason. I'll get it for you. I've got some bond paper, too."

"Good. I'll just sit here at the table and ask you some questions and type up your answers."

The typewriter was an antique itself, but it functioned well. I posed my questions to Fannie as I typed them, then added her answers. It took approximately twenty minutes. Fannie swore to the fact that the statement was the truth, and I notarized it after her signature. When we were finished, she said, "Jason, I have a party of ten people for dinner. Would you care to join us?"

"I'd love to, Fannie, but I'll have to take a rain check tonight," I answered with sincere disappointment.

She nodded. "I understand. Good luck on this case. I can't tell you how grateful I am that you were able to locate my treasure for me." She reached out to clasp my hand.

"Thanks, Fannie. I understand how you feel. I'll talk with you soon."

I reluctantly left the Moose Hotel and returned to Troop S Headquarters, where I gassed up and parked my unmarked car.

Then I climbed to my second-floor office, where I typed up the accusatory information and a criminal warrant. Next I called the Warrensburg region Town Justice, Malcolm Bonner, to inform him of the details of the case. He assured me he would be available at ten in the morning. Before I left the office, I had the dispatcher send a teletype message to the Maine State Police inquiring about any antique thefts that had been reported to them in the Bar Harbor area. It was nine in the evening before I finally left my office for home, where I sank gratefully into bed.

I arrived at Justice Bonner's office a few minutes before ten. All my papers were in order; I always prided myself on my attention to details. I had met the Judge on one other occasion. I remembered that then he had appeared to be in his mid-seventies, with snow-white hair. Now when I entered his office, he looked the same, with a demeanor of clear authority.

"Good morning, Investigator."

"Good morning, Your Honor," I replied respectfully.

We discussed the case for a few minutes, and then I swore and subscribed to the accusatory instrument. Justice Bonner read the charge and the attached statement of Fannie Mullens. After rereading the paperwork, Justice Bonner issued the warrant for the charge of criminal possession of stolen property. I thanked him and left his office.

The dealers were preparing to open their booths when I arrived in Warrensburg. As I pulled into the space in front of Hammond's white truck, he was so busy setting up he didn't even notice me exit my car. He continued to place several pieces of beautiful furniture near the roadway. With the warrant inside my jacket pocket, I walked toward him.

"Good morning, Josh Hammond. How are you this morning?" I asked cordially.

"Jason! I didn't see you drive in. Hang on just a minute and I'll get your pitcher and bowl set for you."

"How have your sales been?" I inquired.

"Haven't sold one item except your purchase," he replied, shaking his head dejectedly.

"Well, Josh, we have a problem here," I said as I reached into my pocket for my identification and displayed it.

"State Police!" he responded, taken aback.

"I'm Investigator Jason Black of the Bureau of Criminal Investigation. I have a warrant for your arrest for criminal possession of stolen property." I went on to inform him of his constitutional rights.

"What?" he asked in consternation, as the color drained from his face.

"That pitcher and bowl set you sold me was reported stolen, Mr. Hammond, and therefore I'm placing you under arrest."

Hammond, already pale, started to shake. I placed handcuffs on his wrists.

"Where's your partner?" I asked sternly.

Josh gazed at me with baleful eyes. "He…he had to return to Maine. When he called home yesterday he learned there's sickness in his family. I believe it's his father."

"What is his last name?" I continued questioning him.

"It's Walters. Damn it! What's going to happen to me, Investigator?" he asked, his voice trembling.

"You're coming with me. I'm impounding your truck and its contents, including the pitcher and bowl set. They will be taken to our headquarters and placed in a secure area. You'll be processed and then we'll visit the issuing magistrate," I explained calmly.

During the trip to headquarters, I questioned Josh further as to his acquisition of the pitcher and bowl set. He kept clearing his throat, and I could tell that he was very nervous. His hands shook and he began to sob. Tears flowed down his cheeks. He asked me what would happen to him if he told me the whole story.

"Josh, I can't make promises, but I will inform the district attorney that you are cooperating with the police."

He became very quiet as he tried to regain control of himself. He finally stopped crying and began his story.

"I have good parents, Investigator Black, and they did teach me right from wrong, but I was backed up against the wall financially. When I had to sell my fishing boat, my childhood friend Charlie and I decided to, uh, go into business. We knew where there was a house full of expensive antiques. The owner was an elderly lady with no living relatives who had been placed in a nursing home. One night Charlie and I drove to her house and, uh, broke in. The rooms were full of valuable stuff—buffets, dry sinks, chairs, lamps, you name it! Most of the pieces were covered with sheets."

"Interesting, Josh. How did you gain entry?" I prodded.

"Through a door in the rear of the house. We pulled around in back so we wouldn't be seen by any passing cars."

"Wasn't the door locked?" I probed.

"Yes, we—well, we used a jack-handle to pry it open."

"Tell me more." I carefully pushed him further.

"We loaded everything we could get into the truck. When it was full, we just pulled the door closed and, uh, left the area."

"You are aware that what you and Charles did by entering the home and stealing the antiques was a crime, aren't you?" I asked.

His face fell even more. "Yes, we both knew it was the wrong thing to do. But, damn it, we were desperate, I guess."

"Will you give me a sworn statement as to what you have just related to me?"

"Yes—yes, I will. I just want all this over and taken care of."

I paused a moment, then continued. "Tell me, Josh, when you and Charles were in the Moose Hotel, whose idea was it to steal the pitcher and bowl set?"

"Sir, it was mine. Charlie went to the restroom and the owner left the bar to go into the kitchen to prepare a meal. I just went over to the piano, picked up the set, and took it out to our truck. When I returned, Charlie was just coming out of the restroom. We sat at the bar and finished our beers. While we were there several people came in. Charlie and I talked for a while and then left." His face showed how painful this memory was.

I could see he was telling me the truth. "Josh, I certainly appreciate your being candid with me. As I said before, you are aware that it was wrong to do what you and Charles did?"

"Yes, sir. It was wrong. I'll cooperate with you fully."

When we pulled into headquarters, we went directly to my office. A teletype message from the Maine Police lay on my desk; it told me they were investigating a burglary of an old home where antiques were stolen. I had one of our uniform troopers stay with Hammond while I made a call to the Maine State Police at Bar Harbor.

"Maine State Police, Trooper Olson. May I be of service?" a man's voice asked.

"This is Investigator Jason Black of the New York State Police. May I speak with one of your detectives?"

"You certainly can. Please hold."

"Detective Paul Richter here. What can I do for you, sir?"

"I'm Investigator Jason Black, Troop S of the New York State Police. Detective Richter, I received a response to a teletype message that said your department is conducting an investigation of a burglary where antiques were stolen."

"That's correct, Investigator," he replied.

"I believe I have some good news for you, Detective Richter. I have arrested a Joshua Hammond for criminal possession of stolen property, which consisted of an antique pitcher and bowl set stolen from the Moose Hotel in Santa Clara, New York. He has made oral admissions to me that he and a Charles Walters broke into a home near Bar Harbor and stole a truckload of antique furniture, for which I am presently processing him. We have impounded the truck and secured it and its contents in our evidence area."

"Good work, Investigator Black. That sounds like it could be our stolen antiques. What about Charles Walters? We are familiar with both of these guys. They were local fishermen who went out of business as the fishing became less profitable," he said, sounding quite pleased. "It looks as though you may have closed one of my cases for me."

"Hammond told me that Walters is in Maine as we speak. The two men were dealing at an antique show in Warrensburg, New York, when Walters was informed there was illness in the family and returned home. Seeing that he has returned to your jurisdiction, Hammond's statement should give you sufficient grounds to pick him up."

"Investigator, thank you for contacting us regarding the apprehension of Hammond. It's almost certain that the antiques you recovered are the ones that were stolen from our area. We do have information about a white truck that was spotted near the scene of the crime," he added.

"Little doubt about it then. I'll send you a teletype when I return from the court. The judge will undoubtedly hold him for your department. We'll let you know. In the meantime, you'll be able to make arrangements to send your officers to our Troop S headquarters."

"We will do that, and thanks again for letting us know. I won't be the one to come to New York, but two detectives from our department should be able to get to your jurisdiction sometime in the morning."

"Sounds good to me. Take care, Detective Richter," I said.

"So long."

I returned to my office and relieved the trooper who was guarding the prisoner. I then took Hammond's photograph and fingerprinted him. After he had washed his hands to remove the ink from the processing, I seated Hammond in front of my desk and took his statement. He again related the events leading up to the burglary and the removal of the antiques from the unoccupied dwelling. He indicated that Charles Walters, his lifelong friend, had been involved with him in the burglary of the house and the theft of the antiques.

Hammond swore and subscribed to the statement.

After this, we left my office en route to Judge Malcolm Bonner's. As we exited the building, I spotted the tow truck pulling into the headquarters parking lot with the truckload of antiques. A uniform trooper led the operator into the secured impound area.

When we arrived at the office, Hammond was arraigned. He entered a plea of guilty before Judge Bonner, who then fined him five hundred dollars, which he could not pay. The judge then committed him to jail in lieu of the fine, where he was to await extradition to Maine. I then transported him there myself.

When I returned to headquarters, I sent a teletype to Detective Paul Richter advising him of Hammond's status and the fact that he would waive extradition and return to Maine with the detectives when they arrived at Troop S. I further informed Richter that he should make arrangements for the return of the truck and its contents to his jurisdiction.

The Maine authorities arrived at troop headquarters the next day around eleven in the morning with a list of the missing items, which matched up perfectly with the list of antiques that were on the truck. Receipts were signed, along with the waiver of extradition papers before the court, and Hammond was taken into custody by Detectives Morey Williams and Oscar Harris. A trooper who was with them would drive the truck back to Maine.

A week later I had the pleasure of returning the unharmed pitcher and bowl to Fannie Mullens. Tears flowed down her cheeks with happiness. I advised Fannie she might want to secure her valuable set in a safer place, and then shared with her the details of the apprehension of the two men who had been her customers the night of the theft.

"Jason, it makes me sick. Look how many years I've had this place and nothing like this has ever happened before." She shook her head dejectedly.

"I know, I know, Fannie. But it's a changing world," I explained.

"I just want to thank you again for finding the set and bringing to justice the people who stole it."

"We all have to be careful, Fannie. You never know who's coming down that highway." I touched her shoulder in consolation. "Now, back to business. Will you please sign this property receipt for me?" I asked. I opened my briefcase for the form and she promptly signed it.

"Take care, Fannie. With your help, justice has been served. Your missing pitcher and bowl set led to the criminals' apprehension and the recovery of antiques valued at thousands of dollars!"

"All because of a good customer with good ears, Jason," she said with a smile. "And a good trooper who listens."

I gave her a nod I knew she'd understand.

"Got any gravy left, Fannie?"

Looney

by David J. Pitkin

When we think of the Adirondacks, we picture vast wilderness tracts or perhaps the hardy men and women who first visited and homesteaded the forest lands. We think of ferocious black bears, wolves, or lynx who snarl at interlopers. Or, perhaps, we visualize the rugged, bearded faces of the woodsmen and trail guides. Here, however, is one of the strangest tales I've encountered—one which seems to combine the elements of both human and animal.

Jimmy Holmes was well known in the Piseco Lake area. He spent his summers on the lake while growing up and befriended many people over the years. His stayed at the old camp his grandfather had built on Point Road, a few miles west of the village. In January of 2001, he mentioned to friends that he didn't feel well, though he hadn't been sick. During Super Bowl week, Jimmy died in his native village of Holland Patent. There were many moist eyes as he was laid to rest.

Lee, one of Jimmy's old friends, visited his family's camp early the next spring, when ice still covered almost all of Piseco's surface. He was quite surprised to see a spot of open water that was only a few feet across, and in the center of that puddle was a large loon. "That's strange," Lee mused, "loons usually arrive as mated pairs in early May, and here it is only late March." But that loon did his solo act all season long and attracted no mate that year. He remained on the lake almost until the end of October, long after the lake's loon population usually migrates to warmer, open waters to the south.

"And that bird was super loud for a loon," Lee's wife, Lynne, added. "Most loons stay within a relatively small area all summer, live and mate in pairs, and are very shy of humans. But this bird was spotted from one end of Piseco Lake to the other. Every time I tried to get a photo of the strange bird, he wouldn't cooperate; though he would swim right up to our canoe when we were paddling out there and didn't have a camera. He was pretty bold," she concluded, "and only swam up to people that Jimmy knew. And, you know, Jimmy never liked to have his photo taken." I was beginning to get her drift, though her reference was startling—was it possible? Was it even conceivable that the departed spirit of Jimmy had chosen to remain on the earth, even if that opportunity required him to live out the short life of a *bird*?

Cheryl, one of my friends who had put me onto this story, had known Jimmy quite well, and suspected he had a crush on her at one time. "Jimmy was a bachelor and only had a few lasting relationships though he was very dear to his friends. That pattern can be observed in this loon's behavior. Lynne once saw him briefly with a female, but it didn't last long. Gee, I said to myself, that sure was Jimmy's style. Of course, there are other similarities," she smiled, "loons love fish and Jimmy loved eating them too."

Cheryl continued, "Then, in February of 2009, I was working in the kitchen in my home in Rensselaerville, New York, when I heard a 'plop' and saw that my son's stuffed loon had fallen off the refrigerator door. There it sat on the floor making the eerie sounds of the loon. I had just been thinking about Jimmy because it was Super Bowl week once again. For us, the Jimmy/loon relationship has lasted over seven years. How would you like to visit Jimmy's camp with me?"

As a teacher of Asian Studies for thirty-five years, I was well aware of the Asian concept of reincarnation, and even the ancient European supposition that the soul can move between species after death, a process known as transmigration. I had come to believe firmly in reincarnation but had never given transmigration much credence. Nevertheless, I am aware of how little I know and understand about life's ultimate rules and purposes, so I was open to hearing some hard facts about the Jimmy case.

The Holmes camp is a beautiful old house with a huge cathedral ceiling. On the day I came to Piseco, there were other house guests and neighbors. One such guest was Penny, a Scottish woman who was on a month-long visit to the Adirondacks. She was sensitive and told me she felt many personalities in the house when she first explored it, especially upstairs. That, however, was the only clue I had prior to my investigation, and, realizing that each individual has a unique perception of the psychic world, I wanted to see what my personal reactions might be.

As I stood at the dining room table I felt someone was speaking to me about excursions—"I loved them," seemed to be the message. I had to ask Lee and Lynne about that—what were excursions, and how did they relate to Jimmy? "Oh, he loved to show people around the lake, both on land and on water. He loved to take people fishing out on the lake," Lee told me. Then I got a name that seemed to begin with the letters D-E-L… but no one there could relate to that. My intuition sometimes reveals spot-on answers, and at other times it leads to an unsolved mystery. Lee and I decided to go upstairs to the balcony that surrounds the camp's interior. As I reached a spot about half-way around, I suddenly felt light-headed and had to reach out to the wall to steady myself—what had come over me?

Penny's teenage daughter, Laura, accompanied us upstairs. As she reached my location on the balcony, she mentioned a similar light-headed feeling. We were standing just outside a bedroom, so I inquired whose it had been. "That was Jimmy's bedroom," Lee told me. I responded that I felt light headed, almost drunk, at that spot on the balcony. Lee gave a wry smile and commented that Jimmy used to love his gin and tonics and martinis in the evening. Had Laura and I tapped into the dizziness that must have accompanied Jimmy upstairs at bedtime?

We then walked into Jimmy's bedroom and I heard (and literally saw) the words, "It's so hard to let go of it all." Those are not unexpected words, as ghosts are often kept suspended between worlds by uncompleted tasks or desires which were never finished when they had a body. Some spirits remain trapped because of strong emotions such as deep love (or hate) for a person or the desire for revenge. None of those negative emotions seemed to be in Jimmy's room—only wistfulness. As I prepared to exit the bedroom, I felt a gentle pressure pushing me out. Jimmy? When I'm "open" intuitively and psychically, I am easy to maneuver. I know that, and I suspect that I more often drift rather than take deliberate steps.

Lee then motioned me to another room. As I entered, I heard a voice say, "Darling." I couldn't tell if it was male or female, but the sensations in that room were subdued and certainly not strong. Lee told me it had been the bedroom of Jimmy's father. That was about it for the interior of the old 1920s camp.

Returning downstairs, I filled Cheryl in on our experiences upstairs. She smiled and said, "Whenever I come up to the lake, I go out to the end of the dock and call out, 'Hello, James' and that loon always shows up in less than thirty minutes. So, what do you think?"

For a person hoping desperately that life in some form continues after death, it might seem to be a formidable case. Jimmy Holmes, who died of an aneurysm at age fifty-two, just wasn't ready to leave the earth. He found an opening and jumped into the loon in order to remain among friends and favorite places on his beloved Piseco Lake for just a bit longer. Maybe, if it is all true, these contacts will allow Jimmy to let go.

Strangely, the loon has been seen less frequently this year, though as Cheryl read my first draft of this story to friends on their boat, the loon started talking to them from the other side of the lake. It moved in their direction, but never approached the boat. "We watched him across the bay for a good half hour," Cheryl grinned.

The Sword and the Stone

Tico Brown

I

The first three deaths took place before Benson was involved. He had been contacted after the local police had failed to diagnose the first two fatalities as homicides. When a third death occurred, Benson, an investigative specialist, was called in.

Walter Smith was the third victim. He and his nephew Marcus arrived at the Adirondack Lodge in the foothills of Mt. MacIntyre on May 14. Walter's face was not young, but not old either. It had the look of a man who had kept his youthful enthusiasm for adventure. Marcus was not old at all, but caring for twins had already begun to line his face. The two had booked their room for ten days. They arrived late that first night, ate dinner at the lodge, unpacked, and went to bed. They rose slightly before noon the next day and headed toward the mountain. The nephew returned alone, rushing down the mountain trail to alert someone to his uncle's death.

Walter Smith's lifeless corpse had been carried down from the mountain by the time Benson arrived. Benson noted the deep, crude slashes in the victim's chest. The local police had found him halfway to the summit, several meters off the main trail. Benson examined the body briefly, turned, and walked to the Adirondack Lodge. The local police chief, Detective Moore, had already gone over the victim's room and interrogated his nephew, but he'd found nothing particularly useful.

Benson entered the victim's room without knocking. It was still filled with Smith's things, which Marcus was packing back into suitcases.

He looked up from his task.

"I'm with the police," said Benson.

"Well, go on," said Marcus, motioning to the room.

Benson opened drawers and rifled through cabinets. He saw nothing worthwhile until he got to the small bookshelf. The larger books caught his attention first—*Adirondack Legends*, *The Bigfoot Omnibus*, *Monsters of the Northwoods*, *Narwhals Lost at Sea*. Beside them were a thick, stapled photocopy of *The Search for Sasquatch* and a battered copy of *Yetis, Yachts, and Yardwork.* Benson shuffled through the pages of *Monsters of the Northwoods* and found entire highlighted sections on the beast.

"Your uncle was interested in Bigfoot?" he asked.

"He was a cryptozoologist, actually. I think he really wanted to nab Sasquatch."

Benson flipped through *Narwhals Lost at Sea* and found nothing underlined or highlighted. He closed the book and looked at the creature on the cover: a whale with a long tusk protruding from its snout.

"Narwhals too?"

Marcus looked up from the suitcase he had been stuffing with clothes.

"Closest living thing to unicorns. Or so he thought."

"So what did the police ask you?"

"They wanted to know what happened. I told them. It's all in the report. He thought he saw something while we were climbing. He went ahead. We got separated. I found him later, all torn up."

"Why did you two come up here?"

"Do you want my reason or my uncle's?"

"Yours."

"I've always liked it up here. I thought about trying my luck at being a forty-sixer."

"How many mountains have you climbed so far?"

"This would've made it an even half. Twenty-three mountains"

"Twenty-three mountains. That's certainly an accomplishment."

Benson's eyes returned to the shelf.

"You need these books?"

"Not anymore. Do you? Take 'em."

"They're going to hold you a little while longer for more questioning, you know," said Benson as he picked up the books. "You were the only one with him, so prime suspect status defaults to you even though they didn't find anything of yours that could've sliced his chest like that."

"You think *I* did it?"

"No," said Benson. "They don't either. It's just procedure."

Benson would have contaminated the upcoming interrogation by telling Marcus about the other two "accidents" on MacIntyre yesterday, so he kept quiet. But Marcus couldn't have murdered anyone while he and Smith were checking in at the lodge.

"Sorry about your uncle," said Benson, turning to go.

"Yeah," said Marcus.

II

Benson went through Smith's books in detail. They offered no key to the murders. Not until the fourth and fifth victims were discovered.

At nine o'clock that night, Mr. Edward Zaretta was found on Mt. Marcy's Van Hoevenberg Trail with severe cuts to the chest and massive head trauma. Zaretta was found alone, but with more than just hiking materials in his possession. Among his belongings were a large canvas bag, a portable optical telescope, a telescope mount, and a leather-bound observation log.

Detective Moore briefed Benson upon his arrival on the scene. They had found the astronomy equipment partially set up, but then knocked over. The body was discovered several meters from the equipment.

Benson asked for a flashlight to examine Zaretta's log. Moore nodded to the forensics officer who had just finished going over it. The officer brought it over and handed Benson two thin latex gloves and a flashlight. Benson slipped the gloves on and opened the log.

The last entry was "Friday, May 14, Algonquian Peak"—yesterday. The two-page entry focused on an unnamed seven-star cluster currently residing in the domain of Taurus. It listed measurements, diagrams, and other scientific notations. Benson turned to the previous entry. It was dated "Sunday, May 2" and involved some other star cluster.

"Why was Zaretta studying this?"

"We don't know," Moore responded

Benson held the book out to him.

"Xerox the last few pages and get me whatever background information you can. Tonight."

Moore nodded, accepting the battered text, and left.

Benson found a large rock in the darkness and sat down. First Bigfoot, now stars. No leads aside from time and location of death.

He looked at his watch. Nine thirty-three and fifty-six seconds. Fifty-seven. Fifty-eight. Fifty-nine. At this time tomorrow, it would be nearly four hundred days since Angela Benson was murdered. She might've known the answer to Zaretta's mystery. Stars were her life, though. Not his.

"Detective Benson," came a familiar voice.

The detective's eyes looked up and met Moore's.

"Sir, you better come see this," said Moore.

Benson followed Moore around the cliff face to a small cave in the mountainside, about ten meters off the Van Hoevenberg trail. Out of the shadows, the police were pulling another corpse, mauled and bloody. Benson shined his light on it and turned away. The victim's chest had been opened up like an autopsy patient's.

"Rigor mortis," said Moore. "Lividity is present and flies are already settling in. Been dead for twenty-four hours at least."

"Who found him?"

"One of the local shamans," said Moore.

Benson frowned.

"A shaman? That's just great."

"We've got him here. Do you want to interrogate him?"

Benson nodded.

An officer brought him to the detective. The shaman was dressed in a denim button-down shirt, black slacks, and a native fox-skin cloak. His face reminded Benson of Walter Smith's—old in texture, but young in spirit.

The man bowed slightly to the detective.

"My name is Mingan," said the shaman. "I am of the Midéwin—what you might call a medicine man."

"So I hear," said Benson. "What happened here? How did you find the body?"

"Have you ever heard the Tale of the Great Bear, Detective? I think it might help you understand."

Benson smelled alcohol on Mingan's breath. He crossed his arms.

"Above our heads is Ursa Major—the Great Bear. The tale is of the same Great Bear, who leaves his cave every year in the spring to hunt. Pursuing the bear are seven great Algonquian hunters—each one of the seven stars in the sky. After a long hunt, they kill the bear and eat it. But that does not end the story. The following winter, the old bear's skeleton lies upon its back in the sky. But its life spirit enters a new bear that is asleep for the winter. Every spring, the cycle begins anew."

All at once, a part of it fell into place for Benson. He understood. He looked at the shaman.

"I knew that the man named Smith was hunting Bigfoot," said the shaman, "Just like the Algonquians hunted the Great Bear. I did not realize that the seven hunters had anything to do with it. Not until the other detective spoke of the seven stars."

"The seven-star cluster in Zaretta's log," Benson muttered.

"The constellation I speak of and the one in Zaretta's book are different, but they both contain seven stars."

"And what about Taurus?" Benson asked, recalling the word from Zaretta's log.

"The ancient bull in the sky. I know nothing of the bull in relation to this matter."

Smith's books, thought Benson. He knew that the key would lie in Walter Smith's books. There had to be something about this Algonquian legend there.

The shaman bowed again, motioning to leave.

"I pray that you will solve the mystery behind these murders."

"Hold on," said Benson. "The local police still have to interrogate you."

"I have no intention of leaving the area."

"But you've got something more to tell me. Some suspicion. Something important."

The white of Mingan's fox-skin cloak glowed with moonlight.

"I have no more information, Detective. Only a theory."

"What is it?" asked Benson.

"Walter Smith was hunting a Great Bear, but he was killed. How many murders have occurred so far, Detective?"

"Three."

"I'm sorry. I mean, how many deaths?"

"Five."

"Out of..."

"Seven."

III

Friday, May 14, Mt. MacIntyre, 9:04 P.M.: William James discovered with his stomach torn open after sliding down a jagged slope.

Friday, May 14, Mt. MacIntyre, 9:47 P.M.: His brother, Harold James, discovered impaled on a small, thick stalagmite inside a nearby cave.

Saturday, May 15, Mt. MacIntyre, 5:57 P.M.: Walter Smith discovered with three crude slashes through his chest.

Saturday, May 15, Mt. Marcy, 8:53 P.M.: Edward Zaretta found with a sharp blow to the chest and head trauma.

Saturday, May 15, Mt. Marcy, 9:12 P.M.: Thomas Farrell discovered in a small cave with his chest mauled and bloody.

"Five victims," Benson said to himself. "All with chest wounds."

They were all murders. All five of them.

Benson lay on his back on his hotel bed and stared at the ceiling. He looked at the glowing numbers on the alarm clock beside him. 1:53 A.M.

Smith's books had not been as helpful as he had hoped.

His mind raced. *Seven warriors hunting a Great Bear.*

Could all five victims have been chasing some Bigfoot myth? It was illogical, but not impossible.

And if they'd been attacked by a creature like that—by a Great Bear? *They should all have similar injuries.*

Was some wild animal on the loose? No, there couldn't be. Grown men would have more sense than to attempt to engage it. And no "creature" would take seven victims in accordance with some myth. No, there had to be a human mind and will behind these murders. There was no other way.

Benson knew his mind needed rest. He reached out for the bottle of sleeping pills on the nightstand. Two pills later, he descended into darkness. As he sank into sleep, tiny pinpricks of light surfaced from the void. Seven stars, somewhere in Taurus. Seven hunters, chasing a bear.

IV

On Sunday, May 16, at 11:13 A.M., Detective Benson entered the shaman's holding cell.

"I need your help," said Benson.

"I foresaw this meeting last night. I dreamed of a large bull in the sky. I am still searching for the meaning of this dream. But for now I believe you are the bull, Detective, trying to remain strong though you really do not know what has been happening."

Benson watched the shaman and said nothing.

"And you have come to me now to determine whether or not there will be another murder. That is the help you require, is it not?"

Benson nodded.

"I have already tried to divine whether or not there will be another murder."

"So you know what's going to happen?"

"I only have an idea. But if my premonition is true, neither of us will be able to stop the murders."

"Murders? You've seen more than one?"

"The last two hunters still seek to hunt the Great Bear. They will meet the Bear, and death shall visit two. But I have seen two possible futures. In one, the Great Bear and one hunter will die. In the other, both hunters will perish this day."

"Where? When?" said Benson.

The shaman shrugged.

"You will not be able to stop what I have foreseen, Detective."

"We won't know for sure until I try."

"It is a rare man that can change the fate of others. But it is not for me to say that you are not such a man. I suppose we shall soon see."

"What exactly did you see in your dream?"

"Both hunters are together now. They will encounter the Great Bear sometime between one and two o'clock today. That is when two of the three will die."

Between one and two. That gave Benson just under an hour and a half.

"Where?" Benson asked. "Which mountain?"

"That I can not say," said the shaman.

"We'll just have to cover both, then."

Benson turned to go.

"I would like my granddaughter, Sooleawa, to guide you, Detective."

Benson stopped. "She knows the mountains?"

The shaman nodded. "She knows them well. You will meet the Great Bear in the mountains. Sooleawa will guide you. I have dreamed it."

The shaman stared intensely at Benson. The weathered Indian hands trembled.

"Sooleawa," he said.

V

Benson left and called Moore, then rushed towards Mt. Marcy. Moore agreed to send a squad to each mountain, with Benson leading one, Moore the other.

Benson's squad arrived seconds before he did. Once Benson appeared, he issued orders. Two of the policemen were assigned to keep civilians from entering the area around the mountain. The rest were to sweep the mountain.

Benson's watch read 1:15. Nothing out of the ordinary had occurred yet. Neither hunters nor a Great Bear.

Had the shaman been mistaken? No, more likely that Benson had the wrong mountain. Maybe he should've met the old man's granddaughter after all. He wished he could contact Moore, but radios and cell phones proved unusable.

By 1:25, Benson and his team had swept the area around the mountain several times. Nothing had happened. He left an officer in charge and went off to hunt the Great Bear on Mt. MacIntyre.

One of Moore's men was waiting for him. The officer brought Benson to the scene of the crime he had wanted to prevent. Encircled by policemen were two men and a woman. Covered in blood.

The first man was Detective Moore. His chest had been torn open like the others. Beside him was an old man. He was dead also, with slashes across his chest. Police were performing resuscitation on the woman. She was still alive.

The detective at the scene told Benson what had happened. Moore had gone straight to the mountain after calling for a squad to meet him there. He had been nearby going over the evidence on his own, so he arrived several minutes before the squad.

The rest of the team had found the scene Benson now witnessed. Both the men had been freshly killed. The woman had likely blacked out from shock. Soon the paramedics would arrive. Once she regained consciousness, they would interrogate her.

The police had not yet worked out a sequence of events. But they had found two items from the scene and sequestered them for evidence. Benson asked to see them.

One of the detectives handed Benson latex gloves. Benson put them on and was presented with a bluish stone and a bloody sword.

VI

On Monday, May 17, Detective Benson entered the shaman's holding cell for the last time. He carried a long, oddly-shaped briefcase.

"I did not realize you would be visiting," said Mingan.

"Your dreams didn't tell you that I'd arrive?"

"I had no dreams last night, Detective. For someone like me, that could be either a good or a bad premonition."

"I'd say it was a bad one," said Benson. "Two more are dead. I have a question for you."

Benson sat on the bench opposite the shaman and opened the briefcase. He removed a cavalry sabre the length of the briefcase. It was sealed in plastic evidence wrap, its pommel and blade guard made of worn gold, its blade, of tarnished steel.

"Have you seen this weapon before?"

Mingan's eyes passed along the sword.

"This," he said slowly, "is an heirloom of my clan. It has been passed from generation to generation for many years. Why would someone use such an heirloom as a weapon?"

"I was hoping you could tell me."

"It is a sacred treasure, not a weapon."

The shaman looked up from the sword at the Detective.

"Who has done this?" asked Mingan.

"We think it was your granddaughter, Sooleawa."

Benson removed a photograph from the briefcase.

"You can identify her, I assume."

The shaman took the picture and stared at it for some time. It showed an Algonquian girl of sixteen or seventeen years, with long black hair, wearing a traditional red robe.

"Her prints were all over the murder weapon," interrupted Benson, "which contained DNA from the two men you predicted would be killed. My bet is that a thorough DNA scan will show that it also contains DNA from the other five murders."

The shaman said nothing.

"What else can you tell me about this sword?" asked Benson.

"It once belonged to a Mohawk, Thayendanegea. One of our forefathers took it from a battlefield, believing it was endowed with Thayendanegea's courage and bravery. We have passed it on as such."

Mingan handed the sabre back to the detective.

"Your granddaughter was calling out a word when she began to regain consciousness. "Chokanipok." What does it mean?"

"Chokanipok is the man of stone in our stories. He is the cruel one amongst four brothers."

"What happened to him?"

"The stories say that he had three brothers, Menabozho, Chibiabos, and Wabose. Of the three, he fought with Menabozho because Menabozho was his opposite: a friend to the human race. Menabozho slew Chokanipok after many fights. It is said that whenever Chokanipok was injured, stones rained down from his body. These stones can still be found on the earth."

"Stones?" asked Benson.

"Yes. Flint. Other kinds of stone. That is where the stories say mountains come from."

"I have one last thing for you to examine," said Benson, removing an item so small that it fit in his closed fist.

He held out his fist to the shaman.

"This was found in your granddaughter's hand," he said, opening his own.

Sealed in official plastic wrap was a roughly-cut sapphire. Speckling the peaceful blue stone were small red shards of chromium. A crude symbol not unlike a simplified Greek alpha was carved onto one face of the stone:

α

"Do you know anything about this?" Benson asked.

"It feels like a stone from Chokanipok, the stone man. I can almost feel his rage and cruelty in it."

"What about the symbol carved into it?" asked Benson.

"I have never seen it before. I have never seen this stone."

Benson put the stone back into his briefcase and closed it.

"The police are going to interrogate you further. We have at least two murders we believe were committed by your granddaughter. They feel you may have some information as to why."

Benson stood up, briefcase in hand.

"I am sorry that you could not change the destiny of those two men," said Mingan.

"At least we have the "Great Bear." No more hunters will die on the mountains."

"Who were the last two hunters who fell to the Bear?" Mingan asked.

"Detective Moore. The man I was working with. And an Algonquian man named Machk. I don't remember his last name."

The shaman nodded.

Benson left the cell and closed the door. Behind him, he heard Mingan's voice, singing softly in his native tongue.

Benson turned and walked away.

The shaman reclined on his cot murmuring the lines of the song.

"Spoken from the sword… handed down from the stone…"

He breathed heavily and fell asleep.

A Silence on Panther Mountain

by W.K. Pomeroy

Silver-gray hair framed a wrinkled face, with unblinking pale blue eyes that stared at Damir, accusing him of something, though he had no idea what. The elderly man could not have been dead too long. His skin was pale, but did not yet have the unhealthy gray pallor of the long dead. No blood stained the stone under the body, nor were there any obvious bruises. A disturbing little patch of rash around the right side of his mouth caught Damir's attention. That rash looked familiar.

Damir had seen enough dead bodies that it only took him a second to get into the automatic, cool displacement of a scientist. The position of the body—sitting on one rock, leaning back against another—almost seemed like a natural resting state. The clothes seemed wrong. It was much too late in the year for anyone who knew Panther Mountain to climb it without a coat. On the ascent itself, a body would generate enough heat that it might not be needed, but resting at the top, the cold would be too much for most people. The feet also seemed wrong. One dark leather moccasin protected the left foot. On the other foot, a blue and green Scottish tartan sock gave contrast to the stone beneath it.

Damir reached for his cell phone and flipped it open, squinting at the screen. "Kleti," he cursed the phone in Bosnian, when he saw that he only had one bar. He did not want to call the police. He had no desire to spend the whole day answering a detective's questions, but he didn't see where he had any choice.

He had punched in the 9 of 911, hoping his signal would be strong enough to get through to the police, when a voice behind him said, "Put it down."

He turned and didn't really see the burly young man who had spoken. He only saw the black barrel of the deer rifle pointed at him. He breathed out his fear, angry with himself for letting someone get that close without knowing they were there. A little voice in the back of his head said, "This isn't how today was supposed to go."

There were already three vehicles parked in the little pullover across from the mouth of the path when Damir arrived earlier that morning. He felt a little surprised that on a weekday this late in the fall there would be that many people awake so early to climb Panther Mountain before sunrise. During the summer, or even the peak of leaf-changing season, it would not have surprised him.

He parked his Hyundai Sonata next to a big Ford Escalade. He slipped a liter of bottled tap water into his ultra light backpack, in a separate pouch from his cameras. While zipping on the arms of his Arctic winter jacket, he noticed the thin coat of frost on the SUV's windshield. It occurred to him that the three cars might not be here for the mountain at all. They could be overflow parking from a party at one of the cabins down the road, though at this time of the year most of those went unoccupied.

Outside the car, he could see his breath form brief clouds of mist in the dim reflection from the waning half-moon. Reluctantly, he clicked his flashlight on, crossed the street, and started up the path.

He breathed in the late fall quiet. It tasted of half-frozen decomposing leaves, hibernating fungus, and the promise of snow to come in the days ahead. Each footstep made the soft crunch of cracking frost on the ground. Damir felt cut off from the rest of the world, and yet connected at the same time. Even when he paused between steps, small sounds came to his ears. Despite the early hour, it is never completely silent on Panther Mountain. There is always wind, or animals, or echoes of voices from camps on the other side of Piseco Lake, which no longer resemble any intelligent human language. This morning seemed a little different. Somehow the soft drone of those foothill noises felt indefinably sad.

Damir experimented with turning his flashlight on and off as he walked. The bare tree limbs did let in some of the moonlight, making long forms of brighter darkness. As the trail became a little steeper, he admitted to himself it was not bright enough for him to make the hike safely, and he let the flashlight remain illuminated.

Without warning, his thoughts turned to Bisera. Her beautiful face floated in his memory. Her dark hair blended in with the darkness of the shadows, the way it had before she dyed it platinum blonde. He almost wished they had never hiked this mountain together. She compared it to his favorite Bosnian mountain, Bjelašnica, although the only real similarity between the two was the gentle slope of the beginning of the trail. Everything else was different, from the maple and pine trees to the varieties of native herbs.

He found himself wondering, once again, if she had found happiness in Boston with her American boyfriend. The thought itself pained him. He wanted her to be happy, and he wanted her to be miserable. He wanted her to come back to him, and he never wanted to see her again. There was little comfort in the thought that it would probably be the latter.

His thoughts were interrupted by laughter, a woman's laughter rolling down the mountain. Between slope and echoes, distances are not always easy to judge when climbing, but Damir did not think it was coming from very far in front of him. With every step the noise came clearer to his ears, and it sounded less and less like laughter.

The young woman sat on a huge maple tree that had fallen parallel to the path, her hands steepled in front of her almost as if she was praying. Damir's flashlight reflected on tears flowing down plump, red cheeks. She stopped crying immediately, wiping the tears away reflexively.

"Hank, is that you?"

Damir moved the flashlight beam out of her eyes. "No. I'm sorry."

He took another step closer to her. He really did not want to stop. She didn't seem injured, just sad. He wanted to get to the top of the mountain in time to get some good sunrise shots. Without the flashlight on her face, he could pretend not to see the deep need in her hazel-green eyes.

He took a step up the mountain. In the darkness, her labored breathing filled his ears. He turned his flashlight back on her. The words came out slowly, with a little more accent than he usually allowed himself. "Are you all right?"

She slowly shook her head from one side to the other. "I don't know. I wish I did. I'm afraid...." It seemed like she wanted to say something else, but she could not make herself say it.

Damir was afraid too. He was afraid this overweight girl was going to keep him here past dawn. He had no interest in hearing some tragic story about a fight with a boyfriend, a lost kitten, or some other small sadness. He had seen and heard all the tragedy he ever needed to before he escaped Bosnia. "There is nothing here to be afraid of." He used his most authoritarian tone of voice.

She tried to peer around the flashlight beam at him. Some of the sadness in her voice was replaced by suspicion, "You're not a cop, are you?"

"No, I am a research scientist." His response was immediate and automatic, if not completely true.

For a moment he considered correcting himself, telling her he had been a biological research scientist specializing in analysis of medicinal herbs in Bosnia, but then he would have to explain that in the United States no one would accept his accreditation. He could go on to explain that he was underemployed as a medical data input technician at Saint Luke's Hospital in Utica. None of that was any of her business, though, so he let the original statement stand.

"I don't know, maybe it would be better if you were a cop."

"I can call the police, if you really need them?" He began to reach for his cell phone.

She hesitated only a split second, "No. I guess what I really need is to find my brothers and my father."

"Are they on the mountain?"

"I think so. My brothers' cars were down there." She pointed down the mountain.

"And your father?"

She stifled a small sob, "I think he's with them."

"You think?"

"He was gone when I woke up. I'm pretty sure they came here together, and I…I know what he's planning."

"What do you mean, planning?" Damir shook his head, annoyed with himself both for asking the question and for how thick his accent had been.

She moved a lock of her curly brown hair out of her face, turning a distraught expression in his direction. "I'm sorry. I don't even know your name."

He sighed, realizing that instead of a tale about a lost kitten, he had assumed the responsibility of helping one. He lowered the flashlight, sitting on the log near her, but not close enough to be threatening. "No, I guess you don't. My name is Damir Hemnon."

"Damir? Is that Russian?"

"No." He tried to keep his tone level, not letting any of his irritation seep in.

"Oh. Well, I'm Gail, Gail Finn. I'm sorry to interrupt your hike. I was trying to get up to the top before my father could…." Her voice trailed away.

Damir let the mountain fill their silence. He resigned himself to helping her if he could.

Gail sobbed twice, then got control of her emotions. "Will you help me get to my father? He'll be close to the top, if not all the way at the top of the mountain."

Damir successfully fought off the urge to sigh. "Yes, I will."

Using his flashlight to guide them, they began to climb the path again. At first neither talked. The loudest sound was Gail's breathing. The thought occurred to Damir that she might be asthmatic. He did not ask.

They moved at a much slower pace than Damir usually liked. Normally, it would only take him twenty to twenty-five minutes to get to the top. Traveling at Gail's pace, it would take at least twice that. He took her hand, to help her up onto a flat rock that functioned as a tall stair in the pathway. He noticed that her hand was soft and warm before he let it go.

She didn't face him as words started to clamber up out of her. "Dad was talking about killing himself last night. You have to understand, my father has been diagnosed with terminal lung cancer."

"Oh, I'm sorry."

"He's been in pain for months already. Sometimes, when he tries to cough, it turns into this strangled scream. It hurts me to hear it. You know?"

Damir grunted something that sounded like agreement.

"Last night we were down at the lodge, and Dad started talking about how this was his favorite place."

"I can understand that."

"He never came up here with me, unless it was back when I was really little, but he brought my brothers up here all the time. It was some kind of male bonding thing."

Listening to the pronounced wheeze of her lungs, Damir could think of other reasons her father might not have wanted her along. They continued hiking up the mountain, until Gail needed to stop and rest again. She sat down on an outcropping of stone, unzipping her jacket with the Hearth Health Foods store logo over her left breast.

"My father said that if he was ever going to…to go out, this would be where he'd want to go."

Damir smiled—and was immediately glad the darkness hid his face.

"It's selfish, and it isn't fair for him to take the time we have left away from us. It just isn't fair."

In an artificially calm tone, Damir responded with the least inflammatory question he could think of. "Is it fair for you to ask him to bear the kind of pain lung cancer is inflicting on him?"

She considered that for what seemed like a very long time. Her breathing got a little smoother. When she found her voice, her tone seemed more rational. "None of this is fair to anyone. He has three grandchildren who will never get to know him."

"You have children?" Damir's surprise came through in the speed of his question. Her attitude and looks seemed far too young for her to have children.

"My Josh is three, the same age as Marie, Hank's oldest. His baby daughter, Tina, is barely six months."

Questions about where those children were now, and who was watching them, ran through Damir's mind, but he did not feel he had the right to ask. Instead he asked, "Are you ready?"

In answer, she used her arms to lift herself up to her feet, and they resumed their walk. Almost imperceptibly, the darkness was turning to pre-dawn gray. Before long, Damir was able to shut off the flashlight for good. In that hazy light before dawn, he could see that Gail might have had a more attractive face under other circumstances and minus about thirty pounds.

Without any prompting, she began talking about her father again. "It's not like we didn't see this coming. He smoked a lot when he was younger, and only cut back as they got more expensive. He kept promising, you know, but he never completely quit."

"It is the nature of addiction."

"I guess additive personalities run in the family."

Damir did not know what to say to this. The trees were beginning to become a little less dense, and a cold breeze gathered strength from being closer to the sky.

"It feels so selfish, but it's also about money. I don't think his insurance will pay out for a suicide. Not that I need it, but it would be good for his grandkids. I mean, they will need to go to college eventually. It would be nice not to have to think about that kind of thing. You don't think I'm being selfish, do you?"

"No."

She peered at him through the dim light. His tight features, almost as hard-edged as the large, shadow-colored rocks around them, gave away nothing.

"You must think I'm a complete wreck." It was more a statement than a question.

With each step, streaks of red and orange added color to the lightening sky. Damir knew he had lost any chance of getting good sunrise pictures.

"We are almost there."

She looked up the path at the rocks ahead. "I need to rest again."

"We are probably only a minute from your family."

"Go…ahead," she wheezed. "Tell them I'll be there in a minute or two."

"They will not know me."

An orange ray of light made Gail's curly hair seem to glow a little. "Just keep my father from doing something stupid."

It seemed like a shame to leave her so close to the top. Damir resisted the urge to take her hand and wait for her to catch her breath.

"I will do…what I can." It struck him that she did not say thank you. He rationalized it by assuming she needed to conserve her breath.

Without her slowing him down, he scrambled up to the first of the clear overlooks in seconds. Someone sat there silently watching the sunrise. The man did not turn toward him when Damir stepped out on the ledge with him. "Hello Mister. Hello? Gail sent me up here ahead of her."

He moved around a boulder to get a better look at the man with silver-gray hair. He decided that if he was already too late, he would have to call the police, despite what Gail wanted.

The deer rifle looked old, with a dark maple stock polished to such a reflective sheen it might have been a display piece. Damir could read the word Remington etched in big Old English letters on the first few inches of the barrel closest to the trigger.

As he sat his cell phone down on the stone, Damir's brain automatically started processing ways he might be able to get the gun away from the burly young man. Most involved getting close to him, and almost all included risks of getting shot or falling if the man holding the gun had any real combat experience. Based on the way he held the gun, where a bad kick might dislocate a shoulder, Damir doubted that he did, but he knew from experience that looks could be deceiving.

"You must be Hank?"

"How do you know who I am?"

Damir forced himself to breath out the remainder of his fear, making his heart slow down to a more normal rate. "I came up the mountain with your sister."

"My sister?"

"Gail."

Hank's large forehead crinkled, "How could she…?"

"She seemed," the American phrase did not come to him immediately, "very determined."

Hank grimaced as if he were in pain, showing off not-quite-straight teeth. "She would have to be." He looked at the cell phone as if it were poisonous. "Step away from it." He waggled the barrel of the gun to direct Damir away from the phone, reinforcing the impression that the man did not have military training.

Damir could hear the slap of leather shoes walking on stone, probably moving down from the next lookout up, where local kids would occasionally have a bonfire.

"Hank, what are you doing?" The shouted question came from a shorter young man, with a face that bore such an uncanny resemblance to Hank that Damir knew they had to be brothers.

The new man's dirty-blonde hair had not receded anywhere near as far as Hank's. It looked like he wore a suit under his expensive, wool winter coat, this in contrast to Hank's faded jeans and plaid lumberjack shirt peeking out from under an old, black leather jacket. The biggest difference between the two was that despite being shorter, and not nearly as muscular, the smaller man's body language radiated confidence, an expectation of not just being listened to, but of being obeyed.

"He was gonna call the cops." Hank indicated Damir by shaking the rifle in his direction.

"So let him. Dad's had his last sunrise." He said it in the same reverent tone that a Catholic might say "Last Sacrament."

"But…"

"But what?" He stepped past his brother, pushing the barrel of the rifle down toward the ground on his way by. "I apologize for my brother. It has been an emotional morning." He thrust his open right hand forward. "My name's Will, Will Finn."

Damir looked at Will's outstretched hand. As he slowly reached his own hand out, he hoped his hesitation did not show. "My name is Damir Hemnon."

"Nice to meet you, Damir."

Will squeezed Damir's hand hard, as if testing his strength. Damir matched it without attempting to overpower the brash young man.

"Can you tell me what happened here?"

Will dropped his hand and took a step back. He reached over to pick up the cell phone. He seemed to consider it for a moment, before handing it to Damir. "It's a sad story. Our dad tried to climb up here to see the sunrise. He hadn't been in great health lately. When he got up here, I think he had a heart attack. He started complaining about his left arm hurting, then he fell to the ground clutching his chest. He said it felt like the mountain fell on him." Will smiled sadly. "He was unconscious before I realized what was happening. Hank tried CPR, but it didn't make any difference. His heart had already stopped beating."

Damir nodded reverently, moving over to look at the dead man's body again. "You are right, that is a sad story." He looked from the body, to Will, to Hank. "And you say the two of you climbed up here with him?"

Will glanced back over his shoulder at Hank, "Yes, we did."

Hank nodded his head in agreement.

"I would ask, if you do not mind, why you felt the need to bring the gun?"

"I ummmm…."

"You never know what sorts of animals you'll run into when hiking in the dark," Will interrupted his brother.

Damir heard her breathing before he saw Gail come up behind her two brothers.

"What's going on?"

"Your brother was just telling me…a story."

"Where's Dad?"

"You'd better sit down, Sis." Hank put a hand on her arm.

"Why? Why had I better sit down?" She turned her head wildly, as if she was trying to look at both brothers at the same time. "Where is he? Where the h…." Her voice trailed off as Will moved aside, giving her a view of their father. "Oh God. Oh my God."

Her legs buckled. For a moment Damir thought she was going to collapse, but she found her balance, stumbling over to her father's side. She punched him in the shoulder hard enough that Damir could hear the fleshy thump. "Why did it have to be this way, Dad? Why?"

"He didn't, Sis. He had a heart attack." For the first time, Will's polished voice sounded genuinely sympathetic.

She put her arms around her father's body, rocking in rhythm to her sobs.

Hank bent down next to them, placing a hand on Gail's back.

Damir felt like an intruder into this most personal of family moments. Then, when Will stood back, Damir moved to get his attention, gesturing with his hands for the young man to follow him.

They moved up the path to the next overview. A tattered brown blanket covered an eight-by-eight-foot square of the ground. Damir kept his voice down so that Gail and Hank would not hear. "Do you want to tell me what really happened?"

Will's face showed surprise, before he covered it with a derisive smirk and snapped, "I already told you."

"No, you didn't."

Will studied Damir's expression, as hard and as cool as the mountain itself, before responding. "What do you think you know?"

"To begin with, you and your brother did not climb up the mountain together."

Will turned his head sideways as if trying to comprehend Damir's words. "What makes you say that?"

"Too many autos. If the three of you had come together, you would have ridden in the Escalade."

"What if we wanted to drive separate cars?"

"That isn't what happened, is it?"

Will shrugged his shoulders, not admitting to anything.

"Your father was carried at least part of the way up here, if not the whole way."

Again Will turned his head away. Damir thought his expression made him look more like Gail.

"That would mean it was your brother who carried him; you could not carry him very far at all, and if you had been with him, you would have picked up his shoe or coat when they fell."

A short, snorted laugh escaped Will's mouth.

"As big as your brother is, I don't think he could carry your father and the gun, which would mean you came up here, after your brother and father, carrying a gun."

"I told you, the gun was in case I ran into any animals."

"Yes, that is what you said."

"Are you calling me a liar?"

"No. You have lied today. That is what I am saying."

"You talk like a D.A. I know."

A realization hit Damir. "You are a lawyer."

"Business law, yes."

"It might be better if you were a criminal lawyer."

"Why do you say that?"

"Because someone in your family killed your father."

Instead of seeming surprised, Will moved aggressively toward Damir, almost growling, "Prove it."

Damir knew he could prove several things, but had not yet completely made up his mind whether he wanted to. "May I ask a question about last night?"

Will nodded hesitantly.

"How did your father threaten to kill himself?"

"How did you know…?"

"Your sister talked a lot on the way up here."

"Of course she did." Will sighed, shrugging his shoulders. "Dad always loved it up here. He said it felt like the top of the world. Last night he was drinking bourbon. Hell, we all had more than a bit to drink. Dad said that if he had to leave the world he wanted to do it from the top." Will looked over the view down at the lake, before looking back at Damir. "Do you get it? He wanted to jump off, but he never got the chance. He had his heart attack before he ever reached the peak."

"Is that what Hank told you?"

"That's what happened, isn't it, Hank?"

This time Damir was not surprised to see that Hank and Gail had walked up on the rocks behind him. Hank still carried the rifle, the barrel pointing down at the ground.

"Yeah, that's it."

"Hank, can you tell me where your father died?"

Hank looked to Will for help, but Will just gazed back at him curiously. "I guess about halfway up."

"He just doubled over there and died, and you carried him the rest of the way to the top."

"Yeah."

"Why?"

"This is where he wanted to die. He said that last night. He wanted to see the sunrise from up here." Hank looked from his brother to his sister.

They both nodded.

"I understand that, but you see I have some…" he paused, struggling to find the English words, "experience with lung cancer. If your father was in the kind of pain your sister said, he couldn't climb even partway up the mountain."

Gail shook her head from side to side. "You don't know our father. When he put his mind to something, there wasn't anything that was gonna stop him."

"Dying stops everyone."

"Not our dad. Even after dying, somehow he got Hank to carry him up here where he wanted to be." Will reached out to slap Hank's broad back fondly.

Damir squinted his eyes, looking for a hint of malice or deception. With a soft certainty, he intoned words intended to provoke a reaction, "Guilt is a powerful motivator."

The three siblings stared at him, at least feigning incredulity. Gail dropped her head first. Hank followed shortly after.

Will's gaze never faltered. "What do you mean guilty. None of us have anything to feel guilty about."

"One of the three of you killed your father."

"Killed? Are you a little slow or something? I told you he died of a heart attack."

"Yes, you told me, but that rash on the side of his face is a symptom of a particular herb called *Arnica montana*." Damir's voice began to take the dry tone of a scientist's lecture. "You probably know it as leopard's bane. It is a basically a cardiotonic steroid, a stimulant that, with your father's compromised immune system, probably mimicked most of the normal effects of a heart attack. A detailed autopsy will prove differently. It will show elevated serum potassium levels, inhibited platelet aggregation, and in all likelihood, an AV node conduction block."

The expression on Will's face showed how much his world was spinning out of control. "What the hell are you talking about? Are you some kind of doctor?"

"He said he was a scientist." Gail's tone was both apologetic and resigned.

"I used to specialize in pharmacological analysis of plants for medical application."

Will shook his head. "I don't get it. What are you saying?"

"I am saying that someone fed your father an herb that was particularly deadly given his medical history, and at this point I suspect the someone would be your sister."

Will's face turned deep red. His mouth opened and closed three times before he turned to face Gail. "What did you do?"

She looked down at her shoes. "He was in so much pain. More than either of you saw, even when you did take the time to visit." She looked down over the lake, which glistened almost silver in the early light. "I'm beginning to understand why he loved this mountain so much."

"You poisoned Dad?" Will took a step toward his sister, his hands balled into fists.

Hank stepped between them. They stared at each other, eye to eye, like boxers before the opening bell. Neither showed any sign of looking away. So low Damir could barely hear it, Hank said, "He wanted to die."

"That's why you snuck him out in the middle of the night to help him kill himself?"

Hank shrugged his shoulders.

"You knew." Damir spoke as the realization hit him.

Hank did not take his eyes off Will. "I saw her put something in

Dad's gorp. I'm not as dense as you two think. I thought I could get him up to his spot before he ate the stuff. I don't think we were more than a third of the way up here before he stopped for a cigarette and ate a couple handfuls."

Damir nodded his head, understanding that this was probably how the leopard's bane made contact with the skin around the mouth, causing the familiar rash.

"I kinda expected him to say something about his dried fruit tasting funny or something. He just puffed on his cigarette and tried to pretend it didn't hurt. He died about ten minutes later."

Will dropped his eyes, but Hank didn't stop talking. "I used the blanket to bundle him up, and I carried him the rest of the way up here for his sunrise. I could have stopped him from coming up here. I could have taken away the gorp, but for our family it had to be this way." Then he turned to Damir, "If you turn us in, we all lose. Gail and I go to jail. My kids lose their father, their aunt, and their grandfather all in one night."

The other two Finn children turned to look at him as well. He looked back at them. Gail's eyes, red from crying, still managed to seem soft. Hank's large forehead looked less threatening. The rifle pointed down at the ground did not impact Damir's thought process any longer. Will's dominant personality seemed crushed by the weight of everything he had learned.

Damir turned away from them, walking deliberately back down to the first overlook. Their father sat there, glazed eyes focused on nothing. "You stole from him the death he wanted. Insurance money will make your lives better, and your children's lives better." He examined the telltale rash, wishing he had been wrong. "It was not right, but nothing you could have done would have been right." He lowered himself to sit down next to their father. "You will need to make sure a thorough autopsy is not done."

Damir felt as much as heard each of them sit down next to him. "The three of you will have to live with what was done here." He breathed in the cool mountain air, closed his eyes, still seeing the reflection of the lake on the inside of his eyelids. "If you can live with that, I can keep silent."

The wind picked up, rippling across the treetops below them.

Gail's voice was almost lost. "We will."

"Yes." Hank's deep voice was easier to make out.

Will spoke last, but most clearly. "It is what we have to do."

The sun grew higher and higher in the pale blue sky.

Damir stood and began the walk down Panther Mountain.

That Old Mountain Spirit

by Paul J. Nandzik

It was the first day of spring vacation, and James William Carlson officially hated his life. This was the time of year his mom took away his video games and banished him to the northern wilderness with his older brother and sister.

"C'mon, Jimmy, get yer ass outta bed," Bobby said as he poked at his eight-year-old little brother through the sheets. Jimmy growled and squirmed, but refused to give up the warmth of his bed. His older brother turned seventeen just last week, and he thought he was the boss of the world, so Jimmy was determined to keep him in his place.

"I don't wanna go," Jimmy whined into his pillow. "Why can't Mom just let me go into hibernation like my biological make-up tells me to?" Jimmy didn't know exactly what that meant, but he knew his brother used to say it all the time.

"Don't be a wise ass, Lil' Jimmy, and don't give me a hard time. If you're not out of bed by the time I'm done brushing my teeth, I'm giving you the triathlon of terror."

The triathlon of terror was Bobby's favorite method of torture. It started out with an atomic wedgie, followed by a wet willie, followed by the sort of noogie that's responsible for causing male-pattern baldness. Jimmy grumbled in defeat. Bobby may have won the battle, but Jimmy refused to let him see that, so he waited for his brother to leave the room before he pulled himself out of bed. Jimmy moaned and shambled like the walking dead as he dragged his bare feet over the cold linoleum floor in search of his "bear feet" slippers.

"Why do we have to go, Bobby?" Jimmy pleaded when his brother emerged from the bathroom with minty-fresh breath. Bobby scowled in annoyance at his little brother.

"Because mom's new boyfriend is a werewolf, and there's going to be a full moon. So unless you want to get gobbled up like Hansel and Gretel, we have to hide in the mountains for the week. Werewolves hate mountains, you know? That's where silver comes from."

"There's no such thing as werewolves or witches or cannibals, Bobby! You're nothing but a big fat liar!" Jimmy shouted, pointing his finger. He gasped as his cheeks flushed and then paled. He didn't mean to shout at his big brother, but it all just tumbled out like his mouth had a mind of its own. It was something he would kick himself in the butt about, except Bobby always beat him to the punch. Or in this case, the kick, which made him stand up on the tips of his toes with tears welling in his eyes.

The morning didn't exactly get any better for Lil' Jimmy. Lisa, his fourteen-year-old sister, came into the room to check on how his packing was coming along. One minute all of his Superman briefs were on top of the stack of clothes he was setting aside for the trip, and the next they were flying through the air faster than a speeding bullet—or at least faster than he could run. Lisa skipped through the house, singing and laughing at the top of her lungs for the neighbors to hear, waving his underwear around like flags at a parade. Jimmy was too upset to make out any of the words, but he knew they were at his expense, and he hated her for it.

Not ten minutes later, the doorbell rang. It was Uncle Frank and Aunt Miami, in their crappy old van that was probably just as old as they were. By the time Jimmy made it downstairs, the adults were already sitting around the kitchen table, talking about all the boring things that adults love to talk about. The steam from the coffee mugs floated toward the motionless ceiling fan and smelled a little like mint chocolate chips.

He was about to say good morning to his aunt and uncle, just like he'd been taught to, but he froze when he heard his mother say: "So I told him his muscles are nice, but he needs to trim his claws and fur. I swear he's more animal than man! But we both took off work to spend a full day at the spa…"

Ohmygod! Jimmy thought. *Maybe Bobby isn't lying after all! Maybe Mr. Ray really is a werewolf!* Jimmy was so frightened that he didn't hear the adults calling his name until after Uncle Frank had reached out and shaken him by the arm a little.

"You look like you done seen a ghost, boy," he said, smiling a little out of the corner of his mouth.

"N-no sir, Uncle Frank," Jimmy stuttered, eyes darting around to find something to focus on besides his uncle's scar. It was a long, thin, pink line that ran under his jaw, from ear to ear, in stark contrast to his chocolate brown skin. But it wasn't just the scar that scared Lil' Jimmy, or even Bobby's stories (he said Uncle Frank was bitten by a vampire and turned into a cannibal when he was in the army). He had command—something his mother never had. The few times Uncle Frank ever yelled at him made Jimmy feel like he was a puppy who just chewed up his master's favorite slippers. But Uncle Frank almost never had to raise his voice. He just gave that look and you knew you were in deep trouble.

"Well, all right, boy. Ain't no spirits supposed to be wanderin' outside the grave anyway. You got all your things packed 'n' ready for our week of fun?"

Jimmy nodded meekly, the words stuck in his throat.

"Good, 'cause we're about done here," Uncle Frank announced before gulping down the last of his coffee. "Let's load up you and your gear." Jimmy bobbed his head timidly and tried not to fidget with his jacket's zipper. "I don't much like to gossip like your momma and Aunt Miami do," he admitted with a hint of a smile and a mischievous glance at the women, who scowled at him playfully.

While Uncle Frank helped Jimmy, Miami rounded up the other two hellions. As soon as everyone's bags were loaded and bodies were buckled in, Uncle Frank started up the van and they were on their way. The engine sputtered and coughed, and there was the faint smell of gasoline that tickled Jimmy's nose.

Jimmy hugged his pillow and yawned as he stared out the side window. The sun hadn't come up yet, and everything was painted a dull gray. He was surprised to see a few cars on the road and could only assume they were prisoner transports for unwanted kids, too.

Over the course of the six and a half hour trip, Jimmy was simultaneously fascinated and frightened by the changes he saw outside the window. In the beginning, there were the familiar, sleek compact cars and towering buildings and waters, but slowly, that all vanished. The water was the first to disappear, then the towers—they were replaced by golden sunlight, old red barns, and fields that swayed in the wind like the incoming tide. The people on the streets were replaced by cows and horses and geese and other creatures whose names he couldn't remember, and the sleek, modern cars were replaced by beat-up pickup trucks, and RVs, and 4x4s with boats and jet skis hitched to the rear.

Uncle Frank pulled over at a small market in the middle of nowhere. Aunt Miami and Lisa raced each other to the lone bathroom, giggling the entire way. Uncle Frank and Bobby just shook their heads and started for the door.

"C'mon, Jimmy, we're gonna pick up some snacks," Bobby called out.

"Good to know."

"You don't wanna come and find something you like?"

"Nope." Lil' Jimmy knew what they were all up to. They were going to get him to hold all of the bags, then "forget" that he was there and leave without him. He wouldn't be that easy to get rid of.

"Boy!" Uncle Frank boomed, half his face scowling.

Bobby stopped. "It's all right, Uncle Frank. I'll stay in the van with him. Just pick up anything sweet for Lil' Jimmy—he's got a mouth full of sweet tooths."

"Well, all right. I won't be a minute."

Bobby walked back to the van and leaned against its side by the open window his little brother had been shouting through. They snickered at their sister, who was doing the pee-pee dance as she waited for Aunt Miami to finish in the bathroom.

"You could have come out, you know," Bobby said, looking at the fluffy, white clouds as they passed slowly overhead.

"Yup."

After a long bout of silence, Bobby grinned from ear to ear. "You want to hear a super secret story about the Adirondacks?"

"Yeah!" Jimmy shouted, nearly jumping out of the open window.

"Okay, but you can't tell anyone I told you, you know?"

"Okay!"

"Okay, so there are these wild barbarians who survived from the ice age. They live in the mountains up north—deep in the belly of the Adirondacks—and they worship Lavagod, who gave them fire to stay warm at night and to light up their caves. They're harmless, really, except the ones that were exiled—just like you—to live in the forests outside of the mountain. Now the worst, most vile ones—even more dangerous than rabid antelopes—they ride on the backs of deer, but not just any deer—man-eating mutant deer that migrated from Lake Erie. They usually live in Canada, but you know where they live in the spring? That's right—right by the railroad tracks by Uncle Frank's camp. So you'd better be careful this week, because stealing little kids like you and feeding them to the mutant deer is their most favorite thing to do."

When Uncle Frank came lumbering out of the store with a few bags hanging from his massive arms, Bobby quickly made it clear that they should act natural. Jimmy rifled through the bags in search of any goodies while they waited for Lisa to finish using the restroom. There were peaches and apples and oranges and a rainbow assortment of vegetables—mostly peppers, he thought. Frowning, Jimmy grabbed a peach and bit through its fuzzy skin. It was no chocolate bar, but it wasn't as bad as he thought.

Back in the van, Jimmy found himself daydreaming about axe-wielding barbarians chasing down small children as they rode zombified deer. The trip was quieter, having one less person arguing over who was touching who first, or who was "chewing like a cow," or being obnoxious.

When the van first went over the grumbling gravel roads, Jimmy nearly jumped out of his skin. It sounded like a monster was under the van, eating its way through the undercarriage. He looked out the side window again, trying to ignore the noise. The sun was setting now, and the trees on either side of the road had a wicked look about them, like they were going to swallow the van whole before it ever reached the cabin at White Lake.

The rest of the night went pretty much the same for Lil' Jimmy. He jumped at the noises in the woods and kept seeing things moving in the darkness out of the corner of his eye. Even the warmth of the campfire and the comfort of the cabin couldn't soothe his fears entirely, although he did feel safer after his Aunt Miami tucked him into bed for the night.

That night, Lil' Jimmy dreamed he was swimming underwater with a beautiful mermaid. She had long, black locks, like the shadow of a Venetian blind; her skin was dull blue, but her eyes sparkled like the sun glinting off the ocean waves.

Jimmy was there with her, under the water. She was singing, but he couldn't make out the words no matter how hard he strained his ears. It wasn't her half-heard words or her melody, but her eyes that pleaded to him. She was in danger—she needed help! She beckoned to him with wild, flailing arms as she descended deeper and deeper into the depths of the water, disappearing into its darkness.

He reached out to catch her hand, but she was already lost to the shadowy depths. Jimmy panicked, and as he swam up to the surface, he cried for his mother, for his uncle, for anyone to help. Then his head hit something hard and he went dizzy for a moment. A sheet of solid ice covered the surface of the water. It was inches thick, and the young boy knew he didn't have the strength to break through. Then all at once he felt the cold water freeze his joints, and his head ached and his vision blurred as he felt something unrelentingly drag him down deeper toward the bottom.

When Jimmy woke up, he felt like a sick animal in a zoo. Everyone was crowded over him, staring with slack jaws and crumpled faces.

"Are you alright, dear?" Aunt Miami asked as she touched his shoulder to comfort him.

"W-what's going on?" Jimmy asked, looking a little spacey. He was on the cold, hard floor next to his bed, and when he started to get up he felt a sharp pain cut through his skull.

"Just relax, boy, and you'll be fine," Uncle Frank commented casually, with an unlit cigar hanging from his mouth.

"Oh, he's fine—he's just milking it up," Bobby was saying as he threw his arms up in frustration.

"Yeah, what a *baby*. Yelling for help like a little sissy girl," Lisa agreed, with crossed arms and daggers for eyes. "I'm going back to bed. Wake me up when the shower's free."

"Why don't you get breakfast started," Uncle Frank suggested to his wife. "I'll take care of things here." After giving a look to Bobby, who promptly made himself scarce, he turned to Jimmy and said, "And you—you just relax, boy."

"But what happened?" Jimmy asked, still confused but a little calmer.

"You musta had some nightmare, boy. Looks like it scared the piss right outta ya before fallin' out of bed and knockin' your head on the floor. You'll be alright though. Even I get bad nightmares sometimes."

"Really?"

"Really."

"What are they about?"

Uncle Frank chuckled a little to himself. "You're too young to be listenin' to stories like that. I got a bad taste of hell in the war, and it's been hauntin' me ever since. Those ghosts never rest, but I let 'em remind me how much I appreciate bein' here with my family—with you."

Jimmy's face lit up as he smiled. He didn't care that Uncle Frank was a cannibal (not like he believed Bobby anyway!). No one ever seemed to appreciate him, and even though Jimmy was small, and even smaller in comparison to his large-framed uncle, he felt like a giant just then.

"Thanks, Uncle Frank," he said as the hulking man carefully lifted him off the floor and over his shoulder, leaving behind the bloodstained towels.

"Now you hit your head pretty hard, boy, but I think you'll be just fine so long as you take it easy. It'll be healin' right quick. Meantime, I'll be waitin' for you right outside the door here, so you just yell if you need me."

Jimmy nodded and closed the bathroom door behind him. He peeled off his soiled pajamas and Aquaman underwear and threw them in a pile on the floor by the toilet. The shower knobs squeaked as they spun, and Jimmy took great care in adjusting them. Just a micro-nanometer this way or that was the difference between icicles and lava. By the time he got into the tub, the water was a little warmer than preferred, but it was still very refreshing.

His head ached a little, and it stung sharply when he lathered the shampoo in his hair. As much as that one spot hurt, Jimmy couldn't help but rub it. It made him a little dizzy and gave him a pounding headache, though.

When he emerged from the bathroom, a cloud of hot mist exploded from the small room. He was wearing dark blue jeans, his yellow baseball jersey, and a Yankees baseball cap.

"I was thinking," Jimmy started as he met his uncle's gaze. "Do mermaids exist?"

"You were swimmin' in there long enough, boy. You don't know?" Uncle Frank was pointing at the bathroom. Jimmy just stared at him blankly.

"Well, I don't know," Uncle Frank said, rubbing his chin and looking a little embarrassed. "I never seen one, but that don't mean they ain't there."

"I saw a mermaid in my dream, er, nightmare," Jimmy confessed. "She had a beautiful voice and wanted me to follow her to the bottom of the ocean. I didn't want to, so she grabbed me and pulled me down."

"Well, that sounds more like a siren than a mermaid."

Jimmy was confused. "Like on a police car?"

"Not really, boy," Uncle Frank said, his amused smile running only half the length of his face. "They're monsters from the old world. I read a story with them in it a real long time ago that said these sirens were beautiful women who lived in the sea. It said these monsters sang irresistible songs to bait sailors—like fishers use worms on hooks. And when they got close enough, they'd drown 'em right there."

Uncle Frank pantomimed a drowning fisherman for effect, but quickly stopped and changed the subject as soon as he saw Lil' Jimmy's horrified face. “Well I, uh, I think Miami has some bacon ’n’ eggs cooked up ’n’ waitin’ with some fresh juice. A meal fit for we three kings.”

Between the thought of food and Uncle Frank’s hard slap to his back, Jimmy forgot all about his nightmare and ran to the breakfast table. The food and juice tasted strange—alien—but he didn’t say anything. He only chewed slowly and looked at his brother and uncle. They didn’t give the food a second thought, and they didn’t drop dead either. Jimmy figured that was a good sign, although he swore he wouldn’t have missed them if they had. Well, he might miss Uncle Frank a little.

Jimmy kept his distance from White Lake that afternoon, even though everyone looked like they were having a lot of fun splashing about and gliding through the waters, arm over arm. Jimmy didn’t feel so bad though—the place was a breeding ground for mosquitoes and horse flies, and despite the bug repellant and his long sleeves, the winged gremlins bit and harassed him to no end.

And every time Uncle Frank caught him scratching, he yelled, “Damnit, boy! That just makes it worse!” But what did he know? He was old and crazy and half his face never moved anyway.

The day passed by quickly, and before Jimmy knew it the mountain was eating the sun on the horizon. His family sloshed and dripped as they took long strides out of the water. In the van, they all shivered under their beach towels while Jimmy struggled not to scratch his bug bites.

By the fire at the camp they made s’mores and fiery marshmallow torches and laughed at each other’s anecdotes and jokes. Jimmy chased his sister around with a water gun as soon as she finished blow-drying her hair, but then Bobby tackled him and gave him Indian burns, which made his arms itch even more.

Once Uncle Frank finished grilling burgers and hotdogs for everyone, he sighed and sat back in his flimsy lawn chair. He had a strange glaze to his eyes that Jimmy wouldn’t appreciate for many years to come.

“Now this is life,” Uncle Frank commented wistfully. “Ain’t no one ’round to write you speedin’ tickets or break into your house for jewelry and change. It’s just nature here. Just nature.”

No one said anything, and Uncle Frank smiled and handed Bobby a beer.

"Yeah, I can't wait to get away from Mom and the city," Bobby said. "As soon as high school's over, I'm going to whatever college is on the opposite end of the state!"

Uncle Frank listened intently, nodding his head in approval, but Jimmy was more interested in studying the Styrofoam cups and dishes as they were enveloped in blue flames and black smog, watching how they dripped and oozed from his roasting stick into the fiery pit of hell.

When it was time for bed, Jimmy changed into his pajamas and went to the bathroom—he didn't want a repeat of last night or that morning. When Aunt Miami came in to tuck him in and kiss him goodnight, she pulled the sheets a little tighter under the mattress, like that would somehow help.

Jimmy restlessly tossed and turned in the bed, unable to get comfortable. When he tried to count sheep, all he could imagine were mutant deer. Mumbling a few obscene curses about his big brother, he turned on his side and stared at the glowing red numbers on the alarm clock on the nightstand next to his bed. It felt like an hour for every minute that passed, but at least, he discovered, he could count sixty seconds without imagining some sort of monster.

The nightlight in the small room flickered and went out, leaving Jimmy in darkness. Despite the wool blankets, Jimmy shivered uncontrollably, so he instinctively brought his knees up to his chest and curled into a ball to keep warm. He only took his hands out of his armpits to wipe the steady drip of mucous from his nose.

A song colder than ice and more beautiful than his mother floated on the air, but Jimmy couldn't make out any of the words. It sounded sad, though.

WHUMP!

Silence.

"Aunt Miami?" the young boy ventured, gripping himself a little tighter. "Lisa?"

Nothing. Only silence.

"My nightlight went out.... Can you fix it?... I'm scared...."

Again—only silence.

"Please?" Jimmy begged, his voice higher in pitch and full of fear.

"Make another noise and I swear to God I'll gut you like goddamn fish!" boomed a deep voice from the doorway.

Jimmy froze as something large flew through the air and crashed in a heap next to his bed. The door slammed like thunder, rattling the windows and the boy's teeth, and probably waking the dead. He held his breath and waited…to be woken up, to be murdered, to hear his name… he waited for anything, and when he was convinced there was nothing, he looked. He knew what he would see. He knew it was the mermaid—or siren—or whatever. Whatever she was, he knew it was her, and when he turned to look, her face was only an inch away.

Tears streamed down her cheeks from her closed eyes. Her lips trembled as she gasped for air. "Help me. Please help me," she pleaded. "God, please!" She wore a plain-looking brown dress with long sleeves and a trail of buttons up the front, except it was torn about the arms and tattered on the bottom, and most of the buttons had been ripped off to reveal a white bodice hiding underneath it all. Her hair was disheveled too, but looked like once upon a time it had been done up nicely.

"It'll be okay," Jimmy wanted to say, but he was afraid, and his tongue wouldn't work. He only stared at her—dumbfounded—even when he heard the distinct sound of raindrops pinging off the roof and windows. The pinging noise grew louder and louder and more and more persistent, until it sounded like the crackling static of an old radio.

The fish-woman pulled herself up to the windowsill next to Jimmy's bed. Her eyes welled with tears as she grunted and drew herself up and back, ready to jump.

"Wait, no!" Jimmy shouted, but it was too late. As the thin pane of glass shattered, gallons of water gushed into the room as if the outside world was flooded. The mermaid fought the current as the nightstand began to float away. Jimmy squeezed his eyes shut as hard as he could and began to recite the "Our Father," while the mermaid sang the same song from the other night.

The other night! Jimmy thought. *This is a dream! Just a dream!*

As soon as the realization came, the vision ended abruptly. Jimmy bolted upright in his bed, gasping for air and holding his stomach with both hands as though Bobby had just sucker-punched him. But Jimmy knew he was alone in the room. Alone in that bed, with lyrics that crept up his spine in a cold chill and echoed in his brain. Except that the lyrics weren't really lyrics at all. They were a gurgling cry for help.

Jimmy watched the first morning rays sweep over him from toe to head while he caught his breath. As the darkness fled blindly, he saw his blood-soaked pillow. Dabbing at his nose with the back of his hand, he knew where it had all come from.

Throwing the covers off his bed, he grabbed the pillow and ran to the bathroom with panicked elephant feet. He had to wash it out before anyone could see! He could hear his brother and sister now: *You're such a baby, Lil' Jimmy. You make everyone's life a hundred times more difficult. Why can't you just take care of yourself for a change? Or take a long walk off a short pier?*

Jimmy plugged the drain on the bathroom sink and filled it up with steaming hot water. He tore the pillowcase off and plunged it into the sink time and again, every dunk turning the water redder and redder as Jimmy's face went pale with panic. He drained the sink and filled it up again. The water was even hotter this time, and Jimmy couldn't tell if his hands were red from the blood or the heat, but he kept on dunking the case into the water and wringing it out. Then he furiously rubbed the bar of soap against the stain, but it wasn't working very well. It was barely faded.

Jimmy's heart nearly jumped out of his mouth when the doorknob rattled.

"J-just a minute!" he shouted, rubbing the soap in even harder.

"Are you all right in there, sugar?" came Aunt Miami's muffled voice through the door.

"Yes, Aunt M-Miami! J-just finishing up!"

Damnit! Why won't this come out?!

Tears welled in Jimmy's eyes, and he sniffled to keep the bloody snot from dripping out of his nose. His heart raced and he was breathing harder, faster. He had to get out the stains!

"James, sugar, you sure you all right in there? Been ten minutes already."

Shaking now, Jimmy let the sink drain as he wringed out the pillowcase one last time. The sham was still stained, and he couldn't stall any longer. He moved to the window, but before he could open it, he was struck with a flashback of his nightmare when the fish-lady broke the window and caused the flood. A bit dazed, Jimmy decided that the window was a bad idea. Instead, he threw the pillowcase into the toilet's water tank, flushing only to mask the noise he made.

Unlocking and opening the bathroom door, Jimmy was surprised to see Aunt Miami's look of horror.

"Oh, my! What happened, sugar?" Aunt Miami asked as she stroked his unkempt bed-head hair and rubbed his back in circles.

Jimmy was confused. How did she know anything happened? But all his questions were answered when she got a wet washcloth and went to work dabbing at his face. In all his panic to clean the pillowcase, he'd forgotten to clean himself up.

Aunt Miami's brows were furrowed, and she was frowning, worrying. It was the same face his mother made that time she picked him up from school after a gang of bullies beat him up at recess. Jimmy's stomach sank with a low and hollow feeling.

"I'm not hurt, Aunt Miami." *At least not before you rubbed my face half off!*

"You shush now, and let me look you over."

"Yes, ma'am," Jimmy conceded, defeated. Anxious to get it over with, he tapped his foot and watched in the mirror as his aunt went to work on his face. Finally, she inspected his skull like an alien headhunter, twisting and tipping it this way and that.

"You look fine now, but maybe we should call your momma," she said, sighing, as she released her hold on Jimmy's face.

"That's okay, Aunt Miami. I'm all right. Really." Not like he'd rather stay in No Man's Land, but the last thing he needed was to go home to an angry mother. She'd probably ground him for the rest of vacation.

"I'll talk to your uncle about it. No one else is awake, so why don't you go watch some TV for now while I make a nice breakfast?"

"Can I just have scrambled eggs and French toast?"

"Sure thing, sugar," Aunt Miami said as she smiled and hugged her nephew, cradling him in her arms for a moment before she walked down the hall to the kitchen.

Jimmy lay down on the couch in the den and sank into its old cushions. He was greeted with the loud crackling of static and black-and-white specks on the screen. The boy grumbled as he flipped through all the channels. Most of them had no picture at all, a few were semi-stable, with the signal cutting out every few seconds, and only two stations were one hundred percent clear (but still in black-and-white). Groaning, the boy turned off the TV, disappointed and bored.

With nothing else to do, he just relaxed there on the couch and enjoyed the mouthwatering smells wafting in from the kitchen. Before he knew it, his aunt was calling him to the table.

"What's wrong? You don't like my cookin', darlin'?" Aunt Miami asked after Jimmy had played with the food more than he ate it.

"No, ma'am. The food's fine. I…I just don't want it."

"But that's what you asked me to make, isn't it?"

"Yeah, but I'm not in the mood for it anymore. Can you make me a bacon and cheese omelet with hot sauce and black pepper instead?"

"Only if you promise to eat it, darlin'—even if ya don't want it no more."

Jimmy nodded his head and smiled. By the time he and his aunt finished eating, everyone else was awake and hungry. Aunt Miami, of course, served the latecomers breakfast. Meanwhile, Jimmy wandered outside and plopped himself down in a plaid, polyester lawn chair with an aluminum skeleton that sent chills through his bare arms and legs.

Branches calmly bent and swayed against the wind, carrying the smell of last night's campfire. Jimmy closed his eyes and sucked it all in through his nose. All those smells—the flowers, the lingering wood smoke, the freshly cut grass—they were somehow exciting and refreshing. Like magic.

"Hey, Lil' Jimmy—we're gonna chop some firewood," Bobby said as he followed Uncle Frank out the screen door. "Come on."

"Nah."

"C'mon, bud. I'll even let you take the first swing. You just can't tell Mom we let you near an axe, let alone use one."

"Maybe later," Jimmy said apathetically. "I'll watch for now. Take some notes."

"Yeah, right," Bobby said wryly, turning his back on his little brother.

Jimmy watched the tree flail helplessly as Bobby and Uncle Frank hacked at the old and dying giant that was covered in moss and vine. They systematically chopped it into little bits and neatly stacked them in a pile next to the cabin.

His eyes drifted away from the powerless trees and their butchers to an anthill by the fire pit. The miniature and frantic black dots seemed oblivious to the air that rippled through the green grass, intent as they were on assaulting the remains of a burned-out marshmallow. Just the thought of the little creatures made Jimmy's skin creep, and he had to wipe his arms and legs at the thought of anything crawling on them.

Aunt Miami hummed a tune while she washed the breakfast dishes and tidied the kitchen. Even though it wasn't even close, the tune reminded Jimmy of the song the mermaid sang in his dreams. The more he remembered the song—that cry for help—the more Jimmy thought he saw things moving out of the corner of his vision.

"Hey, let's play a board game!" Jimmy suggested as Bobby and Uncle Frank walked up the stairs to the wooden porch and headed into the cabin.

"Like what?" Lisa demanded through the open kitchen window, hands on hips.

"I dunno. Monopoly?"

"You always cheat at Monopoly!" she accused, pointing a finger.

"I do not!" Jimmy shouted, looking very hurt. Lisa raised her eyebrows and cocked her head in doubt, but Aunt Miami insisted that everyone play just as soon as the woodcutters were out of the shower.

Everyone had fun with the game, despite Jimmy's blatant cheating, until a strong wind blew the money all over the den. Then it was 52 pick-up, Charades, Uno, and plenty of Uncle Frank's magic tricks. As the afternoon dragged on into evening, it became clear that the games and tricks just weren't cutting it anymore, and everyone went their separate ways for a while.

"Can we go for a walk?" Jimmy asked finally, his eyes lighting up with hope.

"I don't know, boy," Uncle Frank said, scrunching half his face in thought. "The sun's gonna set soon, and you oughta get goin' to bed."

"It'll be a quick one then. Please, Uncle Frank," Jimmy pleaded with the practiced puppy-dog eyes that always got his mother's sympathy. "When's the next time we'll get a chance like this?"

"How about next year, dorkwad," Lisa shot at her brother.

Jimmy wanted this too much to fight with his sister, let alone acknowledge her. He kept on with the eyes and threw in another, "Pleeeeeeeease, Uncle Frank?" for good measure.

Despite his better judgment, Uncle Frank gave in with a sigh and a grumbling, "Yeah, alright."

Uncle Frank grabbed a flashlight while the kids threw on their shoes and coats. Aunt Miami preferred to stay indoors at night, but she promised she'd have a round of hot chocolate ready and waiting for them.

It was a short walk through the backwoods to the abandoned railroad tracks. With Uncle Frank in the lead, the group walked west, toward the orange and red setting sun.

While Jimmy balanced on the left rail, carefully setting one foot after the next, he listened to the rocks grumble under his uncle's heavy feet. The crickets were out still, serenading any potential mate with a chatter that reminded Jimmy of his sister on the phone.

When the last rays of day leapt over the treetops at them, Uncle Frank gestured with his Magnavox flashlight and said, "Alright, folks, turn yerselves around and we'll head back for cocoa."

Still carefully balanced on the metal rail, Jimmy was the last to turn around, and when he did, everything suddenly went pitch-black, like a giant kite blocked out the sun for miles in every direction. His sister's strong, thin fingers curled around his arm and held on for dear life, pulling him off the rusted rail and into the middle of the track beside her.

He heard his brother whisper, “What the hell?”

“Relax,” Uncle Frank said as his flashlight clicked on, illuminating the tracks in front of them. “Just a rain cloud passing by.”

While Uncle Frank led the way back to camp, Jimmy wondered how a rain cloud could block out all the stars, and just when he built up enough courage to ask, the flashlight flickered as it fought to shine, but ultimately died.

“Ha ha, very funny, Uncle Frank,” Bobby said. “You can turn the light back on. Lil’ Jimmy’s the only one actually afraid of the dark.”

“Damn batteries,” Uncle Frank grunted as he blindly fumbled with the flashlight.

“Yeah, we’re not scared,” Lisa chimed in, though her grip on Jimmy’s arm hadn’t loosened any.

“Looks like we’re gonna have to hoof it back in the dark,” Uncle Frank said, surrendering all further effort to make the device work again.

“Really, Uncle Frank, it’s not funny,” Lisa said, her voice trembling now.

“It’s not me, darlin’. Damn thing’s busted. Now everyone hold hands and stay between the rails and we’ll be back home before you know it. The path is just ahead.”

Everyone shivered and gasped involuntarily as an unusually cold wind cut through them to the bone, and something out of this world appeared in the trees about thirty feet away. It glowed pale white like the full moon and, as it drew nearer, its form sharpened into focus.

“That’s her! That’s her!” Jimmy shouted excitedly, pointing and hopping up and down like a Mexican jumping bean on caffeine.

In one fluid and powerful motion, like a ninja master from a Hollywood blockbuster, Lisa pulled her little brother close and covered his mouth with her hand, nearly suffocating him. It didn’t stop the boy’s mouth from moving, though, let alone curb his excitement, but a swift kick to his shin did the trick.

The specter hovered, head twisted almost backwards, as it weaved between the trees as quick as a jaguar. The woods were filled with the sounds of neighing horses and gallops and gunshots and mad shouting. Everyone’s knees buckled, ready to take action, whether fight or flight.

Then the ghost tumbled and fell, just before the railroad tracks. It didn't move.

Jimmy tried to step forward, but his sister jerked him back by the arm, practically giving him whiplash.

"What are you doing?!" she demanded in an angry whisper.

"It's okay," he said. "She won't hurt us."

"What? Jimmy—!"

But Jimmy didn't wait for her. He slipped away from her iron grip and walked toward the motionless ghost. Her glowing body pulsed with every step the boy took, and every step he took echoed the beating of his heart.

When he was only a few feet away, he felt his sister grab him by the arm again. The apparition disappeared then, fading into nothingness. Lisa closed her eyes and breathed in deeply, cherishing the fresh mountain air. Jimmy felt her balance tip this way and that, and now he held onto her to make sure she didn't fall.

"You okay, Sis?" he asked.

Her eyes opened wide suddenly, and water poured out of her mouth in a stream as she tried desperately to speak or breathe. Tears fell from her eyes as her body convulsed, yet she somehow managed to stay on her feet. She gurgled and nearly broke Jimmy's hand, squeezing it as a large fish wiggled its way up her throat and jumped out of her mouth.

Jimmy's face crinkled in disgust as he stepped out of the way of the flying fish. He watched it as it hopped up and down on the forest floor.

"Eeeeewwww!" he said. Before he could turn back to face his sister, he was tumbling backwards against her, but she didn't look like his sister anymore. Branches and leaves tried to hold him up, but it was futile. All the air in Lil' Jimmy's lungs escaped as he landed flat on his back. Then he heard a sharp crack and felt the ground disappear underneath him. He watched the branches disappear above him as he crashed under freezing cold water, breathing it in as he mindlessly flailed his arms and legs. He sank down and down as his sister held him by the collar and stared into his eyes. She sang the same song the mermaid did, and she wouldn't let go. When he hit the bottom of the black lake, his hand blindly reached out and grabbed hold of a golden locket that shined bright white around her neck.

Jimmy got suddenly dizzy, then felt like he'd just fallen from a one-hundred-story building right onto the pavement. He gasped for air and swatted at his uncle, who looked like he was about to kiss him.

"Damn, boy. You alright?" his uncle asked as the boy coughed.

Jimmy didn't say anything as he scrambled to get to his feet and put some space between him and his uncle. Everything was eerily still—the trees, the off-white clouds, the people. The only noise beside his thundering heart and sharp gasps for air was the sound of some awful retching. His sister was hunched over and leaning against a tree. Bobby stood by, helplessly watching her. She must have been dry heaving.

The fish! Jimmy thought, but it was nowhere to be found, and Uncle Frank looked at him like he had ten heads when he recounted the story.

"I dunno, boy. You musta really hit your head hard. You an' Lisa just plum fell over like someone knocked out your lights. You both seemed to stop breathin' and near gave Bobby and me a heart attack."

"What?" Jimmy couldn't believe it. It had all been so real! He swore to his uncle that he could still smell the water and feel the gold locket in the palm of his tiny hand, but the boy was only wasting his breath.

"Best not to mention this to your Aunt Miami. She'll just make herself sick worryin' all night. Understand?"

Jimmy nodded. It was a simple request, and he doubted his aunt would take him any more seriously than Uncle Frank had. So with head hung low, Jimmy followed his uncle and siblings back to camp. While Uncle Frank and Bobby sipped on their mugs of hot cocoa and exchanged jokes around the kitchen table, Lisa and Jimmy gulped their scalding drinks in silence and went to bed.

Jimmy's eyes closed the moment his head hit the pillow. He walked through the forest, the trees towering above him in an explosion of colors. A flock of birds cawed somewhere above the rainbow canopy, and he heard a rumbling in the distance. *Thunder*, he thought, but then realized the ground trembled in fear. *Or is that my knees?* He couldn't quite tell.

The mermaid lay almost motionless on the ground by a dirt mound—a grave, but whose grave he couldn't tell. He needed to get closer to read the rocky headstone. An eternity passed between each step, no matter how fast he pushed himself to run. The whole world was in slow motion.

A giant spider the size of a subway train emerged from the woods. Its exoskeleton, black and fused to the monster's back, was the waist-up body of a man. He wore a plain, brown, long-sleeved shirt with red suspenders and a hat Jimmy recognized from one of his brother's favorite shooting movies.

Between sobs, the mermaid pleaded for mercy, but the monster spider only smiled viciously as it shot its webbing at her. She shouted once in surprise but went back to sobbing as the spider pulled her closer and closer to its chittering mandibles.

As Jimmy pressed on in slow motion, he watched in horror as the spider swallowed the mermaid whole. He heard her muffled calls through the creature's belly, but stopped dead in his tracks when the man on the spider turned to look at him. The thing, yellow eyes flashing, seemed to stare straight into his soul.

Jimmy bolted upright in bed with a shout, grasping his heaving chest. He struggled not to shiver or breathe hard as the sweat dripped off his body onto the pillows and sheets.

After breakfast that morning, everyone piled into the van to go fishing on Uncle Frank's barge. The family sat in silence and looked out at the landscape as Uncle Frank maneuvered the boat to the deeper part of the lake. Turning the engine off and weighing anchor, Uncle Frank opened the cooler and gave a wine cooler to Aunt Miami and root beer to the kids, then took a beer for himself.

Aunt Miami helped everyone put on suntan lotion while Uncle Frank and Bobby fiddled with the fishing gear and Jimmy poked at the earthworms in disgust. Lisa spread herself out across an empty row of chairs to bask in the sun's glory like a lizard.

Between the boat rocking like a cradle and everyone's relaxed mood, Jimmy nearly fell asleep. He lazily watched the sun rise over the treetops until it was at its peak in the sky. Then the boat shook with excitement and action.

"Wow!" Bobby shouted as he yanked on his fishing rod, bending it like a candy cane as the line quivered taut.

"She's a big one! Pull her in, boy!" Uncle Frank shouted from two feet away. He quickly secured his own fishing pole before jumping up with hands too anxious to help.

"Pull!" he kept shouting. "Pull! Pull! Pull!"

Even Aunt Miami and Lisa watched intently.

Bobby nearly fell over backwards as the fish was pulled out of its watery home. Then he regained control, and the fish flopped and twitched helplessly on the fishing line as the proud young man held it high. Aunt Miami was quick to take pictures, and Uncle Frank was quick to be in them with his oldest nephew. It was a true family moment, and under normal circumstances, Jimmy would not have had any interest in it.

Jimmy watched the fish gasp for air, flaring its gills uselessly, dancing as it dangled. He listened intently to the song it sang.

"Do you hear that?" he asked his sister, amazed.

"Huh?" she said, scrunching her face in confusion. But Jimmy wasn't there anymore. He'd leapt over the edge of the boat, the spray from his dive covering her face.

"Hey, what the…!"

Everyone forgot about the two-foot-long drowning trout that—even starved for breathable air—now flopped closer and closer to the boat's edge. Everyone forgot about the pictures and their drinks and stared into the rippling lake, trying to wrap their heads around what just happened.

"Oh, no," Aunt Miami said, frightened. "He knows how to swim, don't he?"

"He just wants attention," Lisa said dismissively, though her eyes said otherwise.

"Yeah," Bobby whispered.

The two siblings shouted at the center of the rippling water, but there was no response. A few bubbles floated to the surface, but Jimmy did not.

Nobody said anything. Everyone just watched the water intently, searching for a sign—any sign. Uncle Frank's knuckles were white from gripping the side railings so tightly.

"Damnit!" he finally cursed as he tore his clothes off and jumped in after the boy.

While everyone else held their breath, Bobby counted the seconds to himself. He started after Uncle Frank dove in. *Fifty-eight, fifty-nine, sixty, minute one, minute two...*

They'd both been down there an awfully long time, and Bobby was about ready to dive in himself when Uncle Frank finally resurfaced. Jimmy was safe in his arms—or at least alive and breathing—and Bobby helped pull his younger brother aboard while Uncle Frank pulled himself over the side of the boat.

Lisa shouted and jumped away from Jimmy, holding herself with one hand and pointing with the other.

"What the hell is that?!" she demanded.

Everyone's eyes followed her gaze and saw the skull—the human skull—that Lil' Jimmy cradled in his arms.

"Not what," Jimmy said between gasps, "but who. This is Esther. Esther Ostrovsky. That was her name. Is." He was smiling like a hyena and glowing like a firefly.

"What?!" Lisa said. "That's totally gross!"

"Honey, why don't you put that thing down? You don't know where it's been," Aunt Miami pleaded.

"Sure I do. It's been at the bottom of the lake for a long time. A really, really long time."

"Boy, listen to your aunt and drop that thing, and I mean NOW!" Uncle Frank shouted. Jimmy jumped a little and dropped the skull, which rolled toward his shrieking sister.

Uncle Frank called the State Troopers on Lisa's cell phone while Jimmy peeled off most of his clothing. Aunt Miami quickly supplied a dry beach towel, and Jimmy shivered underneath it.

The lake and its surrounding beaches were quickly cleared of locals and tourists alike, leaving Uncle Frank's barge eerily alone. The lake was dead quiet until another boat pulled up alongside Uncle Frank's. The smaller boat carried four State Troopers, two of whom promptly put on rubber gloves and inspected the skull before placing it in an evidence bag. The other two asked a lot of questions and jotted down notes on a pad.

"You can't study her bones or file them away in a warehouse somewhere! You have to give her a burial!" Jimmy insisted, when one trooper asked him what happened.

"What do you mean?" the tall man asked as he crouched down to Jimmy's eye level.

"I've seen *The X-Files* before!" he said. "You can't just put her in a box and forget about her! It's not fair!"

"Don't worry, kid," he said. "I'll make sure she gets a proper funeral, and you'll be the first one invited after we contact the surviving family."

"Really?" Jimmy sniffled.

"Really," the trooper said, smiling warmly. "It's been a long day and I'm sure you're tired. Maybe we can talk some more about 'Esther' later."

Jimmy nodded as the man stood up and straightened his hat and wiped away any wrinkles in his gray uniform. One of the troopers escorted the family back to the shore while the other three stayed on the lake. Jimmy saw that one of them had changed into a scuba suit. The officer sat on the side of the boat and fell backwards into the water.

"Me 'n' Uncle Frank are gonna bring y'all back home tomorrow mornin', sugar," Aunt Miami said in the van. "You can see your friends again and play your video games. We're all just gonna relax for today while your mother gets back in town."

Aunt Miami's explanation was met with silence and blank expressions. The vacation was cut short, which meant Mom's personal vacation was cut short.

Surprisingly, when they got back home, they discovered she wasn't that mad. "Oh, he couldn't stand the spa anyway," she said. "And you know I can't stand a man who can't stand a good spa." That meant they probably wouldn't be seeing Mr. Ray around very much anymore.

The next few weeks went by relatively quietly. There was a strange man who wanted to talk to Jimmy about the skeleton, but he didn't wear a uniform—just a suit. He said he was a reporter, but Jimmy didn't want to talk to him. The man wrote his article anyway. Jimmy didn't pay much mind to it, though.

There was another man at the door a few weeks later. Jimmy saw that it was the same officer who had spoken to him on the barge.

"How're you, Jimmy?" the man asked, crouching down to Jimmy's eye level again.

"F-fine, sir. Thank you," he said, backing up into his mother's legs.

"Come in," she said in her friendliest voice, waving the man inside. "Would you like some coffee?"

"That'll be fine, ma'am. Thank you."

Jimmy sat across from the policeman while his mother put the coffee on.

"Do you remember me, Jimmy?" the man asked.

"Yessir. We talked on my uncle's boat."

"That's right. We found the rest of Esther's skeleton at the bottom of the lake. It took some time, but our experts in the lab dated it back over a century ago. We verified her identity and tracked down her last living relatives. They'd like to personally thank you for solving an old family mystery. I'd be happy to introduce you to them at the funeral. That is, if your mother says you can go."

Jimmy looked at his mother, who smiled back at him and said it would be okay.

"All the details are written down here, and I'd be happy to pay for your hotel for the weekend," he said. "Now maybe I could talk to your momma in private for a few minutes."

"Run along now, Lil' Jimmy. Go play some video games in your room," his mother said, never taking her eyes off the officer. Jimmy left the kitchen reluctantly, and instead of going to his room, he crouched behind the kitchen wall, hidden.

"You've got a real special boy," he overheard the trooper say. "He solves ancient mysteries on vacation. I wonder what he'll do for a day job."

"He is a wily one," he heard his mother reply with a chuckle.

"I think your boy has a right to know what we found out about the case, but I'm afraid he's too young to be told. That's your choice. Either way, this here is the police report."

"What does it say?"

"Not much, officially, but as best as we can piece it together, the victim, one Esther Ostrovsky, was kidnapped in the mid-1800s. Her skeleton shows a lot of blunt force trauma. Obviously she wasn't very well treated. We're not sure why she was down there at the bottom of the lake, but we found chains and a weight among her remains. Reminds me of an old mob hit, but Clancy, our lab guy, doesn't think so. The mob wasn't around back then. Anyway, I doubt anyone will ever know who the kidnapper was or why the crime was committed, but I'm glad that girl can finally be put to rest. Clancy says she was only eighteen or so when she died. Such a shame."

The coffee machine finally stopped gurgling, and he heard his mother pour two cups of coffee. A chair scraped the floor and a weight settled into it.

"This is some business," his mother sighed.

"Thank you, ma'am. Yes, it is."

He listened to his mother nervously tap the old wooden table while she and the officer cautiously sipped at the steaming coffee. Chocolate mint wafted through the air, and the two adults talked about all the boring things that adults love to talk about.

Maybe a half hour later, Jimmy heard the scrape of the kitchen chairs. The trooper grunted a little as he stood up.

"I appreciate the coffee, ma'am. The finest I've had in a long time."

"Thank you for your visit, Officer Ramirez. It means a lot to my boy."

"I'm sure it does. It was a pleasure meeting you, ma'am. You let your boy know he can get a good reference out of me when he's old enough to need one."

"Thank you."

There were footsteps, the front door squealing open and then shut, the twisting of the lock, and heavy footfalls down the stairs. The officer was gone and so was the mermaid. She stopped visiting Jimmy's dreams, and he stopped trying to explain what had happened to him on his spring vacation. No one who was there ever forgot about the strange incident, but none of them ever brought it up again either. And that was that.

Warpath

by Gigi Vernon

Stonespeaker had escaped the watchful eye of his new tribe. Even after so many winters, he was not often allowed to wander off by himself. This morning they'd been too busy with a beaver hunt to notice.

Relieved to be away from them, he stirred the creek's shallows with a stick, listening to the water's song and squinting against the sunlight leaping on the ripples. Among the dull pebbles turned to lustrous beads by water and sun, he spied a black stone that would make a fine arrowhead and reached for it.

Voices mingled with the rushing water. A woman giggled, and he recognized Cornflower Woman. Why had she come for fresh water so far from the hunting camp?

Stonespeaker straightened and peeked around trees to look downstream.

"Ouch, you brute!" Cornflower Woman pushed at a young man who pinned her to the bank.

Stonespeaker was about to run to her aid when she giggled again and said, "You're so impatient. Let me lay down the deerskin rug first." The man propped himself on an elbow and flipped a black braid over his shoulder, the familiar, vain gesture of Blue Jacket.

Shocked, Stonespeaker ducked behind a boulder. It was shameful to couple outside where the sun could see. Not to mention dangerous. Cornflower Woman's husband was proud, jealous, and very, very greedy. He would demand many gifts in return for his wife's favors. Or, he might take offense, which he did easily, refuse the gifts, and start a feud with Blue Jacket.

Stonespeaker had no wish to be involved. He hid, his back against a sun-warmed rock, and waited while the lovers grunted and wrestled among the dry leaves. Above, the autumn trees were the shade of pumpkin and squash, and the Sky World, a deep, cloudless blue.

The couple was well matched. Cornflower Woman was comely, but cruel. As war leader, Blue Jacket had led many raids. Scalps and skulls hung in his longhouse compartment, and his captives had replenished many village families.

At last it grew quiet. Stonespeaker checked, then ventured out. It would be dark soon, and he hurried back to the hunting camp. Before he reached it, he met Blue Jacket carving a tree trunk along the trail.

"Where are you coming from?" the war leader asked.

"Cranberry Lake," Stonespeaker lied and indicated the opposite direction from the creek. "Gathering points for arrowheads." He showed the war leader his haul as proof.

"They'll make fine arrows," Blue Jacket said disdainfully. He himself had no need of arrows. He had a white man's musket, the only warrior in the village to possess one. The war leader beckoned him close. "See this record?" His fingers lovingly traced the gruesome pictures and symbols carved into the tree trunk. "This was my raid. Ten winters ago. I led thirty warriors. We burned two of the Tree-Eaters' villages, killed their warriors, and took many scalps." His knife dug at the image of a captive being led by the neck, freshening its blurred edges. "Twelve captives we dragged home over this trail."

The war leader's words were thick with menace. Did Blue Jacket suspect Stonespeaker had overheard him with Cornflower Woman?

Threats were not needed. Stonespeaker would say nothing for fear of the war leader. As if it were yesterday, he remembered the raid on his own people when he himself had been taken captive by a smiling, blood-drenched Blue Jacket. Unlike the defeated warriors of his village, all killed, Stonespeaker was one of the lucky captives. Young and smart, he was adopted and given a new life—as long as he forgot the old one. Showing that he remembered meant torture and agonizing death by burning at the stake. He assumed a cheerful mask with the war leader now.

Blue Jacket fell into step with him. "We'll need your arrowheads. You will need them."

"Why is that?"

"It's time you came on a raid."

Who did Blue Jacket plan to raid? Stonespeaker glanced sideways at the war leader, but he didn't dare ask. His feet were suddenly heavy. He was no warrior. No one expected it of him, or so he thought. The villagers joked that he flinched when his arrow felled a doe.

Over the course of the next moons, Stonespeaker told no one what he knew about Blue Jacket, not even his adopted younger brother, Squirrel. Having no wish to risk more encounters with the lovers, he made no trips to the creek, the lake, or into the forest alone. He hunted and fished with Squirrel or the others.

He avoided Cornflower Woman and her husband, Wolf Claw.

Wolf Claw was disliked by most, but he and Blue Jacket struck up a sudden friendship, hunting together and talking of battles around the fire in the evenings. It was as if the two men had come to an understanding, but if they had, Blue Jacket and Cornflower Woman would have gone about openly together. They did not. Instead, the lovers pretended they were strangers, never locking eyes, touching, or speaking.

Most of all, Stonespeaker avoided the war leader. When Blue Jacket approached, Stonespeaker found a reason to leave. It was not easy. Time and again, he narrowly managed to avoid stalking moose or searching out beaver dams with the war leader.

Stonespeaker grew afraid that the others might notice his odd behavior and interpret it as the disloyalty of a former captive. He became even more helpful and hard working. He renewed his efforts to memorize the tribe's sacred songs and dances, so that he would not make mistakes that would offend their spirits.

Meanwhile, the trees dropped their leaves. The days grew shorter and colder as the Master of Life weakened. In the mornings, the Frost Spirit's breath coated the world. When the first snow came, the camp packed up the venison, the moose and beaver meat, and the pelts, and traveled south on trails through the dense forest known only to them.

Back at the village, Blue Jacket called a war council, where he spoke eloquently. He lamented the pitiful number of beaver pelts they had taken. He argued that the tribe needed more to trade for all manner of good things—knives, hoes, iron kettles, axes, and more of the Whites' muskets.

But Stonespeaker suspected that Blue Jacket had greater ambitions for the weapons. Under his leadership, the Man-Eaters, as the tribe was delighted to be called by their enemies, would earn their name. They would drive away the Tree-Eaters and wipe out the Stammerers, as they called Stonespeaker's own people.

Blue Jacket proposed an ambush. Before the lakes and rivers froze and became impassable to canoes, the Tree-Eaters would make the season's last expedition to trade with the Whites. A war party led by Blue Jacket would attack, kill the Tree-Eaters, take their pelts, and trade them for muskets.

The younger, inexperienced warriors admired Blue Jacket and enthusiastically supported his strategy. Their elders and clan matrons were less keen; they knew the perils of winter warfare. After lengthy discussion, the war council approved Blue Jacket's plan.

In celebration, the young warriors gathered around the fire in the village's center, laughing, dancing, and bursting into snatches of war songs.

Squirrel intended to be among the first to volunteer for the war party. "Elder brother," he said to Stonespeaker, who was standing at the edge of the crowd around the fire, "Come with me. It's time for us to become men."

Blue Jacket overheard. "Yes, both of you must come, especially Stonespeaker, with his skill mending and making arrows."

Stonespeaker did not trust his words. He knew this was a test of loyalty to his new people. In the days before the raid, he feigned a lingering sickness, but when the entire longhouse eyed him with suspicion, he recovered.

Grandmother proudly helped him and Squirrel prepare for the journey, stuffing their packs with dried meat, cornmeal, and warm hides. Stonespeaker hid his reluctance in the shadow of Squirrel's excitement. For the feast the night before their departure, they painted each other's faces with fierce designs and shaved their heads, leaving only a strip of bristling hair. Squirrel insisted on painting their chests and limbs too, even though they would be covered by deerskin.

Throughout the ceremonies and the final leave-taking procession, Stonespeaker warmed his cold heart with the thought that they would fight against the Tree-Eaters, and not his own people.

By the time they set out, the snow was shin-deep, and the war party clambered awkwardly in their snowshoes, single-file behind their war leader. The snow deepened as they traveled north. On the fifth day, they reached a rough hunting camp of bark huts tucked in the hollow of a hillside. They made fires and cooked a stew.

The next morning, Blue Jacket explained how they would ambush the Tree-Eaters when they carried their canoes from Lake-that-is-the-Gate through the woods to Where-the-Mountains-Close-in Lake.

"You two climb up the near side of the mountain," Blue Jacket ordered Stonespeaker and Squirrel. "Find a place with a good view of the woods Between-Two-Lakes. Keep watch. When you spy them, signal with the caw of a crow."

Blue Jacket pointed at four warriors. "You others do the same on the other sides of the mountain. Spread out. If you hear the signal, pass it along." He surveyed the remaining warriors. "Wolf Claw, you and I will scout upwind. You two scout downwind. The rest of you take cover at the bottom of the mountain, out of sight but within earshot."

Stonespeaker's heart lightened. He would be too far away to take part in any battle, and Blue Jacket would be elsewhere. Happily, he climbed, forging ahead of Squirrel. Near the top of the mountain, they found a gap in the bare trees with a good view of Between-Two-Lakes. Any movement would be easily seen against the white emptiness. They settled in. Stonespeaker's eyes burned with the effort of keeping his gaze from drifting towards the rising sun where his own people lived.

A wall of cloud slowly rolled towards them, swallowing them by afternoon. Fine snowflakes like ash sifted down, and the world below disappeared behind a grey curtain. Since he and Squirrel could no longer see, they decided to head down. As they hauled on their packs, a gunshot thundered below and echoed upwards.

"Come on! The battle has begun!" Squirrel bounded down, heedless of rocks and trees.

Stonespeaker followed more carefully.

As they neared the valley, a second shot rang out, louder than the first.

A brash warrior by the name of Man-Who-Sees-Through-Darkness made hand signals, directing them to join the others moving stealthily through the forest, bows drawn, arrows nocked.

Someone crashed heedlessly through the undergrowth towards them. The warriors stepped behind trees for cover. Stonespeaker leaned against a trunk to hold his trembling bow steady.

Blue Jacket staggered into view, panting, his ear and neck bloody. They lowered their weapons and ran to meet him.

"We were attacked!" The war leader braced himself on a tree, chest heaving, unable to speak.

"Where is Wolf Claw?" Stonespeaker asked.

Blue Jacket coughed. Between gasps, he answered, "Killed! By a hunting party of Stammerers!"

Before Stonespeaker caught himself, he jerked his head to see if the Stammerers were still there. Two warriors caught the gesture.

"They tried to kill me, too! But they have bad aim and only nicked my earlobe." Blue Jacket wiped at the blood.

"The curs! Where are they? We will kill them all!" Man-Who-Sees-Through-Darkness shook his war club.

The boast drew forth whoops from the others.

"I frightened them off when I shot my musket," Blue Jacket said and straightened.

"Cowards!"

"We will chase them down!" Man-Who-Sees-Through-Darkness urged.

Stonespeaker eyed the grey sky. "It will be dark soon and the moon will be hidden by snow."

Suspicious gazes turned on him.

"But I know we can catch them," Stonespeaker hurriedly added. He was surprised when the war leader found a log and sat.

"First, I must reload," Blue Jacket said. He scooped up a handful of snow and ate it thirstily. After two more leisurely mouthfuls, Blue Jacket began the complicated, delicate process of measuring out powder, then feeding it and lead nuts to the musket.

When he was at last ready, they set out. Blue Jacket led the way, the others jogging in his wake, weapons ready. In the rear behind his brother, Stonespeaker wondered what he would do if they met up with the hunters. He hoped they did not.

Before long, they came upon Wolf Claw, lying face down in the snow, clutching his bow, the deerskin on his back bloody and sooty from a musket's explosion.

Stonespeaker surveyed the surrounding forest. The trees were evenly spaced and bare. No thickets or pines could have concealed an ambush.

But then how had Wolf Claw been surprised? Where had the hunting party been? How had he been shot in the back?

Convinced the Stammerers were long gone, Blue Jacket and several others began to prepare the corpse. The others, craving the war leader's praise, fanned out to search for the enemy.

Stonespeaker joined the searchers combing the woods Between-Two-Lakes. He dreaded the discovery of a dead member of his former clan, or worse, a wounded warrior who would be taken captive and tortured. A blood-tipped arrow caught his eye, and he picked it up.

With relief that gradually turned to puzzlement, Stonespeaker saw no trail of blood and no footprints or signs of canoe portage. The dusting of snow could not have covered the tracks of even one man let alone a band of warriors.

Man-Who-Sees-Through-Darkness suggested that the Stammerers must have used powerful magic to cloak their escape, but Squirrel and the others scoffed at the idea and decided they'd simply missed the tracks in the thickening dusk. The searchers gave up and turned back as snow began to fall more heavily.

By the time they rejoined the war party, the funeral song had been sung, and the cremation pyre licked Wolf Claw's bones. The greasy smoke tasted of roasting flesh.

The searchers reported their failure, which Blue Jacket accepted without comment.

Stonespeaker asked the war leader, “Which way did the hunting party flee?”

“Towards their villages, of course,” Blue Jacket said in a tone meant to squelch questions.

“Are you sure the hunters weren’t Tree-Eaters?” Stonespeaker asked.

“Yes.” The war leader glared at him.

“But the Stammerers have no muskets.”

“They do now.”

Then why had they shot at Blue Jacket with bows? And why had Stonespeaker found only one arrow?

Wolf Claw’s weapons lay in a heap on the ground. Stonespeaker glanced from the arrow he still carried to Wolf Claw’s full leather quiver. The fletching matched.

Had the two argued over Cornflower Woman?

Had Wolf Claw grown angry, shot at the war leader, and nicked him?

Had Blue Jacket shot at Wolf Claw and killed him? Then fired a second shot to cover up the deed?

Or, had the war leader planned to murder the jealous husband all along?

No; Stonespeaker’s fear and dislike of the war leader had fired his imagination. He flung the arrow into the pyre.

A gust of wind flattened the flames and smoke. Across the blaze, Blue Jacket stared at him, his eyes full of hate. And Stonespeaker knew without a doubt that Blue Jacket had planned to murder Wolf Claw and intended to kill Stonespeaker next before he could tell others.

Despite the cold, Stonespeaker was suddenly drenched in sweat.

“We must take vengeance,” Blue Jacket announced. “Tomorrow we will head for the villages of the Stammerers.”

Jubilant whoops burst from the others.

His legs trembling, Stonespeaker asked, “What about the raid on the Tree-Eaters?”

“That can wait,” Blue Jacket said.

Back at the shelter, the others chattered into the night about the upcoming battle.

Stonespeaker could not eat. Shivering uncontrollably, he rolled himself in a hide and curled against the wall. The others bedded down late. Under his hide, Stonespeaker drew his knife in case he had to defend himself against Blue Jacket. Through the long, sleepless night, he listened to Blue Jacket's snore, watched the fire slowly die, and worried.

By the next morning, a thick layer of fresh snow covered all footprints. They jogged fast and wordlessly south along the shore of Where-the-Mountains-Close-In Lake. At the back of the line, Stonespeaker turned his predicament over and over in his mind. How could he stop the war leader and prevent the attack? If he made an accusation, it would be his word against Blue Jacket's. The war leader was respected by the young warriors. No one would believe an adoptee.

The snow steadily became less deep. On the third day, Stonespeaker began to recognize familiar landmarks. When he smelt the smoke of longhouse fires, he knew it was time to act. He wanted his younger brother to understand his leave-taking, so he whispered the entire story to Squirrel.

Squirrel halted abruptly. "No. He wouldn't do that. Blue Jacket's not a murderer."

In front of him, Man-Who-Sees-Through-Darkness turned and asked, "What?"

Before Stonespeaker could stop him, Squirrel repeated the story, then shouted to the front of the line, "Blue Jacket! Did--"

"Did you murder Wolf Claw?" Stonespeaker cut his younger brother off before Squirrel earned the undying enmity of the war leader.

The line froze. The war leader wheeled and strode towards the back. "Who tells such lies?"

"How was Wolf Claw killed from behind? Why did no one see the enemy, or find their tracks afterwards?" Stonespeaker asked.

The war leader stopped in front of Stonespeaker and tried to stare him down. "I told you. We were attacked."

"You and Cornflower Woman are lovers. You argued with her husband and killed him because you wanted her all for yourself," Stonespeaker said as he took a step backwards.

Blue Jacket turned to his warriors. "He is not to be trusted. He has spun this tale to protect his people."

Squirrel and one or two of the others frowned with doubt.

"I speak the truth," Stonespeaker said, backing clumsily in his snowshoes.

"He's still a Stammerer. We were wrong to trust him."

There were murmurs of assent.

"He's false. He has not become a true Man-Eater." Blue Jacket spat and unsheathed his knife.

Stonespeaker turned, dropped his pack, bounded to the crest of a steep incline, and threw himself on his back, covering his head with his hands. He slid down, bouncing against stones and branches poking through the snow, and came to rest against a tree trunk at the bottom. Bruised, he stood shakily, then bolted into the forest. His broken snowshoes flapped uselessly on his feet, threatening to trip him, and he tore them off and flung them away.

Above, he heard yells. Ignoring the sharp pain in his side, he fled, slipping and sliding in the snow. His feet remembered the way before his mind. They led him to a wood of densely-packed fir trees. He dove in and plummeted along a faint track between branches which whipped and slashed him. If it weren't for the snow, he might have escaped. But his tracks would lead them to him. His only chance was to outrun them.

Terror quickened and steadied his feet. If they caught him, they would not let him live. This time, he would be scalped, carved up, and burnt alive. But he would not allow them to take him again.

And then he realized he was leading them to his village. He stopped, his lungs bursting and his thighs and calves burning. Blue Jacket had caught him in a clever trap, as he had caught Wolf Claw.

The wind carried muffled voices to him. He tore off again, each breath knifing his side. Bursting out of the woods, he crossed a cleared field. An arrow brushed his sleeve and fell harmlessly to the ground beside him. He glanced over his shoulder and saw the war band emerge from the forest and shoot at him.

On the other side of the field, he found a once-familiar path and rounded a bend out of sight and arrow range. Ahead, perched on a short steep hill, was his village, enclosed in its stockade.

He was home. Heart pounding, he lunged up the path and shouted a warning.

Warriors poured out of the stockade, bows drawn. He recognized none of them.

And they didn't recognize him.

He stopped, realizing he looked like a Man-Eater, and called out a greeting. It was too late. Arrows bit his shoulder and leg. He stumbled, then fell into the snow face first.

Both sides promptly forgot him. Arrows flew overhead.

His cheek pressed into the snow, Stonespeaker watched the attacking warriors below send their loose arrows at his village. He hoped he'd given enough warning for his people to vanquish the Man-Eaters.

Blue Jacket raised the musket and took aim. It boomed, enveloping the war leader in a puff of smoke and a burst of flame. The smoke cleared. Blue Jacket collapsed to his knees, covering his bloody, blackened face with smoking fingers. The untrustworthy weapon had exploded in his hands!

His stunned warriors fell quiet and still. Pelted with arrows from above, they slunk towards the trees in retreat, pulling their blinded war leader away.

The defenders leapt over Stonespeaker. Tomahawks and war clubs in hand, they pounded downhill in pursuit.

Stonespeaker smiled. It was Blue Jacket's turn to be taken captive.

Old Family Business

by Cheryl Ann Costa

Adirondack General Hospital Morgue—Friday, 5 April 1935, 12:15 P.M.

I had just finished lunch and I was in the process of greeting my next "patient," the polite term we use for the next stiff. When he passed away on one of the wards, some staff physician made a death pronouncement and filled out the details and time of death on his chart. With that, an orderly brought the patient to the morgue for cold storage.

From there the decisions are rather simple. If the cause of death is clear, we simply release the body to the funeral home of the family's choice. On the other hand, if the circumstances of the death are unknown or questionable, the staff pathologist can make a determination to perform an autopsy. After the untimely heart attack death of our staff pathologist, Dr. Harry Williams, two weeks ago, the tasks of managing the morgue had fallen to me: Dr. Angela Joy Patterson, deputy pathologist on loan from the Department of Surgery.

"Good afternoon, Dr. Patterson," croaked Shelly, the morgue attendant, in her whiskey-tempered voice.

"Hi, Shelly." What I like about Shelly is her military-like efficiency in getting right to the task at hand.

"The chart says he died of a stroke, AJ."

"Well, let's look him over."

When Shelly lifted the sheet, we both immediately saw a couple of nasty-looking scars on his upper torso. Shelly, a seasoned diener, pointed with her gloved finger at a ragged scar in the middle of his right shoulder, “That’s a nasty job of stitching.”

“Sure is, looks like an old gunshot injury, the classic flesh wound.”

Shelly gave it a closer look, “Think he got it in the war, Doc?”

“Don’t know, maybe.” I focused my attention on the two very old, ragged, gash scars below his left breast.

“Looks like he had a knife fight a long time ago,” I commented as I motioned for Shelly to help me turn our patient over. I began a discerning gaze down the man’s neck and back, looking for other new and old injury sites.

Unlike your average hometown doctors who might have a very close and casual relationship with the patients in their practice, surgeons are specialists. Their involvement with a patient is usually by referral, or in the worst case, by critical necessity. For the most part, I have found that the relationship between a surgeon and patient is akin to two ships passing in the night.

“Hey AJ, look on his backside, looks like a well-healed surgical scar.”

“That’s my handiwork!” As a resident staff surgeon at a regional hospital in small and sleepy Plattsburgh, New York, I find that I get a very curious feeling every time evidence of my surgical style turns up again on the autopsy table with some long-forgotten patient.

“You operated on Mr. Baril?”

“Yes, I did, Shelly; if memory serves correctly, he had a shotgun slug in his buttocks.”

Shelly looked fascinated. “When was that, AJ?”

I thought for a long moment. “It was a few years ago, just after I was hired.”

“Did you know that Baril was one of the best-known smugglers in this part of the country?” Shelly queried in an excited tone.

“Nope, I had just moved here from Raleigh, North Carolina. But let’s just focus on the job and perhaps I’ll talk to you about it later over dinner.”

Getting distracted during one of these death certificate exams is not a good thing; besides, I didn’t want to get involved in this conversation just now.

Shelly nodded and refocused on the examination task at hand. “Hey

AJ, look at his feet."

Glancing at his feet, I saw swollen, discolored, ulcerated tissue. For a man of his sixty-three years, with a fatty French-Canadian cuisine and most certainly a habit of drinking liquor to excess, the cause was obvious: diabetes. His thick, glucose-saturated blood would have played havoc with his circulation for years. The long-term result was that his feet had become numb from nerve damage and bad blood flow; the tissue then began to swell and ulcerate. Even with the neuropathy numbness, they must have been painful to walk on.

"What do you think, Doc?"

"In my humble opinion, he's been a coffin dodger for some time now; for his heart, pumping his blood must have been like pumping maple syrup. If a clot in his brain hadn't killed him, I think his kidneys would have given out real soon."

I began to jot down my notes on Mr. Baril's chart. Satisfied with the attending physician's final diagnosis, I didn't see any reason to perform an autopsy.

"Shelly, put our patient back in storage and type up the certificate for my signature."

We found nothing out of the ordinary for a man of his years, beyond a few horrid trophy scars that were a testament to an adventurous life in the smuggling business. After an external examination and a careful reading of his chart, the obvious cause of death for the infamous Mr. Francois Baril was an unremarkable, garden-variety stroke. An understated end, I must say, for someone renowned for illegal exploits that were the stuff of local tavern legend.

Adirondack General Hospital Morgue—Friday, 5 April 1935, 6:37 P.M.

It had been a long day, but at least the afternoon was memorable. My task was a simple medical autopsy on an indigent John Doe, some down-on-his-luck-hobo, who from the looks of him, fell off a fast freight train passing through town.

The amusing part was that seventeen students from the Plattsburgh Normal College biology class were here to observe the dissection of a human body. While a routine autopsy takes perhaps two, maybe three hours, this one took all afternoon due to no less than eight of the students getting sick during the procedure. While the first half-dozen were smart enough to cover their mouths and get out early, there were these two Joe-college guys who tried to tough it out. One managed to puke all over the swinging doors on his way out. The other, much to Shelley's delight, hurled his misery all over our observing hospital administrator. Needless to say it was an entertaining afternoon.

"Hey, AJ, I'm ready for a brew," Shelly said in a cheerful tone. "You ready to get out of here?"

The two of us had just finished our showers and were about to leave the small locker room adjoining the morgue facilities when we both heard the elevator squeak to a stop. We gave each other that look, hoping it wasn't another patient at quitting time. Shelly was dressed and gestured that she'd attend to the matter. "I'll make this short and sweet."

She left the locker room in a huff, forcing a smile as she pushed through the door. I finished drying off from my shower and proceeded to get dressed. A few minutes later she returned. "Just a diener from the Bessette Funeral home to get Mr. Baril," she croaked with a grin. He's doing the paperwork; we'll be out of here in less then ten minutes."

With a sigh of relief I remarked, "Phew, I was hoping it was something easy."

That's when we both heard the elevator make another squeaky arrival. This elicited another pregnant pause as we looked at each other with a grimace of dread. Shelly grabbed her purse and slammed her locker shut, muttering, "Whoever it is, I'm telling them the patient will still be dead in the morning, so they have to come back tomorrow!"

I could hear some murmured conversations in the business area as I dabbed a touch of color to my lips. I was admiring the shade of my Max Factor lipstick when I heard a crash from the reception area and a single scream from Shelly.

"AJ, HELP!"

Immediately, I pushed through the swinging door into the morgue reception area. To my shock, there were two men in dark suits engaged in a fistfight and cussing at each other in French. Meanwhile, on the floor, Shelly was trying to avoid being tramped by the two scrappy men dancing about like wild stallions. I pushed between them trying to break it up.

"Gentlemen, that will be enough!"

Jesus said to turn the other cheek, but I don't think he was talking about two angry French-Canadians. Neither of them hesitated to take a swing, each hitting me in the face and knocking me on my keister as they continued their combat.

Shelly by this time had managed to get to the desk phone and call upstairs for help. Then in a brilliant moment of inspiration, she grabbed a fire extinguisher off the wall, turned it over, and aimed the hose. Instantly volumes of white, watery foam erupted from the nozzle. She doused each of the men and slowed them down a bit, just as two orderlies from the psych ward came rushing out of the stairway. They each grabbed a sloppy, foamy ruffian and put him in some type of hold. Within minutes there was help from other floors pouring down the stairs and out from the elevator. A short time later, the police arrived and attempted to sort everything out.

I sat watching a couple of orderlies mop up the mess from the extinguisher while a nurse applied an ice pack on my left jaw and another on my right cheek.

"You're going to have a shiner, AJ," Shelly observed.

I moaned in acknowledgement; it's not like I had a hot date planned or anything, certainly not in sleepy Plattsburgh. Of course, folks working the wards would be chatting about the big fight in the morgue for weeks.

Shelly walked over to me with an older-looking man in a police uniform. "Doctor Patterson, the police chief wants to talk to you about what happened here." I just nodded, finding it painful to open my mouth.

"It's this way, Doc," the chief said in a gruff voice as he paused to look at his little notebook. "It seems you have a stiff here, a Mr. Francois Baril."

"There's some confusion as to which of the funeral homes these guys work at is supposed to pick up Baril's body," he said with a contented smirk on his face.

I could only stare at the constable in a moment of utter disbelief as Shelly chimed in, “Must be a serious mix up! Chief, who called the two funeral homes?”

Again the chief thumbed a page or two in his notebook. “Well, the Bessette mortuary guy says the daughter; the Proulx funeral home fellow insists that the widow called them.” I gave Shelly a perplexed look as the two undertakers started cussing at each other again on the other side of the room.

“Now what?” the chief groaned. “Bring them over here,” he barked to his officers. Both men were grabbed by the collar and shoved over towards the chief. “OK, what’s the problem?”

A short, pudgy, polite-looking man in a spoiled suit spoke up. “L'officier, I was told to apporter le cadaver,” the short diener reported. “La maison funèbre de Proulx a servi la famille de Baril pendant des années.”

Shelly, a native French speaker, translated. “He says he was sent to get the body and that the Proulx Funeral Home has served the Baril family for years.”

Agitated, the other guy, a tall, skinny blond fellow, spoke up in clear English. “But the Bessette service was called by the daughter.”

The police chief looked at me with a perplexed expression. “What do you want to do, Doc?”

I’d gazed at both men for a few moments when Shorty spoke up. “Docteur, ce qui nous faisons, nous les deux hava un contrat.”

Blondie piped in, “Yeah, we both have a contract!”

At this point, I didn’t care who did the services; all I knew was that this was cutting into my precious Friday evening considerably. I just wanted it settled. I put my ice packs down, got up, and walked through the swinging doors that led to the autopsy room. A few moments later, I returned to the reception area and held up a shiny bone saw and announced, “Gentlemen, suppose we settle this like ole King Solomon; how about I cut the old man in half so each of you can satisfy your precious contracts?”

The chief looked stunned, and I could see Shelly doing her best to contain her laughter. Of course neither of the funeral home reps thought it was funny.

I gave them both a stern look and scolded, “Gentlemen, I suggest you go over in the corner and work this out peacefully; you have ten minutes.”

Both men seemed to wilt as they cowered in a “tail-tucked” manner over to a remote corner of the reception area to work things out.

The police chief spoke in a hushed tone, “Doc, do you really think they’ll come up with an arrangement?”

By this time I had put down the bone saw and was reseated and reapplying the slushy ice packs. I just looked at the chief and nodded, muttering a simple, “yep.” A few minutes later the two funeral home representatives returned with the tall blond one speaking for both of them.

“We have decided that since Mr. Baril is such a well known business man, it will take both of our businesses to do this properly. The Proulx service will prepare and embalm the body and provide the casket. The Bessette service, with its bigger viewing room, will host the wake and the funeral services.”

The short guy from Proulx chimed in, “Les deux services faciliteront le voyage au cimetière pour l'inhumation.”

The tall Bessette representative nodded his head in agreement and translated, “Yes, as my colleague said, and both services will coordinate transportation to the cemetery for the interment.”

Both men, and even the police chief, looked at me expectantly, waiting for my response. I thought about it for a minute and figured that sounded fair. I told the chief that neither Shelly nor I would press charges, and most likely the hospital wouldn’t either, if they kept their bargain. Both men politely agreed. It took another twenty minutes for Shelly and the Proulx diener to get the corpse out to the hearse.

Plattsburgh Diner—Friday, 5 April 1935, 9:05 P.M.

Exhausted from all that had happened, Shelly and I sat nursing a couple of beers while waiting patiently for our supper. The whole day was strange from the get-go, and we both knew it. Shelly and I have that kind of unique friendship that allows two people to sit for long periods without saying a whole lot, but I didn’t think this was going to be one of those times. I could see the wheels turning in Shelly's eyes.

"Here we go you two," Lauren, our waitress, announced in a cheerful way as she carefully set a large serving tray on our table.

"Mashed potatoes, gravy, and pot roast for you, Shelly, and broiled haddock with baked potato and broccoli for AJ."

Lauren asked if there was anything else; we both indicated we could use refreshers on our beers, and she went away to get them and then attend to other customers.

"So tell me about you and Francois Baril?" Shelly asked as she started to pick at her mashed potatoes. I sat for moment staring blankly at my haddock.

"There's not a lot to tell."

Shelly gave me one of those "you've got to be kidding" expressions.

"It was just a brief, chance encounter, nothing more," I remarked as I spread some butter on the haddock.

"AJ, doing surgery on a man is not a chance encounter."

She was right. I figured I better tell her so she wouldn't run off half-cocked and start a bunch of gossip that could get me in a whole lot of trouble.

"OK hon, but this is for your ears only; you have to promise never to speak of it again," I told her in a serious voice. Shelly sipped her beer with an amused look on her face, then asked in a hushed tone, "Good God, AJ, what did you do, have his baby or something?"

I gave her a stern, "this is serious" look. She settled down and nodded her head.

"Yes, AJ, mum's the word," she said; then as an afterthought, she qualified, "Promise."

So I took a bite of my haddock and began to relate how I came to do surgery on Francois Baril. I had been working for the U.S. Public Health Service since I graduated from the Columbia School of Medicine in 1929. In those early days of the Depression, if you had a medical license and were breathing, the Public Health Service would hire you, even if you were a female surgeon. I was assigned to work in the Logan Coalfields of West Virginia, where the patients were dirt poor and sick as hell.

In 1931, somebody who knew somebody in Plattsburgh recommended me for a staff surgeon's job at Adirondack General. Being a gal from the South, initially I didn't relish the idea of living in upstate New York where the winters were purported to be harsh, but I finally decided to take the job. I'd been in Plattsburgh barely a month, living as a boarder in a respectable rooming house on Broad Street run by a Mrs. Edna Miller, when early one Sunday morning, Mrs. Miller came knocking on my door. She had this urgent look on her face.

"Dr. Patterson, please get your doctor things, someone's been hurt and needs your help," she whispered, trying to not wake up the rest of the house.

I was half awake and exhausted from working back-to-back shifts at the hospital the day before. I quickly got dressed and followed her to a cottage behind her house. When we entered the bungalow, she led me to a small bedroom. On the bed was a rather handsome but scruffy man with a few days' beard growth. He looked to be in his late fifties. He was lying on his belly, holding a bloody towel to his right buttock. When he saw me, he remarked to Mrs. Miller in French-accented English, "I told you to get me un docteur! Not this fille."

"She is a doctor," the landlady responded, "Now let her work."

Mrs. Miller motioned to me to proceed. I put my hand tenderly on his and gently lifted his hand and the towel. Finding an obvious gunshot wound, I announced to them that this should be treated at the hospital. They both gave me a look in the negative; the man, struggling with the pain, moaned and said firmly, "No hospital and too many questions."

He knew that if I treated him in the hospital, I would have to report the gunshot wound to the authorities. During my two years in West Virgina, I quickly learned when something had to be done on the sly. I told him I could keep my mouth shut and that I would do my best to treat him, and he seemed to relax. Then I told Mrs. Miller to boil some water so I could sterilize my surgical tools. While I was cleaning up the wound the injured man broke the uncomfortable silence, "Docteur, my name is Francois."

I asked him about the nature of the gunshot and who shot him, half expecting that it had been some jealous husband.

"Mademoiselle, it was a shotgun," he paused for a moment. "The gunner was a revenue man."

I did my best to not be bothered by the revenue man remark, or by the whiskey Mrs. Miller brought to me. I gave Francois four shots; it was during the Prohibition, so I didn't ask where she got it. The whiskey made him a bit less lucid but it soon became obvious the man could hold his liquor.

After Mrs. Miller sterilized my surgical instruments with boiling water, I mixed an anesthetic from a glass ampoule of powdered Tetracaine. Making what I estimated to be a five percent solution, I injected a small amount into a nerve bundle near the wounded area. In a couple of minutes I could tap on and around the wound without getting a reaction from the patient. Again, I told Francois that this whole thing would be better done at the hospital. Again he slurred, "Noo hospit--, no quest--ns."

Using a sterilized glass turkey baster, I irrigated the wound using some of the boiled water. After a few minutes, I found and removed the slug without too much trouble. After a few more moments of probing, I found the corresponding chunk of pants fabric that got taken into the wound with the slug. Again I irrigated and did my best to make sure the wound was clean. I stitched up the wound and my incision with sterilized gut I had on hand in my bag, then I packed the area with gauze and taped the gauze pads with adhesive tape.

After cleaning up from the surgery, Mrs. Miller fixed us some tea, and I sat with Francois for a couple of hours to make sure there were no immediate complications. It was during this time that he told me his last name and admitted that he was a smuggler. His business was bringing things back and forth across the border. He said that since the start of American Prohibition, the majority of his business was bringing alcoholic beverages across the border into the States. He told me that helping him was a crime and that it would be best if I didn't say anything to anyone. I told him that not reporting a gunshot wound was a crime, too, and in the end I would probably be in more trouble than he if it was discovered. He grinned and asked to see his coat. I handed it to him; he fumbled around in the pockets and removed a black leather case. When he opened it, I saw more cash than I have ever seen in my life. A moment later he shoved a wad of bills in my hand and closed my fingers around it.

"Here, Docteur, for your trouble and for your silence."

I didn't look at it; I was too scared. I just put the money in my pocket until I got back to my room, where I opened my top dresser drawer, dropped it in, and closed the drawer.

That evening Mrs. Miller asked me to eat dinner alone with her rather than with the other boarders. During the meal she explained that her house was a checkpoint on Francois's smuggling route. Every few miles on his journey from Canada to Albany, New York, he would stop along the way at the homes and farms of people he trusted to call ahead to the next checkpoint to see if there were any problems like police and revenuer roadblocks along the road. Mrs. Miller said she'd been doing business with him for years. She said he'd come in cut up and bruised before but never shot. She also said that he could be trusted to not give either of them up if he was caught. She put her hand on mine, "Don't worry, Angela, I doubt you'll ever see him again."

When I returned to my room, I locked the door, drew the curtains, and removed the wad of money from my dresser drawer. I laid each bill out on my bedspread; it totaled over six hundred dollars, equal to about two months' salary.

I had not spoken of it since, at least not until then.

Shelly's eyes were as wide as a child's after a good ghost story. She sat in utter silence for a few moments. After taking a swig of her beer she simply uttered, "Good God, AJ!"

Residence of Mrs. Edna Miller—Saturday, 6 April 1935, 11 A.M.

I took a cab over to Broad St. to see my old landlord, Mrs. Miller. I knocked twice, and after a minute or so I saw her face light up when she peeked past the curtain and saw it was me. As she opened the door she called out cheerfully, "Angela, how are you? Please come in."

She graciously offered me lunch, and I gratefully accepted. During the meal we discussed Mr. Francois Baril, whose family she had known for years. She told me that Francois's wife, Madeline, had come from a good French family, the Riendeaus, and that they had raised four fine sons. I casually asked about a daughter.

"They never had a daughter," Miller remarked, taking a last puff on her cigarette and crushing it out. "The couple wanted a daughter but the good Lord never provided one."

I was taken back by that little tidbit of information. So why had someone calling herself Baril's daughter contracted a funeral home to pick up Baril's remains at the morgue? I played things close to my chest as I nudged the conversation toward Miller's relationship with Mr. Baril.

Mrs. Miller pondered for a few moments, then lit another smoke and took a long drag.

"With Francois dead I suppose it wouldn't hurt to tell you some of it," she sighed, a stream of smoke oddly modulated by her words.

"Besides, in a way you're part of it too, so it's in your best interest to keep your mouth shut about what I tell you."

I nodded as she began to relate her story. About ten years earlier, in 1925, Baril came to her and offered her money if she would be a checkpoint on one of his smuggling routes. The money was good and, besides, she didn't believe in Prohibition anyhow. Miller shared a couple of close calls when Baril had to stash his special transport car in her garage just a few minutes ahead of the revenue men.

Miller got up to make a pot of tea for us.

"Why was the car so special?" I asked in humble naivety.

She explained that Baril had a 1914 Lozier, which were high end automobiles that used to be built in Plattsburgh. Baril had paid someone to modify the Lozier by building a secret compartment in its undercarriage. She explained that smugglers would often have special cars equipped with extra heavy suspensions so they would look normal to the casual observer while being weighted down with large loads of Canadian booze destined for speakeasies in New York City.

Miller told me that in all the years she had done business with Baril, there were only two close calls. One time, the revenue men stopped at her house to use her phone during one of their pursuits while Baril and his special Lozier sat quietly in her garage. The other close encounter was when Baril was shot in the backside in '31.

When the tea was done brewing we moved to her large front porch. While sipping our tea I causally asked if Baril had any enemies. Miller stared at me for a pregnant moment, and then put her head back on her rocking chair and said nothing. Fearing I had touched on a dangerous topic, I stopped my rocking and explained that I had signed his death certificate and was wondering if I should have done a full autopsy. I also explained that by all appearances he had died of a common stroke. I started rocking again, as Miller fumbled for a cigarette and lit up.

"Angela, you aren't from around here, so you probably don't know that some of the oldest families in Plattsburgh have been involved in the smuggling business since the American Revolution. Many people in Plattsburgh owe a lot to those smugglers."

Mrs. Miller told me about the Roussels, another French-Canadian smuggling family. Seems that the two families were sometimes partners on big projects and other times friendly competitors. It was like this for Baril's father and one of the older Roussels.

Jean Roussel and Francois Baril went to Catholic school together as young boys and used to drive the nuns nuts with their shenanigans. As young men they both were involved with their respective family businesses, both the legitimate ones and the shady ones.

Seems that back about 1928, some of the Roussels' associates came up missing and were later found dead, floating in Lake Champlain with empty burlap bags tied to their legs. She explained that rum runners transporting booze via the lake used to tie large burlap bags of salt around the cases of hooch. If they were about to be intercepted by revenue men, they dumped the cargo overboard and the heavy salt bags would drag the booze to the bottom. A few days later the salt would have dissolved and the rum runners could recover their inventory when the crates of bottled alcohol would float back to the surface.

It was obvious that whoever intercepted the Roussel people knew this trick and was making a loud and clear statement. Miller said the

Roussels naturally blamed Baril, who had frequent business dealings with Al Capone. I gave her a curious look.

Miller said in a rather matter of fact manner: "From what I understand, Capone made big deals with Canadian distillers and used the well-established regional smuggling network to move booze across the border and downstate."

Taking on a somber tone, she related how the two boyhood friends, Jean and Francois, had a huge falling out that affected both families deeply. She told me that the two families soon became serious competitors with a hateful edge to the competition, and an ugly rumor started to circulate that Jean Roussel swore that Francois Baril would someday "sleep with the fishes of Lake Champlain."

"But I tell you, Angela, Francois Baril swore to me that none of his people had anything to do with the deaths in the Roussel family," she said in reassuring tone.

"He may have been a rogue and a smuggler but he was an honorable man."

When I asked her about old man Roussel, she just shook her head. "Dead for five years now," she said, and she told me the sad story of a simple winter accident. Old man Roussel was at the Plattsburgh Post Office and slipped on some ice on the sidewalk and quite literally broke his neck.

"That poor man died two days later in the arms of his daughter Juliette."

Daughter, I thought to myself. The Bessette Funeral Home diener said that the daughter had called. I wondered to myself if the daughter of Jean Roussel was up to no good, carrying out some sort of vendetta for her deceased father by messing up the funeral plans.

We spent another few hours discussing more pleasant subjects and whiling away a spring-like Saturday afternoon. But in the back of my mind this daughter thing was beginning to nag at me.

The Bessette Funeral Home—Monday, 8 April 1935, 7:12 P.M.

I had spent Sunday on the wards of Adirondack General as the staff resident and on-duty surgeon. The day would have passed as unremarkable except for a local automobile accident; no one was killed, but the car's occupants required some surgery to sort them out. Thank God work gave me some distraction from this Baril business—but not much. Even at work I couldn't get completely away from it. In the doctors' and nurses' break room, the Sunday paper hosted a rather large obituary for Francois Yves Baril, and of course it was the topic of gossip everywhere I went. Apparently anybody who grew up in Plattsburgh knew something interesting about Mr. Baril or his notorious family.

In the obituary, Baril's life accomplishments as well as his civic contributions to the Plattsburgh area were touted as praiseworthy. Since obituaries are more or less advertisements, the family could say just about anything they wanted about him. Because they were a wealthy family, they were able to pull out all the stops, and every child and grandchild was mentioned without exception.

A side bar to the obituary was a small news article about how the local Bessette and Proulx funeral homes teamed up to provide a highly dignified memorial for one of Plattsburgh's more notable citizens. Knowing the truth about that arrangement, I could only bite my tongue.

The Bessette Funeral Home was a majestic Victorian house that was large even by Victorian standards. It was not all that far from my residence, so I decided to walk there in the unusually warm April weather. Shelly planned on attending too, so we agreed to meet outside the funeral home. When I turned the corner of the street leading to Bessette's, I was met by the sight of a sizeable crowd of people on the huge front porch and spilling out onto the front yard. As I approached the property, Shelly emerged from the crowd and walked towards me.

"Hi AJ, what do you think of all this?"

I could only stare in amazement at the crowd of perhaps two hundred people, talking on the porch, milling around the yard, chatting in small groups. Shelly told me that the house was packed and that the funeral directors were giving people twenty minutes inside to view the body and pay their respects to the bereaved family. The people outside were a mix of people who'd already paid their respects and those just arriving.

"Come on, AJ, let's go get in line," Shelly suggested.

After a forty minute wait on the porch, we were ushered into the house by the tall blond diener who had called at the morgue for Baril's corpse. He politely acknowledged us both as he invited us and about twenty other mourners to go inside.

Shelly and I performed the usual rituals, signing the register and viewing the deceased. Francois Baril looked considerably better dressed in his dark, double-breasted suit and lying in his bronze casket than he did the last time I saw him on my examining table. The embalmers at the Proulx funeral home had worked their magic on his corpse, and he looked pretty natural for a dead man.

I took a moment on the kneeler in front of his casket to say a brief prayer and to reconcile the corpse with the man I had done meatball surgery on a few years ago. After paying my respects to the departed Mr. Baril, I made my way over to the family receiving line.

The widow, Madeline Riendeau Baril, sat in a large wooden chair graciously receiving visitors. Beside her in a line were four handsome young men ranging in age from late thirties to middle twenties; I assumed these were the sons.

As I offered my hand to the widow, I simply introduced myself as Dr. Patterson from Adirondack General. She gripped my hand for a moment.

"Docteur Patterson, it is an honor to finally meet you," she exclaimed with a surprised but pleasant look. She leaned toward me and whispered, "Docteur, I want to thank you for treating my Francois many years ago."

Then she looked to her eldest son and gestured. He dutifully leaned over to her and listened to her whispering, then reacted with an interested look. He gave me a brief glance, and then leaned over to his brother, who passed their mother's message down the line.

"Docteur, please join us at our home after the burial on Wednesday," Mrs. Baril said in a dignified tone. She looked to me to be holding up very well under the circumstances.

As I made my way down the line of sons shaking hands and offering condolences, each of them whispered their own thanks for my treatment of their father after his accident. I had no idea that my backroom medical procedure was such a well-known and closely-held family secret.

Shelly and I left the funeral home and walked to a nearby neighborhood tavern, where we had a couple of beers and discussed the more sensational parts of the evening.

Adirondack General Hospital Morgue—Tuesday, 9 April 1935, 1:37 P.M.

Doing double duty as a staff surgeon and the deputy pathologist was starting to take its toll on me. I approached the chief of surgery and asked for a reduced surgical schedule until a new staff pathologist could be hired. He had an appreciation for the hours I was pulling and adjusted the duty rotation to cut me some slack. While waiting for him to show up for our appointment, I thought about the Baril situation. I thought I had this thing figured out.

The late Roussel patriarch, Jean Roussel, promised Francois Baril that he would "sleep with the fishes" during their falling out back in '28. With Roussel buried in a churchyard plot that promise, in theory, died with him, unless another member of the family decided to carry out that pledge. Enter the daughter, Juliette Roussel. In the confusion of Baril's unexpected death, she contracted the Bessette Funeral home to grab the body before the mortuary the family requested could pick up the corpse. "My God," I thought. Was Juliette Roussel really planning to snatch the body of her father's former rival and dump it in Lake Champlain? At first this seemed too shocking to believe, but the more I thought about it, the more plausible it seemed. With the Bessette people employed by Roussel's daughter and in control of the body, anything could happen.

I realized the timeline seemed perfect for this stunt. The Bessette people were going to host the funeral ceremony at their funeral home. Once they closed the lid on that heavy bronze casket, who would know the difference if the body was snatched between the time they wrapped up the memorial and the time the pall bearers carried the casket to the hearse? After all, caskets are almost never opened at the graveyard committal.

"That's it," I blurted out in the deserted autopsy room. "They're going to snatch the body of Francois Baril and dump it in the lake and no one will be the wiser.

Of course the question now was what to do about it. Should I get mixed up in a family feud or just let sleeping dogs lie and not get involved? As a doctor I sometimes have to interpret my patient's wishes. As a pathologist, I sometimes must speak for my patients as well.

I decided it was my place to attend the interment and somehow confirm that Francoise Baril's body was indeed in the casket and was laid to rest in the ground as his family wished.

Riverside Cemetery—Wednesday, 10 April 1935, 10:25 P.M.

The memorial service for Francois Baril at the Bessette funeral home was, in a word, lovely. There was a Catholic priest and a small choir, and nearly a half dozen people got up and spoke kind words about the late Mr. Baril. It was his eldest son who delivered the eulogy. As the service ended, I watched carefully as the funeral directors ushered everyone out to waiting cars and limos. I managed to hide in the rest room until the funeral home was clear of everyone except the employees. The Proulx staff was conveniently outside, leaving the Bessette staff alone with the body. To my surprise, one of the funeral directors simply walked up to the bronze casket, turned in the lace flaps, and carefully closed the lid. Two attendants helped lift the heavy casket onto a cart and wheeled it out the door. As I came out of the restroom, the tall blond diener noticed me and pointed out the open front door toward a waiting limo.

"Doctor Patterson, you better hurry out to the cars before we leave you behind," he urged.

Baril's casket rode in a 1933 Cadillac Chieftain hearse at the head of the long line of cars. It was a short drive to historic Riverside Cemetery.

At the cemetery, the hundred or so mourners gathered graveside and listened to a few words from family and loved ones before the widow put a rose on the casket and left, followed by her sons. After about twenty minutes, everyone was gone except the Bessette staff. I was hiding behind a small mausoleum on a nearby knoll, watching and waiting.

A limo with the Bessette crest on its bumper pulled up. The uniformed driver got out and walked back to a rear door and opened it. A short, red-haired woman dressed in black got out. Just then a black utility truck pulled up behind the limo. Two men in coveralls got out and went to the back of the truck. Moments later the two men appeared again carrying a large packing crate with heavy rope handles on each end. The woman gestured to them and pointed at the grave site. In my mind this was it: they were going to snatch the body; now if I could only catch them doing it.

Unfortunately, my vantage point on the knoll was obstructed by several tall headstones. I couldn't get a clear view. One thing was for certain: Baril's casket was opened for a few minutes, there was some activity, and then it was closed again. I saw the two men carrying the long shipping crate back toward the utility truck.

I quickly made my way down to the grave site, where the funeral director still stood with the red-headed woman and I demanded that the casket be opened. The funeral director gave me a firm, almost perturbed, look and said, "That is impossible, Docteur."

The woman looked at him and in French asked him something that I suspect was "Who's this broad?" He answered her in French and I heard my name mentioned. The woman looked at me with a smile on her face. "So you are the Doctor Patterson who caused so much trouble," she said.

Again I demanded that they open the casket. The woman spoke again, asking, "Doctor, what do you expect to find besides a dead old man?"

I explained that all I wanted to do was make sure that Baril was still in his casket. The woman laughed.

"Doctor, did you expect him to get up and walk away?" she asked. "Didn't you sign his death certificate?"

I acknowledged that I indeed signed his death certificate. Then I asked her who she was. The woman, in a pleasant and dignified way, answered, "I am Juliette Roussel," and then she repeated her question, "Doctor, why do you think that Mr. Baril is not resting in his casket?"

I thought about it a moment; should I reveal that I knew about the vendetta that her late father has promised Baril?

"Miss Roussel, I mean no disrespect to you, but considering the confusion over the body at my morgue and the fact that I heard a story about your late father..."

She cut me off, laughing. "Doctor, did you think I was going to steal poor Francois and dump him out in the lake?"

She went right for the punch line; all I could do was utter a simple, "Yep."

She seemed very amused.

Juliette Roussel walked over and sat on a small headstone, then gestured with a patting motion for me to sit next to her. She opened her purse, took out a silver cigarette case, removed two cigarettes, and offered one to me. While I haven't smoked since college, I figured this was one of those talks that warranted an exception. The undertaker stepped over and lit our smokes, then took the hint when Juliette gestured with her head and went for a short walk.

"Doctor, Francois was like an uncle to me when I was growing up. Our two families were very close," she said, then opened her purse, removed a handkerchief, and promptly blotted some tears from around her eyes.

"But then my father and Francois had a great argument that they never got over."

I nodded and indicated that I was well aware of the tiff. I thought about this a moment and wondered if I was all wrong.

"You mean you never intended to steal his body?"

"No, Doctor, nothing like that," she commented in a somber tone. I wasn't sure if I should believe her, but I figured I would give her a chance.

"Why did you contract the Bessette people to come and tend to the body?"

"You see, Doctor, my father was a hard and stubborn man, and he didn't trust Francois to the end." She took a drag and looked over at the bronze casket.

"When Papa died, Francois took care of the details and did his best to heal the wounds between both families."

Juliette explained to me that, even though both of the patriarchs had been at odds with each other, the women never really lost touch and stayed rather close.

"But what about the issue of those Roussel family members who were drowned in the lake, and your father blamed Francois?"

She took a long drag on her cigarette, shaking her head. "The police found out later the whole thing involved some thugs from downstate and that it didn't involve the Barils at all. My father, being a very stubborn man, refused to believe it all the way to the grave."

As she flicked the butt of her cigarette away, I knew I had to ask one last question. "Juliette, I saw the workmen bring a crate over to the graveside and I could see the casket being opened; what was that all about?"

She gestured to me as she got up off the stone. "Come here, Doctor."

Juliette reached over to the casket, released the latch, and carefully lifted the lid. Much to my surprise, there was Francois Baril. Just as I caught sight of Baril, my nose caught a strange odor. Looking further down, I saw two large lake salmon lying on each side of him, with another lying across his mid-section just below his permanently folded hands. I guess my jaw must have dropped as I snorted a laugh. I looked over to Juliette Roussel for an explanation.

"On his death bed, my father made me promise I would make Francois sleep with the fishes," she remarked with an impish grin. "I simply kept a daughter's promise."

I could only think to myself that I might have done the same if I had been in her shoes. While it seems like a great waste of three perfectly good lake salmon, in the end, who am I to interfere in old family business?

Chanel, 1927

by Angela Zeman

The elderly woman twisted, and twisted again, surveying herself over her shoulder in the mirror. "Perfect, Julia Dayton. And to think you're…" she paused to count, then finished addressing herself, "you're eighty-two come February." The full-length mirror, framed in Art Deco-carved mahogany made a portrait of her slim figure. She wore a white, pleated shirtwaist above a navy, calf-length skirt with a flutter of box-pleats over one knee. Large cuffs fell away from her narrow hands as she raised them to finger the rare frogged, knotwork buttons at her breast. "Lovely," she murmured again. Finding this early nineteen-twenties blouse had been a triumph.

Her legs were necessarily encased in support hose, but daytime hosiery of the era of her costume, when silk cost so dearly, tended to be opaque lisle anyway, with a false flesh color, so the look was passably authentic. Appropriately thick-heeled, navy pumps with a businesslike buckle completed the picture. Julia Dayton delighted in knowing historical details like these, and delighted even more in reproducing them. She patted a rebellious strand of silver hair, restoring it firmly to the knot on her talcummed neck, and turned from the mirror.

Today was Friday, November 11. Her check should have arrived. Still, when she stepped outside, she shivered in surprise. The sun was so bright, she'd thought the air would be warmer. As she made her way to her front gate, she admired the wind-thrashed maples of her neighborhood, thinking how like dancing torches they looked in their brilliant colors.

At the foot of the ancient tree that guarded her gate, she stopped and, for a breathless moment, didn't move. The section of white picket fence that had yesterday supported her mailbox had been smashed and scattered across the narrow sidewalk like pickup sticks. Amid the clutter, the box lay like a crumpled, hollow, tin toy. Gold and russet leaves drifting down from overhead glanced off her body as if in sympathetic caresses. Exhibiting no emotion, she bent to retrieve her mail from the box's wounded mouth, then took a moment to gaze up at her resplendent maple. Fall. New clothes, new colors for the world. She fastened her racing thoughts on pleasure. She always associated fall with pleasure. To her, it was when the new year truly began. She took a deep breath.

Julia returned up the path to her door, picking her way with care so as not to turn a fragile ankle. No money for doctors.

One midnight a month ago, the path between house and gate had been made precarious by an anonymous application of a sledge-hammer to the cement. She hadn't saved enough money to repair it yet. Now she needed to repair her fence, too. In time. Patience, forced on her by the world in which she lived, had long ago become as vital to her well-being as money.

Inside, one of the opened envelopes yielded the expected Social Security check. Her eyes closed for a second of involuntary relief. She fished within her handbag, a black crocheted envelope with a tortoise shell handle she'd purchased for two dollars at the annual Baptist church rummage sale last spring. She withdrew her checkbook and filled out a deposit slip.

She'd need a jacket. Which one would look right with what she already had on? She didn't want to change. Such a lot of fuss, she thought, knowing she'd change if necessary. She did everything necessary. Her posture, her walk, even her hand gestures were designed to enhance the picture of an elegant lady, yes, of advanced years, but still of exquisite taste and style.

Appearance was everything. "Never offer *them* your life as a sport, dear," she'd been instructed. By whom? Sometimes she couldn't recall, but she believed it. Grief, fear, pain, loneliness, and the devastating events in life could be handled more easily if one presented a face of serene control to the world's avid, uncaring spectators.

After choosing a taupe wool jacket with a broad collar and peplum, she left her house again, this time locking the door carefully behind her. Pulling her shoulders straight, she cast nervous glances up the street to see who she might have to pass on the sidewalk. No one in sight. More relaxed, she again picked her way through the crumbled cement to her front gate and, stepping over its pieces, entered the outside world of Trueden Falls.

Drab, diminishing annually, struggling not to disappear entirely from Rand McNally's notice, Trueden Falls had been born as a logging community just after the Civil War. In upper New York State, the Adirondacks had been then, as they mostly still are, a green paradise of lush forests and broad blue lakes, jagged rock laced with waterfalls, and abundant game.

When the Civil War ended, this area seemed to a small group of investors to be especially prime, with seemingly endless stands of mature pines, spruce, and hemlock, conveniently bordered by a powerful waterfall. The group purchased thousands of the acres surrounding that waterfall. They constructed sawmills, utilizing the free water power to run them. Railroads hastened to provide spurs, to carry the millions upon millions of milled boards to the post-war market. Someone built a luxurious hotel; affluent visitors came to hunt, enjoy the lakes, and to spend money. A town grew up around the mills, and then grew fat.

Local history says the group had first wanted to name the mill town Dayton Falls, for Tom Dayton, one of the investors. But Miss Julia's ancestor had been too self-effacing, so they christened it Trueden Falls to honor another investor, James Trueden, a former colonel with an illustrious history of service to his country.

Then in the late nineteen forties, the ravaged forests, never husbanded—and because they were privately owned, never protected by the stringent wilderness laws preserving other similar areas—failed. The railroad abandoned its spurs to rust, and the town lost its reason for existence.

Trueden Falls only now clung to life because a midsized factory had arrived in the sixties, appreciative of the acres of raw, and thus cheap, land and a desperate labor pool.

During one of those declining years, Miss Dayton's formerly prosperous neighborhood became the rusted track's wrong side. Today the once glorious turn-of-the-century houses sheltered mostly bitter and demoralized men and women, stranded, like their houses, by an economy changing faster than their abilities to adjust. Still, a ramshackle house made better shelter than a doorway. Time and innovation hadn't yet caught up with Trueden Falls: bigotry and alcohol were the rampant vices, not crack or more up-to-date aberrations.

Even so, even here, change crept forward: young, double-incomed couples whose occupations were mostly entrepreneurial, or achieved mostly by computer, had lately begun moving into the area, seizing bargains created by the exhaustion of desperate owners. The improvements encouraged an illusion of vitality. A few residents approved. Some residents growled and avoided watching cornices acquire new crisp lines, wood floors new patina, and gardens new discipline, hating this house-proud energy as a reproach to their own shortcomings.

But Julia Dayton didn't know about these conflicts because she was the outcast of the neighborhood. On three occasions, realtors had approached her, lusting for her house. Avid rumor said she'd trained a shotgun on them, but that was unconfirmed. The realtors agreed, though, how hatefully she'd ordered them from her property. "As long as the walls hold," they reported she'd said, "this is my home. It'll stay my home. And by God—I will take it with me when I go." A sprawling Victorian, by far the most resplendent in the neighborhood but shabby despite her efforts, it was obviously loved by her as fiercely as if it were a living thing. The realtors still checked on her periodically. She was old; she could die any day. Her heirs might sell.

In the meantime, Miss Dayton (as she was called despite rumors of a marriage in her remote youth) suffered vandalism problems. Although suffered would not have been her word; endured would be more accurate. Suffering had occurred only at her sudden understanding that the youthful offenders merely amused their elders. And surely, her shattered front walk was a task beyond a child's strength. Her frequently decapitated mailbox, smashed fence, cracked window panes, the rotten eggs and worse drooling down her outside walls, plus other depredations, made tremendous drains on her income and energy, not to mention her sense of security. Nothing done against her had elicited so much as a sympathetic murmur from her neighbors. Neighbors who, she finally realized, had, for reasons unfathomable to herself, probably done the damage. Their enjoyment of her distress shocked her. Recoiling, she became even more a recluse, having begun as nearly one anyway. Exchanging stories about weird Miss Dayton pleasantly distracted her neighbors from themselves.

Until Mr. Rudy Stoner died.

That same Friday night, November 11, the moon waned enough to offer cover to those like Miss Dayton who feel safer concealed. So, happily, she fetched clippers and a basket from the carriage house at the rear of her property and began to putter in her cozily overgrown backyard. She enjoyed the tall ancient trees and lush mature growths that so often graced old neighborhoods. She fingered their barks lovingly as she glided across the soft ground from tree to tree, from rhododendrons to lilacs, wending her way through the fragrant hollows and caves of her yard. She loved it all into flourishing, unable to give it a more material care.

And of course, as was her custom, she finally knelt in the farthest corner: a grassy cove surrounded by rhododendrons and two dogwood trees, nearly dead from strangulation by wisterias, with knotted stems thick as a man's wrist. In spring the fragrant flowers dripped from the dying dogwood branches over the spot, like purple rain frozen before it touched the grass. Bending across a patch of ground discernible as special only to herself, she crooned soft loving words to the only person she'd ever loved, who'd ever loved her back. Jenny, she called her. She visited for a while, discussing her life, as usual not mentioning her problems but dwelling on her pleasures. Her outfit today. The new oranges at the market, how unexpectedly sweet they were. How fall had brought extra vivid colors this year. "Those real estate vultures haven't returned in a while,

Jenny. I think we're rid of them." She laughed softly. "They offer so much money for our house. Where I was born. Where you were born! To think of not being here! Why, this black dirt that keeps you warm surely circulates in my body like blood. This is *our* place in the world. Just think of those who have no place of their own. I can't imagine it. It must feel like they float in air." She bent at the waist and laid her cheek against the swell of cool grass, hands splayed to feel the ground." She whispered, "How could I leave you alone, anyway? This is where we belong, Jenny girl. Rest easy. We won't be moved."

Suddenly, Miss Dayton felt a presence. She froze into silence. She listened, her round dark eyes searching. Long minutes passed. She'd nearly decided it was safe to rise and rush back into her house, when she spotted the deeper shadow. It lay within shadows she'd long ago memorized out of her chronic preternatural wariness. A long horizontal blackness.

She trembled, but accustomed to fear, ignored it. Rising to her knees, she waited. Nothing happened. She regained her feet. Again nothing. No catcalls, no bursts from the bush of something or someone launching itself at her for its own entertainment. Two strides and she looked down. At her feet a man lay sprawled face down, arms flung wide like a crucifixion, body only half tucked beneath the rhododendrons. She bent to touch his neck beneath the ear. Like chilled clay. With concern growing more for him than herself, she heaved his bulky shoulders around to see his face. His eyes were open.

Back to her house she flew, making no sound but a scream of terror in her mind. She slammed her back door, turned the bolt, and pressed herself against it, palms flat against the door at her sides. Her chest heaved, her rasping breath the only noise in the silence. Eventually her panting slowed, and she dragged a wooden chair over from the kitchen table. She sat sideways on it, but still leaned against the door. After a while, her eyes drifted closed, but a vision of the man's shocked stare burst into her mind. Quickly she opened her eyes and wouldn't allow them to shut again.

It was an hour or so before she moved again. Then, steeled with decision, she changed into rough overalls, tall boots, and gloves. She gathered up rags and a bucket and returned to her visitor. She'd decided to call him that. Her visitor.

His body was much larger, longer, and heavier than hers, but she managed to roll him onto his back. Necessity forced her to ignore the sunken, crushed part of his skull. While catching her breath, she delicately smoothed his eyelids closed, for her relief as well as his. Tenderly stroking dirt and blood from his face, she said, "It's peaceful here. You might like that. I—I'm sorry I can't call the authorities to take you to your own family, if you have one. I assure you I've got reasons. But I vow you'll get as much respect and remembrance as if you were my own family. I hope your going wasn't…hard." She paused. *That blow to his head. Of course he'd gone hard.* She tried to remember the expression on his face. Had it seemed agonized? Or was it the open eyes that had suggested pain? She didn't know enough to decide.

In a business-like manner she began brushing down his long-sleeved sweatshirt and nylon shorts. She washed dirt from his hands, legs, and neck with her rags and combed gravel from his short-clipped hair. Then, when she'd done all she could do, she stood with a sigh and began digging next to where she knew Jenny lay. As her shovel chewed at the fine black soil, clouds drifted across the bit of moon, lifting some of her anxiety about being observed.

Exhausted after two hours of steady digging, she decided the hollowed out place she'd made could hold him "comfortably." Alternating lifting and shifting his shoulders and his feet, she maneuvered him into his new home. Gently, to shield him from the dirt, she lay a long linen cloth over him, an old curtain, its bright pink pansies faded now into pale blotches. She replaced the dirt, patting and pressing it into place, topping it with the turves she'd kept whole to make the ground look as undisturbed as possible. She knelt and patted where his chest was beneath his grass coverlet.

"I'll visit you when I visit my Jenny, and glad to do it, too, so don't feel you're imposing. I hope you don't mind we're strangers. You'll never be lonely here, and maybe in time you'll get to love us. God bless you."

Gathering her supplies, she rushed swiftly to her house, locked the door, and went to bed. Her dreams were disturbed that night, but by the following day her habit of taking pleasure in things overcame her distress. By the weekend's passing, except for sorrow that the poor man had lost his life, she thought of him only with affection. Alarm faded as each day brought its new challenges to distract. Her days were full of challenges.

Eleven days after meeting her new friend, a Tuesday midmorning, two young men stood at her door, one tall and burly, one slight and bent in posture. Trueden Falls was the size of town where although they'd never met her, both were well acquainted with the circulating stories, including the local resentment at her origins and the blame that came with it.

Her heart made dull thuds in her chest as she slowly opened her door.

"Deputy Donald Cox, ma'am, and this is Assistant Deputy William Stanton." Deputy Cox extended a worn leather billfold containing a photo ID. His badge was pinned to the breast-pocket flap of his brown shirt, as was Assistant Deputy Stanton's.

She was too flustered to focus on the photo ID, so merely nodded.

"Miss Julia Dayton?" asked Deputy Cox. He was the tall one. Heavily muscled, blonde and blue-eyed. But his voice was soft, almost sorrowful.

Again, she nodded.

"Have you by any chance seen a man in the neighborhood lately, somebody not usually around?"

She looked puzzled, but shook her head no, still not speaking.

"You heard any ruckus lately, maybe at night? Maybe scuffling sounds, or shouting?"

She flushed, remembering the egged windows from Saturday night. The sulfurous smell lingered despite scrubbing. But they wouldn't care, so she didn't mention it. Nobody cared. She shook her head no.

Deputy Cox shifted and glanced at the Assistant Deputy, but Stanton just stared at her. Miss Dayton wore a soft wool shift that day, long sleeved and long waisted, patterned in chevrons of brick-red, brown, and black. It had been pieced together on the bias to flow in curves across her slim body. A work of art obvious even to the deputies, who normally noticed only the brevity of a woman's clothes, not the elegance.

Her silver hair had been caught up into a shining twist with a tortoise shell pin.

"We got a call, ma'am," persevered Deputy Cox, his tone growing even softer in the face of her apparent fright, "saying a man's dead, and his body was seen here."

Finally she spoke. "How terrible."

He shrugged. "But happens a guy is missing, so we—"

"What do you want?" she asked, suddenly insistent.

"To, uh, scout around your place. We could get a warrant if you—" He kept his gaze steady, knowing he'd never get a warrant based on an anonymous tip.

She opened wide the door. "Could I fix some coffee to warm you while you look? It's so chilly today."

The deputies eyed each other in surprise. They'd been led by her reputation to expect arrogance, a snooty attitude, or some kind of obstruction.

"No, we won't trouble you, but thank you anyway. We'll just look quick."

They stepped into a boxy foyer, then through another door of etched glass into a huge, immaculately clean living room. No television, noticed Deputy Cox. Only a bulky ancient turntable flanked by stacks of long-playing vinyl records, covers tattered with overuse. "Scratch-city," he thought, in sympathy with her obvious love of music.

Small bunches of flowers, both fresh and dried, had been tucked into water glasses and subtly perfumed the air. A padded dressmaker's form posed in the middle of the oak floor like a centerpiece on a vast, threadbare, rose and teal Oriental rug. Folded fabrics and sewing tools filled gleaming, mahogany, built-in shelves across the end wall, and an old foot-pump sewing machine sat enthroned in a bow window. A grey and cream dress on a hanger swung from a long-armed coat rack next to a tall floor mirror. No other furniture.

Catching his assistant's eye, Deputy Cox tipped his head towards the staircase. Willy took the stairs two steps at a time. Deputy Cox glanced into each of the first floor's barren rooms and inspected mostly empty closets in which a body might be hidden. Then Miss Dayton and Cox faced each other in silence. Cox could see nothing in her demeanor but patience. Through the ceiling, Willy could be heard thundering down a long hall and into rooms. A door slammed. Deputy Cox winced. He suddenly thought to remove his hat. He pointed at the hanging dress. "Nice."

To Cox's mystification, her eyes suddenly glowed. "Isn't it? A genuine Chanel, created in 1927. See its matching coat on the stool? I'm trimming lilies out of that piece of flowered silk chiffon to make appliqués. I'll sew them to the edges of the dress and coat where they show the worst wear. A picture I once saw—"

She stopped as Stanton appeared suddenly, arriving much more quietly than he'd left.

Willy cleared his throat. "Nothing. Most the rooms're empty, Donnie. An' she keeps 'em closed off. No heat." Stanton's face said clearly that he knew about having to hoard heat and sympathized.

Deputy Cox nodded.

"Outside," said Miss Dayton. "You must look outside, too." Her hands came up to her meager chest and for the first time she looked anxious.

Deputy Cox nearly said no, he saw no point, embarrassed at their obviously unjust intrusion, but then changed his mind. "Yes, right." So they trudged dutifully around the yard, peering into her carriage house, zigzagging through the overgrown clumps of greenery, by now figuring the caller was just another jerk with time on his hands, getting kicks at the old lady's and their expense.

With apologies to her, they climbed back into the old brown and beige Buick cruiser and left.

However, two days later they found it necessary to return. It was a bright golden day, Thanksgiving morning. The two bachelor deputies had hoped for a day of no calls and an early arrival at their clerk/dispatcher's dinner table. Then the phone rang. It seemed the neighborhood dogs were giving unexpected attention to Miss Dayton's back yard. The male caller, saying he spoke for all the dogs' owners, yelled into the receiver, making Donnie wince, "The old bat lured our pets over there to poison 'em!"

When asked why she might bear a grudge against their dogs, the caller, still anonymous, muttered, "They done things to her yard now and again. Y'know how dogs are. Nothin' worth this. She'll kill 'em!"

Donnie hung up and grabbed his car keys. "Uh, huh. Poison dogs in her own yard, broad daylight? Didn't strike me as a stupid woman. C'mon, Willy."

When the roar of the Buick's engine subsided, Deputies Cox and Stanton weren't surprised to hear commotion coming from behind Miss Dayton's house. They plunged through a handful of spectators to find a disheveled and terrified Miss Dayton, wearing heavy unbuckled boots beneath a full woolen skirt, thrusting the straw-bundled end of a homemade broom into the faces of five snarling dogs. None of the animals was larger than a spaniel, but their teeth were bared and their lunges increasingly bold. Deputy Cox snatched the broom from Miss Dayton and walloped the two larger dogs across the haunches so that they tumbled, rolling across the ground like a circus trick. After regaining their scrambled wits, they squealed and ran. The rest raced after them.

Willy flapped his arms at the spectators, hollering, "Beat it, all a' you! Useless bums!" and they fled like the dogs.

Deputy Cox turned to Miss Dayton. To his surprise, she still stood on guard, expression stony, as braced against him as she'd been against the dogs. He considered that maybe she was in shock. Her pale face was whiter than he remembered, bruised under her great round eyes. No sleep for a while, he guessed. He wondered why she hadn't called him herself, and sooner.

They stared at each other without speaking. Her chest heaved so rapidly beneath her heavy sweater that Cox felt he was watching her heart beating. Her arms trembled violently. Miss Dayton saw that he noticed and clamped them to her sides. So small. A pathetic warrior a puff of air could conquer, but fighting off those dogs, he thought. And the neighbors.

"Glad we could help," he said in a friendly tone, as if she had spoken.

She said nothing.

"Hey," began Willy, with rising irritation, "A *thanks* shouldn't be that hard, you coulda got—" but Deputy Cox restrained him with a lifted hand.

"Why the dogs?" he asked, still casual. "Buried garbage? That always attracts animals."

Nothing.

He studied the area. The yard was dim despite the bright sun, deeply shadowed from trees and shrubs that had enjoyed years of unrestrained growth. He almost didn't spot the disturbed patch behind her, but then he did. Of course. Defending it. Whatever it was, it was there. He knew from the look on her face that he'd have to pick her up bodily to move her, so he circled around. She swiveled to face him.

He finally admitted to himself: he'd known since the phone call what he'd find. He'd liked her, and it hurt. For the first time in his experience, compassion warred against his usual revulsion towards offenders. His orderly soul could not adjust to such disorder of thought.

His voice flat, he said, "Ma'am, please go into the house with Deputy Stanton. Freshen up and maybe get a bite. This's gonna be a sad Thanksgiving day." He nodded at Willy, who, unenlightened but trusting, touched her on the elbow to nudge her along. For a bottomless minute she gazed at the disturbed ground. Willy saw Donnie wasn't disturbed by the delay and so didn't hurry her. She finally turned and walked away, Willy following. Defeat lay on her shoulders, in her inward gazing eyes.

Cox watched her go. He wondered what had happened in her life to harden her into this isolated castaway, clinging so fiercely to these few square feet for survival. Then he set the thought aside. More important right now: he needed to see what the dogs had been at. He reached for a broken tree branch to probe with—sturdy, about the thickness of a man's wrist, lying under a nearby dogwood—but drew back before touching it. All his inner alarms said to make it official. He knew he was depending on a hunch with no evidence to confirm it and knew the grief he'd endure if he proved wrong, but he felt the need for a warrant and the attendant proper procedure.

From the cruiser he radioed in a request for the county's one crime scene tech, shared with the surrounding townships. Then he instructed Cathy, the clerk/dispatcher, to bring him some crime scene tape and sawhorses as soon as she could take her attention off her turkey. Her dinner wasn't due to be ready until early evening—and a good thing. Then he called in messages for the Sheriff and a judge. And waited. He hoped he was wrong.

It was nearly two that afternoon before Mr. Rudy Stoner's distressed remains finally emerged, having been officially photographed, scraped, and measured to the extent of the department's limited equipment. The ambulance slid away from the curb, no lights or sirens.

The neighbors had begun collecting again a little after noon, fascinated by the yellow tape fluttering at the edges of Miss Dayton's property. All had been ordered to tie up their dogs or get them shot in short order. The resulting scuffle of hysteria pretty well pulled in every busybody from the neighborhood without exception. After securing their pets, they hung around to watch Miss Julia finally get justice. The ghoulishly appreciative audience had no idea their photos were being taken along with those of the crime site, to be added to the new manila case file housing reports concerning the murder of Rudy Stoner.

The branch nearly used by Cox for a shovel turned out to be elm. Willy's father was a landscaper in the next town and it developed that Willy had absorbed some knowledge from helping out occasionally. Miss Dayton's yard held pines, oaks, maples, and gingkoes, he pointed out to Deputy Cox, but no elms. Same with her neighbors' yards, either side and in back. Pride at this important contribution and the Deputy's praise nearly destroyed Willy's composure, but he compressed his excitement and hung on. They'd had to train a flashlight on it to examine the branch where it lay in the shadows, but were rewarded for their caution by spotting odd stains, maybe blood, maybe bits of brain and flesh. It had been photographed and taken away by the technician.

Deputy Cox finally went to find Miss Dayton. They settled in the kitchen so that he could keep an eye on the backyard through the small-paned windows. He made a mental note about the pink, flowered, linen curtains framing his view. Willy and the tech were now combing through her belongings in the near-empty rooms, searching for God knows what, but justified now to intrude. He studied her lovely face grown old. She radiated aloneness. Her hands cupped each other, perfectly still in her lap. She'd changed into soft slippers and a different dress, a flowing blue that touched her figure lightly. A white lace collar cradled a creamy neck that two thumbs could snap with no trouble. If he'd asked, she'd have told him she wore vintage Yves St. Laurent today.

The kitchen was barren of signs of an intended feast, except for faint yeasty smells of earlier baking. Her oven was cold now, though. Everything in the room was cold, including Cox's dismay.

He steeled himself to objectivity. "Ma'am, did you know this body was buried in your yard?"

She'd been gazing at the scarred wooden table between them. A four-top, it would've been called at the Dining Car Diner. Her eyes didn't lift, and her expression didn't change.

"Did he come here one night? Scare you? He's big, black, maybe you worried he'd be up to something bad? Common bigotry, this white-washed ghetto you live in here. Was it self-defense? He try something, you hit him with that heavy branch, didn't know it'd—" He stopped. He couldn't say 'kill' to that face.

She glanced up at him. Contempt flashed from her glittering eyes, come and gone so fast he wondered if he'd imagined it. She settled her gaze back to the table. "I was here before *they* were," she said, her voice slightly hoarse. With unuse, he guessed. Or fear?

"They. Who's *they*?"

She looked out the windows. Nothing was happening out there at the moment, the yard empty of police personnel. The fluttering tape intimidated the gawkers lining its edges from entering her yard to see the empty grave for themselves. So far.

"No one could blame you for reacting in fear, even if he meant no harm." He cast about in desperation for something more reassuring. Something to encourage a quick confession, to close this case today. "No one could blame you," he repeated lamely.

She remembered smoothing the dirt from his face and worried he'd not rest so easy where they took him. *I'm sorry; I didn't know this would happen*, she told him from her heart. Tears began to well, but she swiftly suppressed them.

He sighed. "No firm ID yet, but a guess is this's the missing man I asked you about Tuesday." A lie. He'd known him the second he spotted those big, wood-shop scarred hands, swollen and discolored as they were. He'd find others to ID the body, maybe force somebody to value life a little more from the horror of Mr. Stoner's state.

Murder was rare in Trueden Falls. What contaminated this town more was its mindless, soul-shriveling, petty neglect of life. Immediately after high school graduation, Donnie Cox had fled. Earned a place on the job in St. Louis, an altogether better place with at least a few people who knew that the latest model of car wasn't a measure of self-worth. But painfully and surely, Trueden Falls had dragged him back. Trueden Falls needed him. He'd long since stopped wondering over his return and decided that his passionate love for Trueden Falls was just one of those unexplainable pieces of himself. It just was, like so much else he didn't understand. So every day he waged his personal war against the disease that made this a sorry, drab place to live. His chest hurt that it was this man who would provide the next lesson.

"My missing man, the man I came here about two days ago? Was Mr. Rudy Stoner. Taught math and shop, coached soccer in his spare time. At Trueden Falls High. Had him myself, when I was there." He looked off unhappily, remembering the endless good-humored patience of the man and his own demands for plenty of it, too, taking for granted it was something he was owed. What a spoiled jerk I was, he mused. Mr. Stoner deserved better than Trueden Falls High. He studied Miss Dayton. But who ever gets what they deserve?

She sat motionless. Cox couldn't tell if she recognized the name or not.

"Any family nearby? Somebody you could call?"

Not a flicker, but he'd expected that. She had nothing but this empty house, that was plain.

He frowned. "Didn't somebody, didn't a girl live here with you before?"

The woman's eyes raised slowly to his. "My granddaughter. Jenny."

He nodded encouragingly. "Where's she? Maybe she can come stay with you. You should have some support."

But she slid into silence again.

He considered putting her overnight in their one jail cell, to keep an eye on her until Monday's arraignment. He dismissed the notion. She'd die of pneumonia inside those damp cement walls.

He leaned towards her, perplexed at himself. Despite his horrified regret over the victim, pity for this likely murderer twisted his guts, confusing him.

He nearly touched her fingers, resting limp in her lap, but stopped himself. "You're in trouble, Miss Dayton. Don't—" he was about to say, don't leave town. But where would she go? Travel costs money, something in obvious short supply here. He wondered where this Jenny had gotten off to. Good luck to her too, for her good sense. And didn't Jenny have a mother?

"What about Jenny's parents?"

"Long dead."

Hell and damn. He ran over a mental list of who could stay here overnight. Not that he thought Miss Dayton would skip, but the law demanded some kind of tribute to form. Gentle, blonde Cathy, the clerk/dispatcher, was his first choice. But the reason Cath worked for the department was to protect herself from her pseudo-religious prick husband, Ned Jeffreys. He liked to kick her in hidden places, although he'd use fists if his choice was limited. And for Cathy to spend a night away from home might attract him to inflict new hell on her, off-premises so to speak, and thus safer for him. Jeffreys was well aware how Donnie itched for any excuse to lock him up and hadn't touched her in some time. Donnie constantly pressed Cath to let him run the bastard in, but she wouldn't. Her religion wasn't pseudo, and it was strict on keeping women beneath the size tens of their husbands, or so she believed. Bible Belt. Donnie often wondered if "Bible Belt" meant, for some, to clutch the holy *un*read book in one hand to free up the other to beat on the weaker, the smaller, the gentler in mind and spirit.

What about Willy? Donnie had first tripped over Willy's long, thin feet four winters ago. He'd been huddled against the Dining Car's glass front door like an abandoned dog, trying to snare heat. Gaunt from hunger, he wouldn't step foot in the diner regardless. No money, he said, and refused Donnie's charity. "My dad taught me I work for what I get. And that's what I do," he said and clamped his lips tight against the mouthwatering temptation of unearned food. It was only after Donnie gave him a five dollar advance to polish his leather holster and boots that Willy followed Donnie into the diner.

By the end of their first meal together, Donnie learned that Willy was from a nearby township, and his father was his entire family. No mother or siblings. No friends, either. And poor luck with jobs. He had no explanation of why this was so, but it had always been true. Job hunting had brought him to Trueden Falls. Donnie realized the boy was slow, but his father's pronouncements of right and wrong had somehow found fertile ground in him and thrived. A few weeks later, with gleaming belts, shoes, car, and a spotless cement block jail cell, Donnie decided he'd never met anyone he could trust so completely.

After maneuvering the Sheriff into creating a new, lesser paying post of Assistant Deputy, Donnie immediately hired Willy. Donnie kept the gun, but Willy had something even better: a hero who never shouted, who never lost patience or temper no matter what Willy screwed up. In return, he did everything with a whole heart, earnest and careful. And happy. Under such circumstances, Willy's slight, bow-legged frame eventually filled out. The filled-in lines in his face helped him to look less than thirty-five and more his true age, which was then eighteen.

Or there was also the County Sheriff. Donnie tried to picture him abandoning his specially-built bed to sit (no extra bed in all those empty rooms) with Miss Dayton over Thanksgiving weekend and failed. Sheriff Quinn, portly and sarcastic, would shred Donnie's ass for suggesting it.

Sheriff Quinn's lifestyle was rich by local standards, as he maintained both a wife and a girlfriend along with a few children on each side. At this moment the Sheriff, if holding to tradition, would be presiding over the Thanksgiving delicacies his wife had special ordered from the supermart. And Donnie knew it was his custom to indulge in a similar bout of gluttony with his other family later this evening. Sheriff Quinn's favorite holiday, Thanksgiving. Not much of a drinker, Sheriff Quinn preferred to eat himself to death. No drugs, either. That would've gotten him bumped from office. Adultery just flaunted his virility.

County Sheriffs were elected every three years. After Quinn's customary unopposed run, it was his job to appoint staff to keep the peace in the small towns that littered his county. As few staff as possible, so as not to strain the budget that also paid his own salary. After each election, the Sheriff resumed occupation of his modern, air-conditioned office. (He'd moved from the derelict Town Hall to Trueden Falls's most deluxe office complex after his first year in office.) There he pursued his constitutional mandate—collecting back-owed taxes for the county and its townships—which returned to him a percentage for his trouble. Few in Trueden Falls could rightfully avoid his heavy-handed visits, although arrangements had been known to be made that could be mutually beneficial.

Trueden Falls' staff had remained static for some years. Donnie, Willy, and Cath. Few cared to earn less than the waitress at the Dining Car, so the three suffered no competition.

So the Sheriff and Cath weren't even options. And Donnie was the only one who could handle incoming trouble without help. Willy would stay.

"I don't suppose you got a lawyer?"

Her eyebrows rose almost imperceptibly, but she still didn't look him in the eye.

He went to search for Willy. He would stand guard duty on or near her front porch until Donnie came to escort her to court Monday morning. Willy could handle it. He was used to sleeping out in all kinds of weather from his various evictions. Donnie instructed Willy, then left, leather holster belt creaking in the icy air.

Next chore, Mrs. Stoner.

The Stoner house was a red brick box with white shutters, at the moment stained orange-gold by the rays of the setting sun. Signs of loving care showed in the perfect curve of weedless lawn fluorescing in the evening light, although it could stand a good mowing. Indoors, silky cherrywood molding, curved and delicate, lined each turn and curve on the walls, doors, and ceiling, a pain-in-the-ass feature for which a professional carpenter would charge more than a teacher could pay. Ceiling-high shelves, also cherry, hand turned to graceful curves along the edges, spilled over with well-read books. Homemade, but pleasing.

Mrs. Stoner's housekeeping fell far short of matching her husband's efforts. To her pardon, however, Donnie remembered that her husband had been missing for nearly two weeks. She seemed ill, her pallor greenish under her pale yellow skin, her clothes smelling of unwashed body. She was tall, ungainly, her hair pulled back into a stiff, toffee-gold ponytail, with some kinked straggles poking like curved wires at her oddly bulging eyes. Donnie ached to push them away, thinking they must hurt. Too many bones and too little flesh, he thought. She bit at the nails of her big hands. Donnie noticed her cuticles were bleeding. Her hands trembled.

"Just fishing to uncover new facts, Mrs. Stoner. To help us search better. When did your husband first go missing?" asked Donnie, his small spiral notebook and mechanical pencil out.

She stared at him until he wondered if she were drugged. He started to repeat the question, but she interrupted and said, "Friday. A week ago last Friday. I called, don't you remember?"

Donnie thought back. "That would be Friday, November 11?"

She shrugged.

"What made you first think something was wrong?"

"He didn't come home to shower." Again, the stare. Like a raccoon caught in the beam of a headlight.

"Shower."

A long pause. He relented, added, "Why don't you assume I don't know anything and tell me everything you can think of, okay?" Truth, he knew nothing except Willy telling him Rudy Stoner had gone missing. He made a note to himself to review the written report.

She frowned. "He ran every morning. At the track."

"The high school track?"

"Yeah. He was always back by seven. To shower and get ready for work. He didn't come back."

"Mrs. Stoner—"

"Denise," she blurted, then added a nervous smile.

Concealing his surprise at this sudden animation, Donnie nodded agreeably. "So he didn't come home; then what? Denise."

"I got worried. I told all this to somebody at the police station." She gnawed again at the skin around her thumbnail.

"He ever go off unexpectedly before?"

She shook her head vigorously. "He was always here for me. He took care of me. I—I have problems. Things are wrong with me. I had four miscarriages. I'm not strong." She looked away, tears welling. "I can't hold a job. I've tried and tried, but I get sick. He just says don't worry, I have him—" She clenched her fists. "He would never leave."

Donnie revised his notion of a drug habit reducing her to what he saw. He imagined her dependence frightened her and guessed she must be very worried indeed.

"Do you need a doctor, Mrs. Stoner?"

She shook her head. "Got plenty of those, Rudy made sure." She burst out suddenly, "Rudy, he was the best."

Was. She guessed? Or feared.

Suddenly she leaned forward, strain pulling her features into a grimace. "I need money. Any ideas about that?"

"You have savings to fall back on? Insurance?"

"No savings. Doctor bills took all that. Life insurance on Rudy. He worried about me if something happened to him. But he's just missing, not dead, isn't he? I need something to live on *now*. I have expenses."

"Like what, Denise?"

"Food, for one thing."

In surprise, Donnie scanned the mess in the living room, which included grocery sacks with contents spilled out like a cornucopia, as if she'd had the energy to shop, but not to carry anything as far as the kitchen. Half-eaten food left out on a dining room table was visible through a wide, arched doorway that led to a kitchen.

"What about his next paycheck? Surely the high school would give you some sick pay owed."

"In due time, they said."

"Need medicine?"

She shook her head sadly. "Never mind."

"Ma'am, you got family nearby, a friend to come stay with you?"

"Just Rudy."

A damned lonely town. Maybe that's what made people's spirits so small. Loneliness.

He promised to let her know if he got news and left without telling her of her new state of widowhood. Somebody from the school could ID the body. He'd send Cathy to Mrs. Stoner when the ID became official. A woman was required with a woman, anyway. Sometimes procedure was a friend to fall back on.

Monday morning, Donnie noticed for the first time the patterns in the smashed areas of Miss Dayton's cement path to the front door. He mounted the two steps to her wide porch, gave Willy's comatose sleeping bag-wrapped ribs a nudge with his toe. "Guard duty means you're supposed to stay awake, Deputy. At least in daylight."

While Willy struggled to unzip the bag, Donnie examined the damage again. Sledge hammer, he guessed, adding to his list of observations about Miss Dayton's life in this neighborhood. God.

He had no need to knock on the door; she opened it first, ready in her mended, flower-trimmed Chanel coat and dress. She was pulling a heavy, long wool coat over it all. Their exhalations clouded the air between them. It was colder today than yesterday. A local record.

"Willy explained about today, what to do," she said, her voice breathy with anxiety. Her face, though, looked serene.

Donnie gazed down at the slow-stirring Willy with pleased surprise. "Well done, Willy," he said, knowing the strain behind Willy's efforts. Willy beamed, bleary eyed.

"I left you coffee on the counter, Willy," said Miss Dayton briskly. "Fresh this morning and heavy cream, like you like, and some apples if you want them. I think it's important to eat well, don't you?" she asked Donnie defiantly, as if he might object.

Donnie stared at Willy.

Willy reddened. "You bet, Miss. And thanks. Fair to starving about now. I'll lock up for you, don't you worry."

In a dank corner of the Trueden Falls Town Hall, which had been built in 1911 and ignored ever since, two levels above the Deputy Sheriff's ground floor office and jail cell, dozy old Judge Persons came to attention. Even though he was never much good early in the morning, he sensed a reappointment media vehicle in this case and scraped himself together. He mumbled briskly over the police reports while the small party before him, both seated and standing, watched. He asked questions. During the answers he downed vast cups of evil-smelling coffee, replenished by his underworked clerk. A top-ranked reporter from the *Weekly Sentinel*, jittery with excitement, snapped photos of each participant one at a time and scratched out a note after each shot.

Two male and one female civic-minded (as they called themselves) neighbors had unexpectedly appeared, neatly clothed, eager, and uninvited. Deputy Cox could not imagine how they'd learned of the hearing, but here they were. After noisily pushing themselves into the notice of the confused old judge, who seemed to think they'd been subpoenaed to testify, they were allowed to add character statements to the record. One by one, each squirmed self-importantly in the oversized oak chair nearest the judge and declared in sanctimonious tones how for years, thanklessly, they'd borne with her odd ways and "watched out for" the vicious old lunatic. As each dismounted the witness chair, he or she paused for the newsman's photo. They left behind an impression that, in their opinion, Miss Dayton would continue to kill until restrained.

Her own testimony was sparse, unemotional.

Bank statements revealed that her income consisted of two checks per month—Social Security and a VA benefit check from her long dead husband's military service. No savings. She admitted that her only family was a granddaughter named Jenny, but would say only, when pressed, that she could expect no support from her.

After deliberation, the judge appointed a public defense lawyer on her behalf: Phil Roberts, a thirty-one-year-old, pudgy ball of zeal in a decent blue suit, white Celtic skin, and too much black curly hair, with long-lashed eyes like a girl, which Willy remarked on, earning a frown from Donnie. Briefed in advance by the bored clerk, Roberts had been waiting at the back of the room. He came forward. With Roberts' agreement (he had no other cases at present), the judge remanded Miss Dayton for trial in two weeks' time. The court docket was rarely crowded this time of year, the low temperatures cutting into most public nuisances' and thieves' comfort levels.

Roberts immediately asked permission for Miss Dayton, in deference to her age and obvious frailty, to remain at home until trial. He added, "And without bail, as we all stand witness to her financial distress." Seeming electrified with relief, Judge Persons agreed at once to the motion. As the apathetic prosecutor gaped, his attention finally engaged, the judge pounded his gavel and bounded off his chair, aiming for the men's room with a newspaper under his arm. Donnie guessed Roberts had perceived how frightening Miss Dayton's frailty might seem to the elderly judge, an echo of fears for himself, and was impressed.

Phil Roberts and Donnie eyed each other. They appeared roughly the same age. Donnie decided, after digging through memory, that Roberts might have attended Trueden Falls High. Where'd he been since high school?

Roberts, ushering his client out of the courtroom, signaled Donnie he'd be calling soon. Donnie nodded. He ordered Willy home to wash and sleep so he could repeat his guard duty tonight on Miss Dayton's front porch. Awake through the night, this time, sleeping by day. Donnie didn't trust the quality of support her neighbors might offer, although he wasn't sure he should worry, Mr. Stoner being black.

Soon, Phil Roberts sat smiling across Miss Dayton's rough kitchen table, cradling a cup of excellent coffee in his palms to keep warm. He hadn't taken off his top coat. Miss Dayton seemed untroubled by the inadequate heat, now that she'd wisely changed into a voluminous garment of wool, he observed. But he, despite the layers of fat on his short frame and the cashmere blended into his thick overcoat, was freezing.

"I'm originally from here in town," said Roberts agreeably. His "get acquainted" mode. The old lady looked withdrawn, as if she had much to think over and would prefer to be alone. Which was probably true, he thought, philosophically. But his job required her to talk, so talk she must.

"I can get you more heat for the house, by the way," he added.

She looked up, startled. "I can't afford—"

"I know. That's why you can get it. You can't pay, so you pay less than the ones who can afford it. I'll take care of it."

Her eyebrows, silky wings of shiny black, lifted at him, impressed. "Really?"

"No problem. Say. Your granddaughter, didn't she go to Trueden Falls High?"

Her gaze dropped to the untouched cup resting on the table before her. Her imperceptible breath wafted its warm, nutty aroma into the still air.

"You know," Phil continued. "I think I remember her. She had your eyes?"

Beneath the creped layers of aged skin, Miss Dayton's eyes looked to him like glistening olives. Round, a smudge of brown in the black, no discernible iris, swimming in flawless opaque white. Phil couldn't remember ever seeing a person her age with such clear whites of her eyes. Her lashes were dark and straight, stabbing downwards, a protective awning as silky as her eyebrows. Striking, with the silver hair.

Phil's memories expanded of the dreamy, wonderful girl with just those eyes, Jenny Dayton. Quiet, but smart enough to drift through Trueden Falls High classes with little effort. He bet her grandmother, if she loved her, had been happy she left town. Look at her options around here. Females hadn't even made it into the top ten "discriminated against" list yet. The best young people vanished as soon as they accumulated bus fare to anywhere else.

He had. Worked and borrowed himself through law school in Bloomington, Indiana. Moved from there to Michigan, tipped by a professor that the Detroit area offered money and jobs to a man who didn't mind scrambling. He didn't mind. Paid off his last student loan three years ago August.

Until, telling himself he needed to feel needed, and for God's sake, this place needed *something*, he'd just recently returned. Omitted from his reasoning was the wedding he'd fled a few months ago. He wanted that memory excised like a cancerous tumor. Someday he hoped to stop dreaming about it.

When the Presbyterian minister had asked him to repeat, "'Til death do us part," an abrupt revelation, maybe born from the idea of being with the same woman until death, had choked off his response. Unable to stop himself, he leaned toward her until their eyes were inches apart. Misinterpreting this move for admiration, she flashed him her familiar photo-op smile but, soon bored, let her gaze drift. Staring at her, searching her face, he knew with sickening clarity that by standing there, young and pretty, she was giving him her best. His hand dropped hers. He began to perspire.

Seconds passed. Facing him in a cloud of Vera Wang gown, physically perfect, she waited with growing impatience. The minister pointedly cleared his throat. Phil Roberts could only stare, mute, while he suddenly replayed in his mind as if hearing it for the first time how the crowning glory of her entire life had occurred eight years ago, when elected president of her university's leading sorority while still a sophomore. A Chi Phi Mu record, she always insisted to listeners, as if it were the Pulitzer Prize and she its least known recipient, deserving of better publicity. She also bubbled over with excitement when musing over her next-best expected triumph, which would be when *her daughter* entered the University of Michigan sorority (a given, as a legacy of her mother, who'd set the record...blah, blah). Surely her precious daughter (a carbon copy of *her*) would someday equal that achievement! Go Big Blue!

For the first time, he asked himself what lay beneath that satiny caramel tan? What magic beat within that heart, what feverish ideas fired her brain? The question was only self-flagellation, because he knew the answer. Had always known but hadn't cared to face it until this moment. Time would bring no complexities, no awakenings, nothing but cosmetic ruin to the perky sheen that had so attracted him, although with his expected income, surgery was always available. Her soul, her being, overflowed with a solemn dedication to year-round tennis and summer golf practiced religiously twice a week under the supervision of coaches, because that's all daddy could afford. After marriage to him she would increase to five lessons a week, a blissful prospect.

Memories of her cherished triumph buoyed her daily as if she'd been crowned just yesterday. Was this Barbie? God, he begged the chaste cross behind the minister, am I *Ken*?

Galvanized by his questions, terrified of the answers, he crossed Detroit's city limits an hour later—alone—perplexed at both his horror and his ungainly flight. She'd been angry. Her mother had been furious. He didn't care. In sweaty, abject fear he ran. He shuddered, thrust back into this memory for the thousandth time. He gripped the cup tighter. Move on, he warned himself.

Back home. Okay, yes, Trueden Falls was home. For now. No decision was stone yet. Never had to be, for that matter. Meanwhile, nobody remembered him, and he had a practice to build. So he'd applied for and gotten the unpopular, unwanted post of Public Defender. It was a start. He wanted passionately to start again. But to start what? To end up where?

He smiled at Miss Dayton and tried to remember more about Jenny. He couldn't. Miss Dayton seemed unaware he was still here. He sighed. His toes were numbing in his Cole Haans.

His last reserves of geniality chilling along with his feet, he asked, "What do you do all day by yourself?"

She shrugged, still within herself, and answered absently, "Read. Housework. Listen to records." She looked up. "I sew. Costumes."

"Costumes?"

She smiled, faintly. "Dresses."

"How about curtains?"

"Certainly, curtains." Her smile vanished, maybe remembering Mr. Stoner's shroud.

"Doesn't sound too boring."

She tilted her head at him, frowning. "I'm never bored."

"Ah, yes. Boring people get bored, I remember hearing that myself. Did you know Mr. Stoner?"

She shook her head. "Never met him before."

Phil quit the soft chat. "Before when, before you killed him? Before you buried him, for you almost certainly buried him. Or before the cops showed you his decomposed body?"

She didn't answer.

Inwardly he groaned. She'd said in court that she'd never known him alive, a statement open to vast interpretation that he, as her would-be defender, had crossed his fingers over, and the prosecution must've slept through. He needed to ask, now, though.

"Miss Dayton. Had you ever met Mr. Stoner before you buried him?"

She raised troubled eyes to his. After a moment, she asked, "Do I have to talk to you?"

"Pardon?"

"If I refuse to talk, do I go to jail after all? I mean, would they take me away from here to stay in jail until time for my trial?"

He glared at her, stood. "No. You can keep your mouth tight as a clamshell and still stay in your house. But you'll be doing yourself a favor to confide in me, since I'm the only one on your side in this town."

"You're required to be."

"What?"

"On my side. You don't care what happens to me. It's just your job to act like it. You'll get paid whatever the verdict. What if I'm as crazy as the neighbors say? Can so many people be wrong against the protests of one?"

"If you protested, I never heard it. Time to defend yourself, Miss Dayton. I can't do this alone. You lay down like a weak kitten, they'll convict you, guilty or not. Nobody likes you."

"So is law a popularity contest?" Her breathing was level, indifferent.

Roberts searched her expression for a clue to her thinking. "Look. My integrity would cost the government a hell of a lot more than my salary, if it were for sale. You have to trust somebody, and I'm not the worst choice you might make. Had you ever seen him before? Did you know him? Know *of* him?"

She picked up her coffee, although surely it was cold now, and sipped.

Furious, he plucked his briefcase from the floor and buttoned his coat. "Ma'am, if convicted, you'll definitely have to leave your house." He walked out the door, leaving her sitting at the table with her icy coffee. What if she was indeed as crazy as her neighbors claimed? But her popularity question stung, pricking him to worry. A sophomoric question. Wasn't it?

Still angry, although some of it directed at himself for ineptly handling a frail old woman, he stopped at the utility offices and enrolled her in the federally-assisted fuel program. He kept his promises. Well, as long as he was careful what he promised, he did. Again he pushed Detroit out of his head.

Later, Donnie filled him in on the facts as he knew them. He also told Phil about Mrs. Stoner, the state she was in, and that for motive, she had the most reasons to keep her husband as healthy as possible. A few phone calls had revealed that Stoner's insurance, even with its double indemnity clause, would keep her far less well than his income had. As Donnie finished, both fell silent, eyeing each other.

Donnie muttered then how unsettling it was to him, sympathizing with an alleged murderer. He grinned wryly. "My black-and-white ideals of justice seem to be acquiring shades of grey. It doesn't sit comfortably."

Phil thought about that. "At least you know what your ideals are," he finally said, and left.

The day after Miss Dayton's court appearance, the *Weekly Sentinel* printed a letter to their Editor-In-Chief from the leader of a white supremist commune that subsisted on a ramshackle farm on the outskirts of town. The leader claimed credit for Rudy Stoner's death. "Purifying the School for Innocent Children," ran the header, repeating a phrase from the letter's text.

Phil took the paper to show Donnie.

Donnie read it, chuckled grimly. "Last thing those maggots would do is bury the body. They'd hang it from the stoplight at the Main and Highway 37 Bypass. They don't allow their larvae to attend public school, anyway. Might inspire the kids to trade hardscrabble labor for indoor plumbing and video games. Somebody out there's got a certificate for 'home teaching.' I always suspected it was bogus."

Phil mused, "Nice of them to try to take the heat off an old lady."

Donnie snorted. "Think I'll write that in a letter to the editor. Last thing they want is to be accused of something nice. Yeah, I'll do that."

Phil's case was heading nowhere fast, not that it had ever started. It lay on the floor like a dead thing nobody could identify or wanted.

A few forays around town revealed that Miss Dayton led the life of a hermit. No clubs, no church, no meals away from home. Not that

Trueden Falls offered much more than the Dining Car Diner. Library books in volume, the titles revealing her deep fondness for sewing and couture. And home repair books. Phil puzzled over the number of repair books listed on her record. No car, so she walked everywhere, not hard in a town this size. Healthy. The town's only general practitioner, a slight, overworked, but still energetic man in his early seventies, admitted he hadn't seen her within memory but hadn't noticed, being so busy. "Everyone should do so well!" said the doc, recalling her only faintly, but impressed.

Walking must suit her, Phil mused, and he decided to walk more, himself.

A visit to Mrs. Stoner left him, like Deputy Cox, bereft of motive or a list of enemies. When mentioning to her that she and her husband might be resented for the color of their skin by a certain element in this backwater, her mouth twisted as if remembering an old frustration. "Rudy liked it here. But money's a problem," she added, suddenly tense.

Phil slid forward on the sofa, his comfort hampered by the scatter of canned foods roosting there. "Won't your insurance company advance you funds?"

Tears formed. "They said no cash until the case is settled. They got to find that old lady guilty."

Phil suddenly imagined Miss Dayton bashing in the head of a big man like Rudy Stoner. Unfortunately, it was all too believable. The autopsy had revealed no self-defense wounds. The woman looked too harmless to scare a rabbit, but seemed all steel under that powdery skin. She could've given that elm branch at least one good home-run swing, cracking that skull before Stoner figured out what she was up to. And then there was the kitchen curtain shroud.

"The trial's soon, Denise," Phil said. "And it'll be a short run," he added wryly, thinking of his empty briefcase. "You won't have long to wait."

"Better not. I got expenses." Denise pulled her feet up to tuck under her long body in an overstuffed chair that matched the sofa. She reached over her shoulder for a pack of Marlboro Lights lying on the TV, and picking one, lit up.

"What expenses?" asked Phil, perplexed. "Insurance pays off the house for you, doesn't it?"

"Other expenses." She breathed out smoke.

Phil leaned towards her, tipping more groceries towards his thighs with the movement. "Denise, what do you do all day, here alone?" he asked suddenly, remembering Miss Dayton. Two people, so solitary.

She let one arm flop listlessly. Gazed around as if she'd suddenly arrived at an unfamiliar place, then shook her head. "Nothing."

Phil repeated, "Nothing?" He looked around at the mess. "You're not fond of housekeeping."

She snorted. "Who is?"

He puffed out his cheeks, then expelled air, thinking. "Mmm. You know, I could use a drink. Got anything on hand, Denise? A beer?"

Denise blinked at him in surprise. She shrugged, letting her gaze drift. "We don't drink."

"At all?"

"Oh, birthdays. I like champagne sometimes, but who can afford it?" she asked bitterly.

"Seen your doctor lately?" pressed Phil.

"Yes."

"Bet he says you're real stressed, doesn't he?"

Denise's eyes connected with his for a surprised second. "Yeah. He said that." She shrugged. "But how can I help it?"

"Did he give you any tranquilizers?"

"A few. I don't like them, though. Make me dizzy."

Phil pressed on. "You knit? Have any hobbies? Sewing, ceramics? Collect baseball cards?"

Denise grimaced. "You crazy? No. Takes money, anyway."

"Too bad. Hard to imagine you just sitting here all day. You're an intelligent woman. Do friends stop by? Do you read? Is there anything I can bring you to help you pass the time?"

"No," she answered shortly. "Everything's too damn boring."

Phil sat back, perched his ankle on a knee, expression baffled. "I know what you mean. I took up law for the excitement. Like acting, but in a courtroom." He flinched, hearing himself. *Ken* wins a suspect's confidence! "Better than factory work." Well, that was damn sure the truth.

Denise finally gave him her attention. Her eyes burned at him. "This town's dull," she said. "It's hard to live in all this nothing-shit. Fields and empty roads, and seventeen shades of white."

He dropped a twenty on her smudged coffee table and left.

That afternoon he crossed paths with Donnie, who was surveying the high school track yet again for signs of violence.

Donnie muttered, "Having no notion where Stoner was killed is a real problem. Miss Dayton could never have dragged his big body to her yard from here. From anywhere. The tech, however, thinks he wasn't killed where he was buried. Maybe."

"Did she lure him to her yard?" Phil speculated.

Donnie's eyes squeezed shut in frustration. "Could be. Stoner was one of the good guys. He would've gone to help an old lady."

Elms dotted the edges of the school property. But then, elms could be found in many places. Donnie never realized so many elms grew in Trueden Falls. The murderer could have acquired a branch of elm anywhere. Maybe while out walking, Miss Dayton had spotted it and admired its heft. The significance of no elms growing in her back yard diminished, taking with it some of Phil's defense argument.

Interviewing Mr. Stoner's peers at the school, even some of his students, gave Phil nothing more than a picture of a man so steadfast in character that even in Trueden Falls the color of his skin was discounted. No bad habits. A hobby of working on his house. Supportive and protective of his wife. No more debts than the next guy. A superior influence on the coma-brained children floating through his classes. Cheery and contented in his self-created niche. Phil was as much awed as he was irritated. "Funny that this paragon ended up dead," he said to Donnie, with whom he was rapidly becoming familiar.

Four days after the arraignment, Phil caught sight of children pelting his still uncooperative client with cement chunks pulled from the crumbling street curbs. After he leapt from his Acura, scattering the brats, she had scurried home, not bothering to thank him.

At Phil's request, Donnie then switched Willy from night to twenty-four-hour guard duty. From then on Willy stayed at Miss Dayton's side. The deputy swiftly acquired use of a spare bedroom in her old house, although his bedroll was still necessary. But plenty of heat now. (Again, no gratitude.) To both Donnie and Phil's amazement, Miss Dayton and Willy had taken to each other. "Willy's gotten a grandma out of this," Phil teased. But Donnie, knowing Willy's burdensome need for constant kindness and endless patience, found his newly grey ideas of judgment greying even more, and he was troubled.

Phil concluded after six full days of fruitless investigations (added to Deputy Cox's similarly fruitless efforts) that to find Jenny might be helpful, if not vital. At the very least, she might get the old lady to tell her side of things. So the search for Jenny began.

The town, as usual, caught on. And suddenly everybody remembered Jenny. How pretty. How sweet. Smart, too, and not wild, meaning she hadn't "given it away," like many. But now that you mention it, she never dated, did she? Was she a lesbian? Surely not, but then… Imagine, a girl with her looks.

Her grandmother probably hadn't allowed boys around. Kept an iron grip. Afraid she'd lose her built-in nurse and housekeeper. No wonder Jenny'd snuck out of town, nobody noticing. While the old lunatic slept, must've been.

"Nurse?" questioned Phil as rumors flew. Cathy kept him as informed now as she did Donnie.

"The old lady, she was sick a lot back then. The cold bothered her, if I remember," said Cathy.

Phil returned to the doctor and asked. He looked up her records, then agreed, the cold *had* hurt the woman, worse every year. Rheumatoid arthritis, weak lungs and heart. Yes, quite often Jenny would have to nurse her along through bronchitic winters. "Devoted, though," added the old doctor. "Those two were spirited. Had a good time together. Nice to see."

"You didn't get the impression Miss Dayton kept Jenny under her thumb? Looks like she hasn't needed any care since. Maybe she was exaggerating her problems, trying to keep Jenny home?"

"Mmm, y'know, people sometimes rise to the occasion. Maybe she made more effort when the girl left, and it strengthened her in the long run." He shook his head. "I know what you're talking about, though. It was what, six, eight years ago Jenny left?"

"Eight," said Phil, short-temperedly, reminded it was now December 3. Eight days gone already. Six days to trial. What case?

Then two of Miss Dayton's neighbors dropped in at the Town Hall. Cathy immediately radioed Donnie, who had been cruising the three Swifty Convenience Marts, showing himself to discourage those who considered the quick-stops as personal ATM machines. He picked up her call and rolled, the big Buick thundering through the quiet streets until he reached the Town Hall.

He found a thirtyish couple shifting and fidgeting in the open space in front of Cathy's high-platformed desk. Cathy was keeping a wary eye on them, her annoyance perceptible only to Donnie. Her pencil tap-tap-tapped on an IRS form she was using to correct Willy's withholding taxes. Theirs was a mutual-support operation.

Before Donnie could ask, the couple burst into simultaneous babble, each vying for the deputy's attention. "Everybody knows you can't find Jenny Dayton." "Not a trace." "Nobody remembers her leaving." "It's not possible."

Finally, the wife held up a hand and the husband's mouth clamped shut. "We've been thinking," she stated.

And you think I haven't, added Donnie to himself.

"These days," she declared, "with checking accounts, credit cards, phone bills, records like that make it easy to find a person."

"True. But it's not likely Jenny had a credit card when she left," said Donnie mildly. "No job. No income. And no phone. At least, not in Trueden Falls."

The woman blinked. "No phone?"

"The Dayton family built that house back in '86. 1886," he clarified. "No phone installed. Ever."

She made an "O" with her mouth. "I thought people *had* to have a phone," she said to her husband.

Donnie waited.

"Mortgage, leases, taxes?" ventured the husband.

"No mortgage. A small equity loan was taken out twelve years ago, to finance repairs to the house. Miss Dayton still pays on that and also pays her taxes. Nothing's been found in Jenny Dayton's name. So far." Not their business, but he didn't mind corking some of the gossip with actual information.

A flush crept up the woman's round, paste-colored face, a face that make-up would have improved. "Well, still, we think you should dig up Miss Dayton's yard some more."

The little hairs all over Donnie's skin stood up on end. He peered at the woman, then at her meek husband. A small paunch strained the buttons on the husband's coat, which was of nicer quality than any Donnie had seen except on Phil. "What'd you say your names were?"

"Laura and Steven Maccles," intoned Cathy from her desk, eyes still on the IRS form.

"And you folks do what for a living?"

"I sell insurance over in Pine City," said Steven Maccles. "My own agency, so I can make good deals!" he added sprightly, alert for business.

"I'm a nurse at County Hospital," said Laura mulishly. "And I've seen a lot, so I'm not naïve, don't you think it."

Donnie nodded at her amiably, not interested in letting her know what he thought. He ushered them out without listening to their excuses for squealing on an old lady, which seemed to bother them. Predictably, they balked, but finally left.

"Personality can either gloss over a load of sins, or air them out on the front porch unnecessarily," he commented to Cathy. Meanwhile, Cathy, who never needed to have things spelled out, dialed the judge's office and handed the receiver to Donnie. Minutes later, as Donnie jogged upstairs to fetch his warrant, she called the local volunteer fire department and asked for two men with shovels to meet Deputy Cox at Miss Dayton's back yard. Donnie said he'd let her know in a bit if she should call Miss Dayton's lawyer. And if the lawyer was needed, then so would the part-time crime scene tech. Cathy nodded.

On a hunch, Donnie had instructed the digging to begin near Mr. Stoner's former grave, so discovery hadn't taken long. The ground had been hard to move, nearly frozen from this week's unusually low temperatures.

The flesh had long since gone back to the dust from which it had been formed, if the bible be literally believed. The thin-boned skeleton disconnected its parts at the first touch, leaving the Medical Examiner counting tiny hand and toe bones to be sure he got them all.

Phil peered at the skeleton. "Small. Like a child's bones," he said. The Examiner gave that an abrupt negative.

Donnie brooded, silently grieving for this lost girl, forever lost now. When he glanced up, he saw the pink flowered kitchen curtain drop back into place. He wondered what Miss Dayton was thinking about now.

They blocked off the area again, using the uncollected saw horses and tape from the last digging. "You'll have to wait for the autopsy report," said the Examiner, "to know whether a crime's been committed. Other than using residential land for burial, that is."

A crime, but low on Donnie's priority list at the moment.

Donnie and Phil jointly decided not to consult Miss Dayton until they had the corpse's identity and manner of death. "Let her simmer," Donnie muttered bitterly. "She hasn't opened up yet, why should she now, even with this second body adding to her troubles?"

"She doesn't trust us," Phil shrugged. "The woman trusts nobody. And the more I learn about her life, the less I resent it. All she's been able to cling to seems to be this old house. And far as I can tell, it's the only thing in her life that hasn't let her down."

He and Phil drove off in their separate cars to meet at the Dining Car. They found a booth with no maple syrup tracks on the red vinyl and sat. After swiping crumbs from the table, Donnie called to the waitress, a compact, natural redhead in her forties who'd astonished him by never marrying. She liked being at the diner so much, she said, marriage would just interfere. The crossroads of Trueden Falls.

Donnie gestured at Phil. "Hey, Barb. New man in town, Phil Roberts. Attorney."

Barb grinned wide and gave him a nod. "Welcome, sucker."

"You're too kind. I'm from here, actually."

"Nah. Nobody's from *here*."

"You don't remember me, but nobody could forget a woman like you," leered Phil, winking at her.

"Those *eyelashes*!" Barb squealed and swanned her way back to the counter.

Both ordered tea. Hard to screw up a tea bag. Donnie was amused to see this evidence of like minds. While they waited, Phil enlightened Donnie about the blind alleys he'd run down and the useless details he'd learned. "The victim was loved by all. If you ignore the bullshit stories, Miss Dayton could be a model for model citizens—except for her burial habits and that damning curtain, which still doesn't make her a murderer. Denise Stoner doesn't drink or do drugs. Unless some brat killed Mr. Stoner in revenge for an F in math, I can't think of one damned reason he's dead, or find one damned suspect for killing him!"

When the teabags and hot water arrived, Donnie fanned the case file papers between them like a card game, but his attention soon drifted from the too familiar reports. Phil dunked his bag rhythmically while he picked among the papers.

After a while, Barb came over and leaned against Donnie's booth cushion, nudging him with a nicely rounded hip. He looked up at her, surprised. She asked, "Checked anybody into your downtown suite lately?" Leaning over his shoulder, she poked at Donnie's nearly black, neglected tea, then removed the tea bag for him.

Donnie blinked. "The cell? Maybe some spiders, why?"

"Thought you mighta arrested Hooker. Not been in his corner booth for some days. Man of habit, Hooker. Seen him around?"

"No," Donnie said flatly. "And who cares?"

She laughed, a bit uneasily. "Well, fact is, I bagged a big one on the Atlanta/Steelers game. He owes me money." Hooker was the only bookie in town Donnie hadn't been able to run off. Card games, guessing the minute the sun would set on Christmas Day, but mostly sports. Whatever you wanted to give him money for, he'd take it. His flexibility served him well, but he did like eating at the Dining Car.

"When'd you last see him?"

She scratched her nose with her ballpoint, counting back. "About… ah, geeze. Few weeks ago."

"Before or after we dug up Mr. Stoner?"

She thought. "Now that's funny. That's the day I first missed him, I remember now. We all waited to see how he'd figure a betting angle from it, and he never showed."

"Barb." He glared at her until she flushed. She knew his opinion of gambling and the riff-raff it attracted. "You want me to find and bring back a leech this town is better off without? No. Unless you won enough to change your life."

She flushed.

After a pause, Donnie sighed. "Shouldn't be too hard. He's too lazy to start somewhere new, with so many here on his books. Probably just went south for vacation. I'll look around."

The size of Barb's relief told Donnie the size of the pot.

"Jesus, Barb. You ever gamble again in Trueden Falls, I'll be fluffing that pillow in the downtown suite just for you. That's a promise."

"Aw, Donnie, it was just a fly—okay, okay." She scuttled away.

Phil focused on Donnie. "You see this?" He pointed at the pile of paper.

"What?"

"Nothing, that's what. Where's Mrs. Stoner's missing person report?"

"Oh, it's—" He searched through the pile. He searched again. "Um, I think we got an oops here. And that's Willy's middle name. By God, I assumed Cathy talked to her, not Willy."

"Maybe she didn't write anything down?"

"Cathy? Hell'd be a snow cap before she made an error like that."

Phil canted his body to fit the banquette curves, spread his arms over its back. "So how did you learn Stoner was missing?"

"Willy told me. Never thought to ask for a report. I knew Stoner, didn't need to read about him." Donnie compressed his lips.

"So you've got nothing in writing?"

"Hell, can't be." He started through the pile of papers again.

Phil held up a finger. "Hang on." A moment later, he held up a dated phone log notation, initialed by Willy, that Rudy Stoner hadn't been seen at home, was considered missing. "Does this mean Mrs. Stoner talked to Willy on that day?"

Donnie scanned the paper. "Looks like it. Still, he should've made out a full report. Willy tries hard. It'll upset him to find out he didn't do something right." He slid the sheet around. "Hey. This is from November 14. That was a Monday. I swear she said he disappeared Friday, November 11."

Phil frowned at the paper. "Could Willy get the day wrong?"

"On a report, sure. But this is the daily log. We can cross-check the other entries to confirm the date. Cathy probably saw Willy's entry and made this copy for the Stoner file. Original's probably where it ought to be, still in the book, knowing Cathy."

Phil mused. "Mrs. Stoner's a nervous, vulnerable woman who needs her husband. Wouldn't she panic and call the police an hour after he was due home? And the school probably called her on Friday to see what happened. They'd need to hire a substitute for his classes. They must've been as alarmed as his wife when he didn't show up. He was known to be totally reliable."

Donnie pursed his lips. "Willy could've screwed up. Or maybe she remembers the day wrong from being upset. A loose end. Want to go with me to tie it up?"

Phil didn't answer at first, too busy watching Barb. Donnie grinned at first, seeing this. Then a thoughtful look crossed his face.

At Mrs. Stoner's, Phil cringed as he was forced to nest in a pool of neglected laundry. He hoped it was clean. Two cushions over, Donnie got the spot still awash with canned goods. Phil glanced around the messy room. Worse than before. Produce had wilted. Was she eating? She didn't look fed.

Donnie hunched forward, dangled his hands over his knees. "Denise, did your husband disappear on Friday the eleventh or Monday the fourteenth? We're finding a discrepency here. Did you call us the day he disappeared. Or did you wait a few days, and then call? I haven't got it straight, could you help me out?"

Denise rubbed the skin between her eyes with the hand holding the cigarette. "I, uh, I don't really remember. I was so messed up over him not being home."

"The morning he went missing—did the school call here, looking for him?" asked Phil.

Denise stared at Phil. "I don't—well, sure they did. I think I told them that they shouldn't expect him at school." She gestured with the cigarette in her bony hand. "That's logical, isn't it? Didn't come home to change, wouldn't go to work in his sweats, would he?"

Phil said, "Denise. Did you use those exact words?"

Denise shrugged.

"Because maybe the school would think nothing was wrong if you put it so casually, in that tone of voice?" He ended on a questioning note, but Denise didn't comment. "Well, okay," he said to Donnie, "I'll call the school. They had to get in a substitute, they'll have a record."

Donnie said, "Come to that, maybe Miss Dayton can be persuaded to tell us when she buried him. Confirm that date, at least. Assuming he was buried within the same twenty-four hours he died." He turned again to Denise. "Sure you can't tell us exactly what day he went missing?"

She drew heavily on the cigarette, then exhaled smoke with a jerky negative motion of her head. "Sorry. I'm just not sure."

Phil sat back and folded his arms, as if to yield the floor to Donnie. Donnie asked, "Denise, you know Barb, don't you? Waitress at the Dining Car? Took a bet with a bookie named Hooker, won some major cash. On a football game! Her whole life'll change, that's how much money she won."

"Now *that's* exciting, isn't it, Denise?" asked Phil, arms still folded.

Denise caught her breath, glowing with sudden interest. "Hell, yes. Should happen to *me*."

Looking at her, her defective body curled up in her soiled chair in her lonely house, Phil had to agree. He leaned forward, said, "Say, I'm thirsty. The Dining Car's tea didn't do much for me." He surmised she wouldn't move to fetch him a drink, and she didn't disappoint him. "You mind I get myself some water from the kitchen, Denise?"

She shrugged.

He extricated himself carefully from the sunken cushion so he wouldn't dump clothes onto the floor. "Can I get either of you anything?" he asked.

Her lanky arm waved him away.

Donnie began a long disjointed explanation of when she'd receive her husband's body for burial and the reason for the delay. She appeared to be thinking of something else, which was just as well, as he winged his way through some nonsense forensic rules. Soon he began thinking, what was Phil doing back there, taking so long! He should've gone himself. Well. Except he'd get in a world of trouble if he did. He began rubbing his palms together nervously and chattered on about Mr. Stoner's classes he'd taken when a child himself. Denise had totally tuned him out.

Finally Phil reappeared in the arched doorway. In his hand was a piece of lined, yellow, legal-sized notepad paper, much wrinkled and scribbled on. He waved it at Donnie. "On the floor by her bed. Like everything else that's not in here."

Phil dropped it into Donnie's palm and plopped down again among the laundry. Denise saw the paper, bolted up straight. She gripped her knees with her two hands, quivering. "You went in my bedroom?"

Donnie spread the paper across his broad knee and read it silently.

Phil said, "You're a slob, Denise. A dirty, lazy human being. My mother would've grounded you until you learned to throw trash in a trash can, not on the floor. Didn't you have a mother?"

"Yes." Her reply was a whisper.

"Have a father, too?"

"Yes."

"Were they good to you? Loving, kind parents?"

"Yes."

"And Mr. Stoner did everything for you, he loved you so much."

"Yes," she sobbed.

"So where did you learn to love gambling more than your husband?"

Her eyes stared so fixedly, Phil worried that she might be in shock.

Donnie sat forward on the sofa. "Denise. You sure pissed off whoever wrote this crazy note. It's from Hooker, right?" He glanced at Phil. "Barb can confirm his writing, but it's got to be. Look what he says."

Denise swayed in the chair but said nothing.

Donnie held up the paper. "Look how much he says you owe him, this rat shit! Your husband'd never be able to get that much together if he worked all his life, and another life, too, would he, Denise? Even if he sold his house. But he could…by dying. This note mentions how much life insurance you got coming. Now, how'd he get that personal piece of information? Then he claims it's all his, all but the pocket change."

He tucked the paper neatly into a breast pocket. "He calls you some not very nice names for not phoning my office the Friday morning Rudy went missing, as instructed. You waited until Monday. Willy did get the day right. What held you up, Denise? Were you paralyzed with fright, 'cause you knew why your husband never showed? This note from Hooker, now you knew he was a murderer, must've scared you silly."

He turned to Phil as if making conversation and added, "That anonymous call, telling us to check out Miss Dayton's house for a dead man. Hooker again. When Miss Dayton buried him, she *really* screwed up his plan!" He looked soberly at Denise. "Snake Eyes for Hooker. You wait three days to call in the missing person report, and Miss Dayton buries him to avoid trouble."

Phil mused in a low voice, "Can't collect insurance money if no corpse is found, as Denise already pointed out."

Denise's lower lip quivered.

"You got a gambling habit, Denise," persisted Donnie.

She shook her head, a jerky movement.

Donnie ignored it. "I can see why Hooker wouldn't want to be seen near you, but why'd he write a note? Why didn't he just call?"

Nothing.

Making a guess, Phil reached over, picked up a nearby phone, listened to the receiver. "They cut your service? Non-payment?"

Nothing.

Donnie laid his hand gently on the back of her neck. Her skin was icy, bloodless. "That insurance, with double indemnity for murder, would pay off Hooker okay. What were you going to live on after that?"

Her face crumpled and she began to sob, still upright and stiff. "I don't know. I couldn't think. Hooker, he said he'd stake me to start over. Do better next time—" She choked on her own words, then cradled her face in her hands. Donnie watched her cry.

"So Hooker attacks Rudy on a dark morning at the deserted high school track," Donnie said. "Hauls him to Miss Dayton's, along with the elm branch, the murder weapon. Lets her take the blame, with her reputation for being nuts and all. Plus, a white woman all by herself and Rudy being big and black. A natural conclusion in certain circles, right?" He nudged Denise.

Keeping her face hidden in her hands, she pulled away. "Hooker didn't ask my opinion."

"Pretty vicious note, Denise. Says he'll carve it outta your face, if he can't get Rudy's money," commented Phil. "You could use that in your defense."

Donnie swiveled to look at him. Phil raised his palms. "Public Defender. Maybe she didn't know what he was going to do?"

"I *didn't*!"

Donnie turned back to Denise. "Then how'd Hooker know about the insurance?"

She wiped her broad palm across her eyes, then looked up. "I mentioned it. Like collateral for a loan. Thought I could convince him to carry me a while longer, I could win a few times, pay off the debt. Didn't have a notion that he'd do something like…"

"Like collect the insurance himself." Donnie stood and told her to find a coat so she could come with him. Phil trailed out the front door behind them and, even though Denise seemed unconcerned, locked it behind his new client.

That same afternoon, the autopsy report for the second skeleton dug out of Miss Dayton's back yard arrived. Adult female, no foul play detected. Donnie puzzled over the report, sorting out the technical phrases. Then he called Phil and arranged to pick him up a few minutes later.

"Miss Dayton," began Phil.

She was seated at her kitchen table between the two standing men.

Donnie leaned against her sink, hoping to look trustworthy, or at least unintimidating. He heard Willy's spirited whistling from an upstairs room. Grateful Dead. Willy was a champion whistler, which was fortunate because he sang like Janis Joplin with infected adenoids.

Phil tilted his head towards the back yard, glancing through the windows. "We guessed who the second person is, buried back there. It isn't your granddaughter, Jenny Dayton. Is it?"

She lifted her olive eyes to his. Again, he marveled at how clear they were. "May I touch you?" he asked. He reached a tentative hand to her cheek. She didn't move, but seemed to steel herself. He fumbled with blunt fingers at the edge of her jaw, then slowly, surely began to peel whisper thin latex away from soft firm skin. Eerie seconds passed as she emerged from his efforts, blinking at shreds he'd left behind on her eyelids, calmly waiting for him to finish.

"Youth is a state of mind," she finally said, startling him.

Phil looked at the fragments of latex dangling from his fingers like rubbery spider webs. "Looks like youth is knowing how to use stage makeup!"

"*Who are you*?" Donnie softly asked, tensely.

"I'm Miss Dayton. Of course."

"Jenny? Or Julia?"

She lowered her eyes to her lap. Her hands lay one on each knee, but with weightless grace, not frozen and gripping with fear like Denise.

"Sometimes I believe I'm Julia," she murmured. "But it's just that I forget for a while. It used to upset me to forget, but then I thought maybe it was better. Less chance of mistakes. But don't worry. I know who I am. I am in full possession of my mind."

Phil crouched to get closer to her. "Why did you become Julia?"

She smiled faintly at him. "To keep the checks coming, so I could live in our house like all the other Daytons. Grandmother taught me everything so I could manage when she was gone. When she died I buried her. We wanted to stay close to each other, so that was all right. We planned it together."

"Couldn't you get a job, make money?" asked Donnie, relieved that she at least sounded stable in spite of the life she'd made for herself.

She shrugged. "Doing what? Factory line work, waitressing at the Dining Car? Minimum wage would feed me, but how would I pay for electricity? Heat? And…and sewing supplies."

"And repairs of vandalism damage," said Phil.

She nodded. "Social Security and my grandfather's VA pension covers expenses if I'm careful. It is *our home*. The Dayton house. We were here before everybody. Before *they* came."

"*They* being your neighbors?" asked Donnie.

She gazed at Donnie, perplexed. "I've never understood why they ha…hate me. Are they jealous? Have I offended them? Please, if you understand what went wrong, tell me. All these years I still can't figure it out."

Donnie shook his head. "I don't know either. Honest to God, I'd give anything to fix it." Then he stepped closer to her. "But you've broken a few laws, Miss *Jenny* Dayton."

She glared up at Donnie with sharp intelligence. "So I'm to go to jail after all? And I'll get what, two or three years for fraud? And lose my house. Well, that will satisfy *them*. Maybe."

Donnie stared at her, then at Phil. He shifted his weight from one foot to another. "Well, damn," he finally said.

Phil shrugged. "I don't mind." And he was pleased to notice that he really didn't. "But she needs a new plan," he said firmly.

After the trial of Denise Stoner and Jerry Hooker came to a sordid, avidly-attended conclusion in late February, old Miss Dayton left her house in the care of Assistant Deputy William Stanton. He was to house-sit while she recuperated from her ordeal in a Florida nursing home of a complicated name, difficult for Willy to remember if asked. But nobody asked. As these things go, Miss Dayton soon perished there and was buried in the same city to save costs, she having no family to object. Willy could hardly be restrained from going to Florida, he was so devastated.

Charges pending against her for improper use of residential-zoned land for burial were set aside. Most agreed it was improbable she'd buried the bodies anyway, a frail lady of eighty-two. The second skeleton's identity puzzled everybody, but with no reason to suspect foul play and no budget for more extensive tests, the desire for answers gradually withered. The anonymous woman was reinterred as a Jane Doe in the public cemetery, with only Deputy Cox, Willy Stanton, and Public Defender Roberts in attendance.

With inexplicable timing, young Miss Jenny Dayton suddenly returned home. When informed of her grandmother's demise, she gently evicted Willy, then withdrew from public scrutiny for a while.

Phil, Donnie, and Willy visited her often enough to cause some buzzing around the neighborhood, but with no signs of misbehavior the gossip fell to a grudging trickle. With the arrival of spring in Trueden Falls and the nearer towns came newspaper ads and flyers advertising "Opening Day" for a reasonably-priced custom clothing designer salon. The services included style and makeup tips.

When Jenny Dayton revealed that she had made many of her grandmother's exquisite clothes, the tide of customers through her doorway expanded into a river, until the neighbors complained she was running a business in a residential zone. So she opened a shop near the Dining Car Diner.

A subdued Willy stuck close to Donnie until mid-March, when he began tagging along behind Miss Jenny, as he insisted on calling her, on her shopping trips, carrying her bags as he'd done for her grandmother. It wasn't long until he asked, kneading his hat brim between nervous fingers, if he could fix up the carriage house as an apartment and rent it from her. Miss Dayton had been as close to a grandmother as he'd ever known, he said, and maybe Miss Jenny wouldn't mind if he stayed around, in honor of her memory. He could make himself useful in the yard, fix things, and maybe scare the vandals away for good. Miss Jenny understood and told him she didn't mind sharing her grandmother with him. She'd always wanted a brother.

Just like old Miss Dayton, she liked to walk everywhere. She did many things just like old Miss Dayton, including treating Willy's shortcomings with kindly patience. So, although the old lady could never be replaced in his heart, Willy's grief eased.

Every day in her shop Miss Dayton wore many things designed by Yves St. Laurent, by Dior, by Jacques Fath, Ricci, and Givenchy. But her favorite was the taupe and cream Chanel dress and matching coat edged with silk flower appliqués, a 1927 design.

Blackfoot Joe

by Dennis Webster

Sheriff Bernie Block stood with his arms folded, his stiff tan police hat pulled down to his brow. The Bigfoot floats paraded down Main Street in front of the hundreds of townspeople, spectators, and tourists gathered on both sides of the two-lane road. He yawned. August sunbeams toasted his bare forearms. He looked at his watch, glad that there was little time left in the annual Lumberjack Hollow Bigfoot Festival parade. In a few days the festival would be over. Normally, the town got by with its several dozen residents and sporadic tourists from the Adirondack Railroad, but the August festival brought in a thousand visitors every year. This meant extra work for him and his deputy. The town elders loved the event for the tourist dollars that poured in, helping Lumberjack Hollow in the lean seasons of spring and fall. Winters brought snowmobilers and summer brought hikers, canoeists, and mountain bikers, but the bulk of travelers went to Saranac Lake or Lake Placid, with a small number of random tourists plopping into Lumberjack Hollow. Other than Cricket Lake, which was more like a sizable pond, the only other thing going for the town was the abundance of supposed Bigfoot sightings.

The call came over his radio. "Bernie? Sheriff?"

He tipped his hat back, then turned away from the sun, for it hurt his eyes. He took a step back from the crowd. "Yes, Angela."

"How're things looking over there?"

"Deputy, I asked you not to call me unless there's somethin' to be callin' me about. So don't call me unless there's somethin'."

"Yes, sir. Over and out."

Bernie chuckled as he placed the radio back on his leather belt. His rookie deputy was full of piss and vinegar. He looked both ways and walked back behind Lacky's Pub. The few deer roaming around the dumpster paused, gazed languidly at the Sheriff, and strolled away. He took out a cigarette, snapped a match with his thumbnail, and inhaled while shaking his head. Generations of humans feeding the deer had made them unafraid. He took a deep drag and suddenly sensed eyes on him. He wheeled to his right and found himself staring into the ketchup-and-mustard-smudged faces of two young tourist boys, around ten years old, both wearing one of the "I walked with Bigfoot" T-shirts sold in Ostrander's store. Bernie quickly threw his butt to the ground and tamped it out with the heel of his boot.

"What you boys doin' back here?"

They both fidgeted, first staring at his hat, then down to his badge, finally gaping at his gun.

They answered together, "We have to go to the bathroom."

"This ain't no outhouse, boys. Public bathroom right around the corner."

They ran off. The Sheriff regretted that the boys had seen him smoking. He took his job as Sheriff of Lumberjack Hollow seriously, and he knew he was a role model with a bad habit. He shook his head and went back out to watch the rest of the parade.

He always stood at the beginning of the parade route by Lacky's Pub, and he assigned his Deputy, Angela Barnes, to stand near the Lumberjack Hollow volunteer fire department. In the past, he was all that was needed when it came to law enforcement. He so rarely arrested anyone that the jailhouse cell had dust bunnies. However, the festival attracted some of the weirdest and scruffiest conspiracy theorists and cryptozoologists from across the country, all bringing their grainy woodland photos, plaster foot casts, and growling tape recordings as supposed proof of Bigfoot. That's why he hired Angela.

Sheriff Bernard Block didn't believe in such mythical creature nonsense. He was thirty-five years old, had hunted the rugged Adirondack

Mountains his entire life, and had never seen anything other than black bear, deer, fox, rabbits, and an occasional moose. He'd certainly never seen a nine-foot, woodland-strolling, mountain-hippie Bigfoot. But he did appreciate the festival and the money it made for the community. It allowed the town to have two new squad cars for him and Angela and a new pump truck for the fire department.

He leaned against the pole as the parade was concluding. Here came the honorable, the rich, the one and only Harold T. Willingham III in his silver Rolls Royce, ending the parade as always. The old man had started the Bigfoot craze when he was a boy, long before Bernie was born. Everyone knew the story. Harold's grandfather, Harold Sr., had founded Lumberjack Hollow and owned the sawmill over on Cricket Stream, at the mouth of Cricket Lake, that had stopped operating when Bernie was nine years old. The story, as told in Lumberjack Hollow, was that in 1935, Harold had been lollygagging around the campsite in the latest wood clearing created by loggers, when he wandered deep into the pines, was accosted by a Bigfoot, and wet himself. The lumberjacks laughed at the boy for peeing his pants and were docked a day's pay by Harold's father, Harold Jr. The boy supposedly had scratches and a fistful of chestnut hair yanked from the chest of the beast, but neither Bernie nor anyone else had ever seen the hair. It wasn't even in the museum that was a part of Moll and Jed Ostrander's Bigfoot Museum and Gift Shop.

Harold T. Willingham III, who never married, lived in the only house on Cricket Lake. He allowed free and open access to the lake for swimming, kayaking, canoeing, and paddle boating, but allowed no powerboats or jet skis. With the sawmill long since gone, Bernie often wondered how the hermit lived. He only went into town for the parade or a rare appearance at Lacky's Pub for a beer and Rueben. He was well liked but reclusive, and the town respected his privacy.

"God bless him," said Bernie, waving at Harold, marveling that the old man was driving the Rolls himself at his age.

Bernie was about to doze off standing up when the roar of an engine drew his attention. It was a dark green Land Rover, barreling towards the back of the parade. He ran out into the middle of the street with one hand up, while resting the other on his Glock pistol in its holster. The driver of the Land Rover slammed on the brakes and skidded to a stop inches from Bernie. The vehicle, adorned with plates from Washington State, had barely stopped when the driver jumped out and took a step towards him.

"Stop right there, Mister," said Bernie as he unsnapped the strap holding his weapon in its holster.

"Don't you know who I am?" the stranger said as he took the large cigar out of his mouth. "I come in peace, Mr. Officer, sir." He saluted.

Bernie lowered his hand, took off his hat, and wiped the sweat from his brow. "You're gonna hurt somebody drivin' like that. And, no, I don't know who you are."

"I'm Blackfoot Joe."

The stranger smiled through his Grizzly Adams beard. He wore a light brown leather jacket with fringe, matching pants, and boots. He looked like something right out of the Northwest Passage, a mountain man with a tan crusher pulled down to his ears.

"You part of the Donner party leftovers?"

"That's pretty funny."

"I'm Sheriff Bernard Block and I can't have you creating trouble in Lumberjack Hollow. There's spectators all over here and you drivin' like that." He ran his hand through his blonde hair with its early flecks of stress gray.

"Sheriff? What's the commotion?" buzzed Angela on the radio.

"I got it. Some stranger is drivin' crazy. I got it covered. Just watch the kids trying to go into Lacky's for a beer."

"I'll tell you who and what I am. You'll never forget my name when I'm through. In case you didn't catch it the first time, it's Blackfoot Joe. I'm a blended machine. I'm quarter Sioux, quarter Welsh, a fifth wolf, and a little bit of somethin' else."

"Whatever you say. If you're here for the parade, you just missed it. The Bigfoot Festival has a few more days. Park that vehicle and try to stay out of trouble."

The mountain man grinned at him and nodded. Bernie found the man obnoxious but compelling. Just then he heard a car behind him and turned to see the silver Rolls Royce coming to a halt.

"This must be my employer," said Blackfoot Joe, taking off his hat and pulling his long, greasy hair behind his ears. The window lowered slowly and Blackfoot moseyed over.

"Hello there."

"You must be Dr. Blackfoot Joe," said Harold T. Willingham III in a weakened octogenarian voice, "the notorious Bigfoot hunter."

"The one and only. You must be Willy."

"Absolutely, my good friend. Please follow me to the house so we can share a cognac and you can begin your quest."

"Sure, boss." Blackfoot Joe smiled at Bernie and slapped him on the shoulder as he walked by. "Thanks for the talk, Barney Fife." He shoved the cigar back between his lips and smirked at Bernie, then got in his car and followed the town patriarch down to the dirt access road that led to Cricket Lake and the old man's mansion.

Bernie just smiled and shook his head as he walked to the post-parade gathering in the fire station parking lot. He could smell the barbecued chicken before he got there. Angela met him halfway, walking in her police academy trained, robotic style. She had her dark brown hair pulled into the tightest bun he'd ever seen. Her sapphire eyes were slits of seriousness.

"Sheriff. What was all the commotion?"

"Just some friend of Harold."

"He has a friend?"

He leaned and whispered so no bystanders could hear him. "Let's be sure we keep an eye on Lacky's. Teens love to sneak beers, then hide behind the pines directly in the back."

"Yes, sir. I'll do it right now."

"Good. Then come see me at the barbeque."

"I'll get right on it, Sheriff."

He chuckled under his breath. She was reliable and a good officer but a little over-the-top. He probably was the same way when he first started.

He always walked and moved more slowly than Angela. His rookie helper was fresh out of college and the police academy, ready to arrest every jaywalking mammal in the town. He admired her passion, yet he knew he had to get her seasoned and mellowed or she'd blow a gasket. This was Lumberjack Hollow, not the streets of New York City, but he figured she'd start to realize that before too long. After all, the former Angela LeBlanc had only lived in Lumberjack Hollow six months when she met, fell in love with, and married the hot-tempered Joseph Barnes—or Barnsy as everyone called him. People thought it good that Barnsy settled down with the new deputy; perhaps she could tame the wild beast.

Bernie stopped to admire the incredible ingenuity and skill of the teenagers and other Bigfoot enthusiasts who used nothing but papier-mâché and toilet paper to transform flatbed wagons and tractors into professional-looking floats, all in tribute to a made-up creature.

He turned toward the chicken barbeque—the Fire Department's biggest fundraiser of the year—and went to the rear of the long queue of Bigfoot Fest visitors. Almost as soon as he got in line, Tom, the fire captain, came up to him with a plate loaded with chicken, an ear of sweet corn, baked beans, coleslaw, and a fluffy bun.

"Here ya' go, Bernie," said Tom.

"Nope." He held up his hand. "I can wait in line like everybody else. Besides, no freebies. How we gonna buy new ladders and hoses if you give the food away?" He smiled.

"Gotcha." Tom returned the smile and went back to the front of the serving line.

As he stood there, Bernie thought about how ridiculous it seemed that the town made so much money off of what was essentially a hoax. He'd seen the plaster foot-casts in Ostrander's as well as the books, fuzzy photos, and such. He did appreciate the fact that the town had its niche, a thing that made it unique. It was harmless fun. Even the bikers, when they came to town, were respectful and cooperative, not like some other cities' festivals he'd been to when he was in college. He got to the front of the line and was surprised to see his wife, Julia, and daughter, Barbara, waiting for him.

"Daddy!" yelled his little girl as she jumped into his arms.

"Hello, my little Barbie doll." He hugged her tight before setting her back down. He took off his hat, leaned in, and kissed Julia. "What a pleasant surprise."

"We got you food over there," said Barbie, pointing to the far picnic table. "Let's go."

His large hand engulfed hers as his five-year-old led him over to their Styrofoam plates piled with food and three bottles of Saranac root beer. He waited for his wife and daughter to sit before he planted himself.

"I'm starving. I've been patrolling and watching the parade all day." He picked up his ear of corn and chomped away.

"Looks like a great crowd this year, honey."

"You bet. We were blessed to have this fantastic weather. Looks like the Ostranders are selling a lot of Bigfoot trinkets, and I bet the fire department will sell all these chicken dinners. It's nice to see you." He reached out and took Julia's hand. He loved her jade eyes, which Barbie had inherited. His wife was into the entire Bigfoot craze, so of course she was here in the middle of the wackiness. "I love you, sweetheart," he said as he leaned in to kiss his wife.

He was amazed at her abilities. She'd been a psychic in a past life and her clairvoyance always flared when he least expected it. It's what had kept her in Lumberjack Hollow. She claimed the woods had special powers, and she truly believed in Gougou. He was a skeptic but loved her nonetheless. She was his opposite—and little Barbie had the best of both of them.

"Ewwww," said Barbie, scrunching her mouth and squinting her eyes. "I'm eating, Mommy and Daddy!"

They all laughed and went back to eating their ears of corn. Bernie didn't say anything until he was finished and had wiped his buttery face and hands with a wet napkin.

"I'll be home late, Julia. Angela and I'll be watching this nonsense till last call."

"I know. Barbara wants to see the Bigfoot stuff; we'll head home after that." Julia held her hands up and shrugged her shoulders.

"Is it real, Daddy?" Her eyes were wide.

"Some people believe so. You'll have to look at the plaster footprints and decide for yourself."

She nodded her head, gave him a hug, then took her mother's hand. "Let's go, Mommy. I wanna see the g'rilla."

He shook his head and laughed. "Call me on the cell phone if you need to. I probably won't be home till three in the morning, so don't wait up for me."

"Please, be careful. I love you."

"I love you too, sweetie." He kissed her, then waved them off while he started to pick up the plates and mess. That's when Angela showed up.

"You have a nice family, Sheriff," she said, and then it was back to business. "I stopped some hippies from stepping on the flowers in front of the library."

He just nodded as he threw the plates in the trash barrel. She seemed to love her work more than anything, more than her husband, even. He remembered when he was that way, but that was before he met Julia.

"I'll go walk around while you get something to eat. When you're finished, go to Lacky's. Call if you need me."

"Yes, sir."

Blackfoot Joe had trouble keeping up with Harold T. Willingham III as he followed the Rolls in his Land Rover down the bumpy dirt road. He could see the mansion on the water's edge a good hundred yards before they halted in front of the two-story brick structure. He liked the Victorian look with the turrets and tall, thin glass windows.

He climbed out of his Land Rover gnawing on his cigar. "That's some driving there, Willy," he said. He admired the old man's recklessness with the valuable Rolls Royce.

"You can't take it with you, Dr. Blackfoot. Please, come in the house so we can discuss business."

"Sure thing, Willy."

While Blackfoot Joe admired the old man's agility and quickness, he wanted a different path for himself. He wanted to be a Roman candle, living a hard-charging, spectacularly ridiculous existence. Ever since getting his Ph.D. in Evolutionary Anthropology at Washington State University, he'd been hooked on Bigfoot.

He was impressed with the sprawling foyer as he followed the old man inside the unlocked house. That it was unlocked made him feel good. These Adirondack people seemed to be honest, fair, and decent citizens, much like the rural people of the Northwest. He knew with the one gesture that the stories he would be told would not be fairy tales. Honest folk like these didn't lie.

He took off his hat and scratched his scalp as he stepped into the living room. It had a wall of windows, offering a beautiful view of the glistening lake. Loons flew overhead, and the pines across the way swayed in the summer breeze.

Harold left, then walked back into the living room carrying a small wooden box with a padlock on it. He put it on the coffee table and motioned to his guest to sit across from him. Blackfoot Joe nodded and sat down, then started to bounce his restless leg up and down. He hated idleness.

Harold poured glasses of cognac and handed him one. "You know why I brought you here?" he asked as he took a string with a small key on it from around his neck.

"Of course; to find your Bigfoot." Blackfoot Joe stroked his beard, and then sipped the cognac.

"Yes. You'll get that one hundred thousand dollars I promised you if you capture one. But remember, it must be unharmed. Bring it into town and we'll get photos and some blood and tissue samples, then we'll let it go. First, here's the cash advance we discussed. I hope two thousand dollars covers your expenses?"

"Sure thing, Willy. I drove all the way from Washington State. I hate flying."

"Did you bring equipment?"

"I have a tranquilizer gun to take the beast down. I'll have to shackle it until I can get back in there with a vehicle to haul it out."

"You must treat it with the utmost respect, Dr. Blackfoot. It must not be harmed in any way. I want it released as quickly as possible."

"Not a problem. But, if I'm under attack, a dead Bigfoot will have to do."

"I will not pay you for a dead animal."

"Why do you care, Mr. Rich Man? I thought you wanted proof? I've been called a crackpot my entire life, like I'm sure you have."

"I saw one when I was just a boy." Harold took the key and unlocked the wooden box. He took out a tuft of brown fur and handed it to Blackfoot Joe. "I was exploring in the woods just a few miles north of here, while my grandfather led a group of lumberjacks cutting down hundred-foot pines. Those were great times," he reminisced. "They'd haul the big logs to our sawmill and slice them into boards. Trucks would take the boards to the railroad to go to Utica, and then they were shipped on the Barge Canal to lumberyards all over the state." Harold's eyes watered at the memories.

"That how you got all this money?"

"Yes. My family loved the Adirondack Mountains. My grandfather moved up here from Hackensack and never looked back. He founded Lumberjack Hollow and built this house on Cricket Lake with his own two hands. Most of the townspeople are direct descendants of the hard-working woodsmen he hired."

"I'm sorry, old man. Let's get back on track. You've seen a Bigfoot?"

"Absolutely. I was bored, so my grandfather told me to look for some sticks that'd make good furniture. You see the handmade chairs in this room? My grandfather and father made most of them with sticks picked up off the floor of the woods. Anyhow, I was looking around and was a little lost when I smelled something funny."

"You smelled it?"

"Yes. It was sort of like a skunk but not quite. I heard a twig snap and I turned around and saw the monster. It had a child not much taller than me that ran and hid when the mother growled. I was scared. I fell backwards. Gougou—as some Indians called Bigfoot—chased me when I got up and ran. Her breath was on my neck. The ground shook under her feet. I fell over a small ridge and banged my head. When I came to I was in the arms of the mother Bigfoot. I looked into her brown eyes and could see love."

"What?" Blackfoot Joe tried not to laugh at the crazy fool, but there was no denying the fur he held in his hands.

"Her little one was walking next to us and gently patted my head. I started to pet the mother's chest and shoulder. She purred with joy. That's how I got the fur. She set me down on the ground at the edge of the clearing, nudged me with the back of her hand, and I ran back to my grandfather."

"You had the fur. Didn't anyone believe you?"

"No," said Harold, pounding his fist into his hand. "My grandfather thought I'd made it up to excuse wetting my pants. He was a sweet but no-nonsense kind of man. The men in the camp laughed.

Ever since then, people have mocked me, but others have claimed to have seen these creatures too. The Native Americans have many legends. The explorer Champlain discovered what the Micmac Indians called Gougou, the Iroquois called the Stonish Giants, and others called Slippery Skin."

"Yes, I know these Native American names well. They have many other names for the same creature: Windigo, Tornit, Atshen, Witiko, Kokotshe, and the most popular, Sasquatch. We can have this fur tested but we'll still need better proof that this animal exists. I'll track this Gougou and bring it to town for all to see. Then your festival will have real meaning."

"That's all an old man can ask."

Bernie walked up and down Main Street until the sun was a mere sliver of light across the top of the pine trees. The parade participants scattered, going to the campsite at the edge of town or to the Water's Edge Hotel (that wasn't near the edge of any water). The rowdy, fun-loving ones went into Lacky's for beer and burgers. Bernie was still out there when Blackfoot Joe came rolling back into town. He was pleased the Bigfoot hunter was driving slowly this time. He watched as the man parked his Land Rover and went into the Ostrander's store. Bernie looked at his watch. The store was about to close.

Blackfoot Joe slowed down when he saw the pesky sheriff standing in front of the pub with his arms crossed. “Damn, small-town copper,” he muttered as he gnawed his cigar. He wanted to check out the Lumberjack Hollow Museum that he’d heard about from other Bigfoot hunters who’d come to the Adirondack Mountains. None of them ever came back with any evidence, but then again, they weren’t Blackfoot Joe, Ph.D.

He parked in front of the museum and walked in, shaking his head at the jingle bells that hung on the knob, announcing his arrival. He glanced around at the T-shirts, mugs, shot glasses, and baby bibs with Bigfoot on them. He marveled at the toys, stuffed animals, and plastic, molded action figures.

He went over to the counter, where a gray-haired lady waited for him with a welcoming expression on her face. An indifferent younger man sat next to her on a stool, staring at his flipped-open cell phone. Blackfoot Joe took the unlit cigar from his mouth and smiled.

“Are you Blackfoot Joe?” Moll asked.

“But of course.”

“It’s an honor having you here.”

“I know.”

“I’m Moll Ostrander, this is my son, Oz, and this is my museum. Let me get my husband; he won’t believe you’re here.” Moll ducked behind the shower curtain.

He glanced at the young man in the baggy, gray, hooded sweatshirt, who looked both irritated and embarrassed to be there.

“So, you believe in this crap?” said the young man without looking up from his phone.

“Of course I do, young man. I’ve hunted Bigfoot my entire life.”

The boy looked up and laughed. “Nice outfit, dude.”

Moll returned, pulling an older man by the hand.

“This here’s my husband, Jed. Jed, this is Dr. Blackfoot Joe, Bigfoot hunter extraordinaire.”

Jed stepped over and reached his hand out. “Nice to meet you, Dr. Blackfoot.”

"Of course," said Blackfoot Joe, grinning.

"What is the best evidence you have in here, Moll?"

Oz spoke up, "Her stuffed animals."

"Hush your mouth, son. I have a few pristine pieces, Dr. Blackfoot," said Moll as she went to the glass counter and came back with an eighteen-inch plaster cast of a footprint, a photograph of a Bigfoot in the Adirondacks, and a lump of something.

Blackfoot Joe picked up the plaster cast and held it in front of his eyes, squinted, and viewed it back and forth. "This is an obvious fake. There are no dermal ridges or any indication that this is anything other than a hoax." He dropped the plaster foot cast to the counter with a thud. Moll and Jed Ostrander and even their smart-mouth son looked stunned, mouths agape. "And look at this so-called photo. It's so vague and grainy, it may as well be a photograph of the Fiji Mermaid. What's this, a clump of dog shit? You find any random scat and pass it off as Bigfoot dung?" He snapped the poop apart, sniffed it, scrunched his nose, then tossed the crumble on the counter.

A few tourists and townspeople gathered within earshot, pretending to browse at the T-shirt rack.

"What makes you such hot shit?" snorted Oz.

"I'll tell you what." Blackfoot Joe took the Gougou chest fur out of his breast pocket and waved it. "Old man Harold gave me this. It's worth more than this entire crummy museum. Real proof, not tourist draws of obvious fakery. More genuine than the China-made airport presents you overcharge for."

"Sir, I'll ask you to leave," said Jed.

Blackfoot Joe smiled as he tucked the Bigfoot hair back into his pocket. "I'll take this book." Blackfoot Joe threw a twenty on the counter and grabbed a copy of *Monsters of the Northwoods*. "Goodbye, fakers." He waved the book at them as he went out the door, leaving behind a steaming, shamed family.

Sheriff Block hadn't spoken to Angela in a while, so he decided to go into the pub and park himself in the corner. When he walked in there were a few parade participants sitting at the bar, still wearing their Bigfoot costumes, drinking large mugs of beer, apparently unaware how ridiculous they looked. Bernie mumbled to himself as he waved to Whitey Wallace, the owner of Lacky's. He didn't understand the nickname, since Whitey had squid-ink black hair. Then again, the only things that really made sense to Bernie were a hearty handshake, a man's word, and the love of his family.

He ordered a root beer and stood against the back wall noticing Angela, frozen in the corner like a statue. She looked at him and nodded. Just then, the doors banged open like a bull rammed them, and in walked Blackfoot Joe with a large, metal bear trap slung over his shoulder. The entire place went silent as they all watched the mountain man mosey towards the bar, then slam the trap down on its surface, making everyone jump.

"I'm Blackfoot Joe and I want to buy a round for everyone!"

The bar erupted with cheering and backslapping. Bernie looked over and saw Angela laughing, covering her mouth with her hand. He was used to her professional decorum when doing police work, so it threw him off. Laughter from a cop pissed people off more than a scowl. Bernie had broken up many fights caused by a simple joke. He watched as she stopped smiling and wandered a little closer to the group gathered around the Bigfoot hunter.

Whitey came over with another root beer, but Bernie waved him off. Blackfoot Joe jumped up on the bar and gestured for everyone to hush.

"I know some of you recognize me from the Animal Channel. For those who don't, I'm the famed Bigfoot Hunter of the Northwest. I'm the one who took the video footage at Spokane. I'm the one who recorded the grunts in Vancouver. I've been brought here by your benefactor, Master Harold T. Willingham III, to not only find proof of the beast but to capture him. I will parade Bigfoot right into this bar. Willingham gave me a bounty, so the drinks are on me."

Everyone whooped, cheered, and laughed when Blackfoot Joe jumped off the bar and downed a mug of beer, foam dripping and running through his lengthy beard. Bernie had to give the man credit—he was dramatic. Bernie had never seen anything like Blackfoot Joe in all his years as Sheriff—or even in his youth. He'd seen every Adirondack mountain guide and Bigfoot fanatic around, but this man was a different breed.

A crowd gathered around Blackfoot Joe. Bernie wasn't paying attention when Deputy Angela Barnes wandered too close and Blackfoot Joe swept her into his arms. She elbowed him off and took a step back. Before Bernie could swoop in, Angela's husband had entered Lacky's and was parting the crowd, headed for Blackfoot Joe and Angela. Bernie flew into the fray, but it was too late—Barnsy had smashed his fist into the jaw of Blackfoot Joe, catapulting the man backwards, leather fringe and hair flying, a modern caveman falling backwards onto his rear end.

Bernie was shoving people aside trying to reach them, when Blackfoot Joe stood up and unsheathed a foot-long Bowie knife. Everyone cleared away, even Angela. Meanwhile, Barnsy smashed a beer bottle on the bar making a jagged, amber shard. The two were circling when Bernie stepped between them and held his arms up.

"Both of you put your weapons on the floor. Now!"

"I'm gonna' kill the sonofabitch," said Barnsy.

"I've killed beasts like you but none quite so feral," responded Blackfoot Joe.

"What're you sayin'? I'll kill you!"

"Barnsy, now!" The Sheriff looked the man in the eyes. He shook his head from side to side, refusing to stop, so Bernie turned to look at Blackfoot Joe, who slowly set his massive knife on the floor, stood up with his hands in the air, and took a step back. Bernie placed his boot on the blade and nodded to Barnsy, who threw the broken bottle over the bar and against the wall. "Put your hands on your head and turn around." Barnsy listened.

Bernie couldn't see his deputy. She'd shrunk back into the mumbling crowd. "Walk backwards towards me." Bernie took out his handcuffs and snapped them on Barnsy. The now silent, hot-tempered husband turned around and glared with rage into the eyes of Blackfoot Joe.

Bernie picked up the knife and asked the mountain man, "You want to press charges?"

"No, Sheriff."

"Well, I'm taking him in for the night to cool off. I want you to skedaddle to wherever you're stayin'."

Blackfoot Joe nodded and took one last swig from his mug before attempting to get back his knife.

"Sheath your weapon. Take it out again and I'll own it. Take that trap as well. Now go." Bernie nodded as the mountain man took the large knife and slowly sheathed it.

Blackfoot Joe nodded and walked through the crowd, smacking the door on his way out. Bernie knew the man was angry; he'd known many Adirondack guides who loved their knives more than their wives.

"He comes back in here, Whitey, you call me."

"Sure thing, Sheriff."

"Angela!" shouted Barnsy.

Bernie walked his deputy's husband out to the squad car and put him in the back. When he shut the door he finally saw his assistant, hiding in the shadow of the bar, peeking round the corner. He went over.

"I'm sorry, Sheriff."

"You should know better, Angela. What were you thinkin'?"

"I was just listening to his stories about hunting Bigfoot. That's all. I got too close. When you had it under control I came outside. I can't arrest my husband. Can I take him home?"

"No. I'm locking him up for the night. He's lucky that guy didn't press charges. Or worse, put that sword in his gut. Come see me at the station in the morning. You're off duty now, deputy."

"Yes, sir."

Barnsy didn't say a word until they got to the Lumberjack Hollow police station.

"You can let me go now, Bernie."

"You're drunk and need to cool off. I can't have you messing up the festival by killing somebody. One night in here and you'll be fine. Or, I can take you to see Judge Brown."

Nobody wanted to see Judge Brown. He'd put Barnsy away for a month. They went into the one-story brick building that had a large processing office, one tiny bathroom, and one cell with a cot. Bernie could only hold someone a short time until he'd have to call the state troopers to come and pick up the prisoner. He took off the cuffs and locked Barnsy in the cell. Then he called Julia, who told him their daughter was sick and asking for Daddy. That put him in a bad spot. He couldn't leave Barnsy alone and it would be inappropriate for Angela to guard her own husband. He finally decided he had to put his family first, even if it clashed with his duty. He stood up and Barnsy came to the door of the cell, smiling.

"I'm letting you off with a warning. I'll give you a ride home."

"Thank ya', Bernie."

Bernie knew he shouldn't be doing this, but his little Barbie needed him. He had known Barnsy his entire life. He could trust the sober Barnsy but not the drunk one, and that was the conundrum; Barnsy was always drunk. He was a bit like Otis of Mayberry, but with a rattlesnake in his ear and a badger in his throat. Bernie didn't say much to Barnsy until he dropped him off in front of where he and Angela lived. Her squad car was parked. Silent.

"Go to bed and sleep it off."

See the swipe. Watch the slash. Blood poured out of his mouth, and Blackfoot Joe felt his teeth grind and gnash as he fought the attack. He fell to one knee while trying to get out his large Bowie knife. The swings came at him in brutal, powerful blows, with feral ferocity. He couldn't get to the tranquilizer gun that he'd left in his Land Rover, and just as he tried to pull his knife blade free of its sheath, a smash to the wrist made him drop it. More strikes, more pain, and no way to defend himself. He held his wounds as he fell to the ground, getting clawed and pummeled as he rolled onto his back. He stared through the pine tree tips at the star-spotted sky, the view blocked by his attacker looming over him. He snickered at the ridiculousness of it all. His vision clouded with expanding blackness, and with his last wisp of breath he uttered, "Gougou."

Bernie spent the night getting in and out of the chair next to Barbie's bed, putting the back of his hand against her forehead, pulling the covers back up to her chin, and comforting her as best he could. Finally, still wearing his uniform, he fell asleep and slept until the smell of coffee raised his nose hairs. He opened his eyes to Julia smiling, waving a mug of coffee in front of him. Light was peeking between the curtains, and he could see that Barbie was no longer in her bed.

"She's downstairs eating toast. She's back to normal," Julia said as she handed him the mug.

"Good." He smiled and followed her out of the room, playfully slapping her on the rump. She smiled and wagged her finger at him as they made their way into the kitchen where Barbie was eating her toast, humming a tune.

"How's my little cutie?"

"I'm all better, Daddy."

He leaned down and kissed her on the forehead. She wiped it away and he smiled. Bernie looked out the window, sipping coffee that burned his tongue, and saw Angela getting out of her squad car. He smiled over the lip of his mug; she seemed back to her usual self. He said nothing as he went to the front door, opening it before Angela could knock.

"Sheriff, we got a dead body." She had a few loose hair strands hanging out of her bun. He'd never seen a speck of anything out of place on her.

"Give me a minute."

Bernie went back into the house, put the coffee mug on the stairs, and grabbed his hat and gun belt. No shower, no shave, no tooth brushing. He kissed Julia and Barbie and went out the door. He walked down the steps into the morning sun, pulling his hat down to his ears. He looked at Angela and didn't speak. Her hat was on the ground, and she was picking grass blades off her lower pant cuffs. Normally, Angela was meticulous about her appearance. Seeing the body must've thrown her.

Angela picked her hat off the ground and twirled it in her hands. "It's that Blackfoot person," she said. "The Ostranders were taking out the Bigfoot dawn patrol and found him in the woods, shredded."

"Barnsy?"

"He's home sleeping."

"I'll follow you," said Bernie. He got in his patrol car, wanting a smoke. He stayed a car length behind as they drove through town, passing a large group of people standing in front of the Ostrander's Bigfoot Museum. They were tourists, waiting to pay their admission charge and be taken through the woods to the abandoned site where Harold T. Willingham III had seen the Bigfoot. The Ostrander's tour was excellent, but they never ran into anything.

Bernie and Angela pulled off the pavement onto the dirt road that went by the abandoned town dump, where black bears used to feast when he was a lad. They stopped where the road bottlenecked down into a wide footpath.

Bernie got out of the squad car and joined Angela, who was holding her hat down on her head to keep the morning wind from taking it.

"It's just around this bend."

They walked down the path side-by-side. He could hear voices before they went around a crook in the path and saw a group of tourists standing back, with Moll and Jed Ostrander closest to the body. Their faces were ashen.

Bernie cleared his throat, "Did anybody see anything? Did anybody touch the body?"

"No," answered Jed. "We were starting our Bigfoot tour and found him like this. Looks like Gougou mauled him."

The crowd of onlookers murmured and mumbled, uttering odd grunts.

"Jed. Get all these people out of here. I'll come to your store and talk with you later." He waved his deputy to the side and spoke softly, "Angela. Go get the crime scene kit and call the county coroner. Call the ambulance but tell them to run quiet."

She looked at him blankly. It caught him off guard.

"That means without the sirens. With the Ostrander crew going back to town, everyone will know soon enough. I don't need the entire festival descending upon the scene. Okay?"

"Yes, Sheriff," said Angela as she headed off.

Bernie stood back and looked over Blackfoot Joe. He took out a cigarette, struck a match, and puffed until an ember glowed orange on the cigarette tip. Then he moistened the match and put it in his front pocket. He looked and pondered. The man was face down in the trail. His clothes were ripped. Shredded, revealing damaged skin underneath. He was spread eagle, arms and legs akimbo, looking wilder in death than in life.

Angela returned with the large, yellow tackle box, stepping back as Bernie snapped it open, chasing away a swarm of black flies with his hand. The town sprayed annually, yet the flies were never under control.

He took out the cigarette and spit on the tip, putting it out, then shoving it in his pocket. He knelt down and took out the latex gloves, snapping them on. The Adirondack Train whistle caught his attention; he guessed it was probably taking Bigfoot enthusiasts up to Lake Placid. He took out the Polaroid camera and handed it to a pale-looking Angela. She held a hand over her mouth and gave the camera back, then ran to the side of the trail and threw up violently into the tall grass. He stood silently and waited.

She turned back, wiped her mouth, and said, "My apologies, Sheriff. I've never seen a dead body before."

Her eyes were red-rimmed. Her tight bun of brown hair had wisps sticking out and waving in the morning breeze. He understood. Nothing in an academy classroom can prepare you for your first death experience in the line of duty. He remembered thinking it would be no different than what he'd watched on television or in the movies, except it was real, not fake—but in person, it's difficult. He knew he had to be stern with her.

"Deputy, please."

"Sorry." She snapped back to attention and seemed back to her old structured self.

"Take photographs of the body and the surrounding scene before I touch anything."

He waited until Angela had taken several shots and asked her to step back, then he went in and waved away the flies that were buzzing around the corpse. Blackfoot Joe was face down, so Bernie grabbed the body by the shirt and pant leg and pulled towards himself, rolling him onto his back. There was a shocked look on the dead man's face. His eyes were wide open, with bits of grit, leaves, and grass stuck to them;

his hands were frozen claws, his mouth agape. It almost looked like the Bigfoot hunter died of fright, but the blood-soaked jacket and shirt spoke of a different demise. His clothes were sliced as if a large claw had slashed across over and over again.

The sheriff reached inside the unbuttoned jacket and found a billfold in the front inside pocket. When he took it out and opened it, he found it was empty. He removed the driver's license and looked at the birth date. The grizzled-looking hunter was actually only forty-five years old.

"The paramedics are here," said Angela.

Bernie nodded and placed the wallet into a brown paper evidence bag. He taped plastic bags over the dead man's hands. After that, he snapped off the gloves, threw them in the tackle box, and took out another cigarette. As the paramedics bounced the gurney down the trail, he took a drag and spoke as he exhaled. "This is a crime scene. Take the body to your vehicle to wait for the coroner, but don't touch anything else. I'll be there in a minute."

"Yes, Sheriff."

He watched as the paramedics lifted the body of Blackfoot Joe and placed it on the gurney, covering it with a white sheet that flapped in the morning breeze. The paramedics struggled to get the gurney back down the bumpy dirt trail to the waiting county coroner. The flies moved along with the scent, except for the few that buzzed around the blood-stained earthen path. He had Angela take more pictures, and then they put on fresh gloves and carefully searched the tall grass on both sides of the trail, looking for any evidence.

As Bernie looked up, he could see the county coroner, Dr. Silver, calling him over.

"Keep looking, Angela."

"What am I looking for?"

"Evidence." He didn't know himself what evidence might be found, but there had to be something.

As he got closer, Bernie could tell by the look on Dr. Silver's face that it wasn't good. Before they spoke, he waved away the bystanders who were rubbernecking on the fringe of the crime scene.

"Hello, Doc. Thanks for coming out," he said, flicking his smoke to the ground, stepping it out. He took off the new pair of gloves. "Do we have a black bear attack on our hands? It seems he was clawed to death."

"Not quite, Sheriff. Come here."

He stepped up as Dr. Silver peeled back Blackfoot Joe's shirt, revealing multiple puncture wounds to the chest and stomach.

Bernie said, "Stabbed."

The coroner nodded. "Yes, sir, stabbed. It was a large blade knife. You can see the defensive wounds on his hands. Almost certainly this one to the upper chest was the fatal blow. Even without an autopsy, I can tell it severed the aorta. He was dead before he hit the ground. Unless Gougou can work rudimentary tools, I'd say we have a murderer loose in Lumberjack Hollow."

Bernie checked the knife sheath attached to Blackfoot Joe's belt; the large blade was missing. He watched as they covered the body and put it into the ambulance. Nearby was the green Land Rover. Bernie hadn't found any keys, so he decided to check the vehicle out. But first he backtracked and told Angela to search for the knife. The killer might have thrown it into the woods after the slaughter. He put a fresh pair of gloves on and walked slowly around the vehicle. He grabbed the door handle and found it was unlocked. No alarm went off as he leaned in and took the keys out of the ignition. Curious. He went around back and opened the hatch. It held all manner of gear that must have been for Bigfoot hunting, yet Blackfoot Joe had gone into the woods without any of it. He was killed not that far in. Bernie wondered what the mountain man was up to when he was murdered.

He opened the passenger door and picked up a brown sack sitting on the floor. He took out a paperback book with a drawing of Gougou on the front cover. "Monsters of the Northwoods," he said as he looked at the binding. It was a book on Bigfoot sightings in the Adirondack Mountains. Stuck inside was a little paper receipt that he took out. He whispered, "Ostrander's."

The ambulance and the coroner drove off. Angela quickstepped up the path. "Sheriff, I didn't find the knife but I did find this. It was in the grass a few feet from the body." She held up a crushed cigar sealed in a plastic evidence bag.

"Good work, Deputy." He gritted his teeth. He knew he had to ask her a tough question. "Where was Barnsy last night?"

Her face dropped. "You don't think he did this?"

"Were you with him?"

"He ran an errand but he wasn't gone long. He didn't do this. I left home this morning when it was still dark and he was passed out drunk. I went to the station first to do paperwork, then the body was found and I came and got you."

"Keep looking for the knife and any other evidence."

"Please, Bernie." Her bottom lip trembled. Her eyes moistened. He knew this was tough for her to think about.

"I need you steady on this, Angela. I'll have to call the State Police in Ray Brook if you can't hold it together, because I need someone to guard this crime scene and continue looking for evidence. Can you do this?"

She looked down at the ground and exhaled slowly and steadily. When she brought her face up, she had the stern professional look that made him hire her in the first place. He nodded. She nodded back. Bernie went to his squad car and sped off to see Barnsy.

Bernie was worried about Barnsy's temper. If he'd murdered the Bigfoot hunter in a jealous rage, who knew what else he could do? Desperate men were dangerous. He pulled into the gravel driveway of Angela and Barnsy's modest little yellow house that had no garage, no view of the lake. Even the view of the Adirondack peaks was blocked by enormous pines that were mere feet from the sides of the house, making the morning sun a stranger to the damp, mossy ground. In spite of that, Angela had landscaped with flowers and shrubs which were trimmed and lined-up meticulously.

He went up and tapped on the door, unsnapping the leather strap that held his Glock in the holster as he walked. The sheriff was in hot pursuit of a murder suspect, so he knew he didn't need a warrant. He turned the knob and crept in, but the door squeaked. "Barnsy?" he called. The dog came running in, wagging his tail, and jumped up on him. "Hey,

Blue. Good boy." He petted the yellow lab, and then set him back down. He gently slapped Blue's ribs, saying, "Some guard dog you are. You'll love a robber till he leaves." He had never been in his deputy's house. It was small but neat and immaculate, just like her.

Bernie crept toward a closed door with his hand on his pistol. "Barnsy?" He peeked in and saw Barnsy passed out drunk on the bed. He eased up and waved his hand at the alcohol scent. Blue went over and licked Barnsy's hand, but Barnsy didn't budge.

Bernie was worried about him so he gently lifted Barnsy to his side to be sure he was okay—and gasped at what he saw. Blood covered the white sheet and Barnsy's white T-shirt. Under him was Blackfoot Joe's enormous Bowie knife. Barnsy huffed when Bernie rolled him back onto his stomach, letting Bernie know he wasn't dead from drink. He took out his handcuffs and snapped them onto Barnsy's wrists. As he sat him up, Barnsy came to. He reeked. Bernie knew the drunkard needed a bath, a cup of coffee, and a lawyer.

"Sheriff?"

"Come on, Barnsy."

"What? I'm not going anywhere."

He pulled Barnsy to his feet and turned him around. "What do you call that?" asked Bernie as he pointed to the bloody knife.

"What is that?"

"We found that Bigfoot hunter dead this morning. He was stabbed."

"This is bullshit! I didn't do it, Bernie."

"I advise you not to say anything until you get a lawyer, Barnsy."

"Why? Just because I threatened him in Lacky's? He was trying to pick up Angela. You've known me all my life. You know I'm not a murderer."

"Angela said you went to run an errand."

"What? What's she talking about? Sometimes I sleepwalk drunk. I probably went outside to take a piss."

"What's wrong with a toilet?"

"I like to piss outdoors."

Bernie shook his head. They walked outside as Angela pulled up.

"Christ," said Bernie as he tried to get Barnsy quickly to the squad car. Angela jumped out of her car before it was stopped.

"Oh-my-God! What did you do?" She held her hand over her mouth.

"You know I never left last night, Angela. You're my alibi. I never left. I went out to piss. Some sonofabitch set me up."

Bernie put Barnsy in the car and shut the door. The man was weeping drunk and slumped onto his side.

"Angela, stay out here. Don't touch anything. Hand me the camera and evidence bags."

"Yes, Sheriff."

He was worried about proper procedure. Angela was a mess, yet his pride made him reluctant to call in the Essex County Sheriff or the New York State Police. He was afraid they'd take over and make him look like the small-time Adirondack cop that he was. He might be small-time but it didn't take a genius to figure this one out. Yet it all seemed too damn easy and convenient, like the peanut butter and jelly were already mixed together in the jar.

He donned gloves again and took pictures of the knife on the bloody sheets. He took the knife and placed it carefully in an evidence bag. Then he rolled up the sheets and put them in a larger bag.

"Those were expensive." Angela was shaking her head as he looked up at her.

Bernie's heart leapt as he spoke, "I asked you to stay outside."

"It looks like my husband is a killer. I thought I heard him leave in the middle of the night. I don't know how long he was gone. I fell back asleep."

"Angela. Please don't talk until I get to the station and I'm ready to take the official report."

"Okay. I'll meet you there." She started to cry and quake.

"Hold yourself together. I want you to stay here until I call you down to the station."

"Okay." She brushed her fallen hair away and Bernie wondered about the dirt under her nails. She'd searched the woodland crime scene with gloves. Her getting involved could get her fired. He wondered once again why she married Barnsy. She was prim, proper, neat and excellent in her duties. He didn't understand why such mismatches happen.

Bernie walked outside and lit a cigarette, then leaned against the hood of his car and puffed. He took off his hat, scratched his head, and wiped the noontime heat from his brow. Then, putting the lit smoke in the corner of his mouth, he took out his cell phone and called Julia, who answered on the third ring.

"Hi, honey."

"Bernie! What happened? I heard there was a man dead in the woods?"

"Yes. That Wildman from the West. Instead of finding Gougou, the bad ass Bigfoot hunter found a knife in his belly."

"Is there a killer on the loose?"

"Well, it looks like Barnsy did it. I just arrested him at his house. Passed out drunk. I really can't tell you anything else."

"Oh my God. Poor Angela."

"I know, honey. She's upset. I'm leaving her to rest in her house till I need her."

"Your daughter wants to talk to you."

He waited until Barbara got on the phone.

"Hi, Daddy."

"Hello, Barbie doll."

"Mommy and I are baking Bigfoot cookies. Here's Mommy."

He winced as the phone shuffling noise hurt his eardrums.

"Sorry about that," said Julia.

"Honey, I'd feel better if you skipped the festivities and went over to your parents' house."

"You don't really think Barnsy did it, do you?"

He hesitated. There went her damned sixth sense. "No, I don't. Will you go there? I'll call you later."

"I love you."

"I love you too." He hung up the phone, dropped his cigarette, and crushed it out before moving on. The summer had been hot and dry, and he couldn't afford to start a forest fire. He got in the squad car, shut the door, and looked at Barnsy in the rear view mirror.

"I was set up."

"Barnsy, please. I asked you not to talk."

"I don't want no God damned lawyer. I passed out drunk in that bed and didn't wake up till you were there. I think Angela did it."

"Watch yourself."

"She wanted to go with that hair bag."

Bernie was irritated at the accusation. "Enough," he said, growling it under his breath. He shook his head to clear his thoughts. He had a gut feeling that there was something suspicious. Angela had dirt under her nails, grass in her hair, and was mussed up when he saw her. That was way out of character for the normally well-groomed Angela. It made sense—she'd be rid of her abusive lout husband. But how could she have the strength to overpower the large Blackfoot Joe? He wondered if she used her official authority to lure the man to his death. She had the police training in takedowns. He felt guilty for thinking it. He shook it off as he pulled up to the police station. He quickly walked Barnsy toward the door as tourists and random townsfolk gawked. He noticed Whitey in the crowd, and gestured to him to follow him inside.

Bernie walked Barnsy into the holding cell and sat him on the cot. He wouldn't take the cuffs off, just in case Barnsy wanted to try suicide.

"What do you need, Sheriff?" asked Whitey.

"I'm deputizing you. Just watch Barnsy. Don't let anyone in. If Angela shows up, call me."

"Okay."

"If he tries to hurt himself, call me." Bernie wrote his cell number down on a slip of paper.

Whitey was in his usual bathrobe and slippers. He'd tend bar in the getup like he was the Hugh Hefner of the Adirondack Mountains, except he didn't have the looks, charm, money, or women.

"What about my bar?"

"I won't be long."

He knew he didn't have much time to find the real killer before he'd have to charge Barnsy. His first stop would be to see Harold T. Willingham III. Within a few minutes he was at the house on the lake. He spotted the old man fishing and paused to look at the rippling Adirondack water, wishing he were out there himself, snagging some lake trout. He loved to fish but never had time for it.

"Officer?" asked Harold. He had a stringer of lake trout, their white bellies in contrast to their dark backs. The old man had on waders and a fishing hat covered with flies that Bernie admired for their craftsmanship.

"Mr. Willingham. Sorry to bother you, but we found Blackfoot Joe dead this morning."

"Was he mauled by Gougou?"

"No sir. It wasn't a Bigfoot. He was stabbed."

"Did he locate one? Did he acquire any evidence?" The old man got excited and took a step toward Bernie.

"No. He had nothing. As a matter of fact, he left all that fancy Bigfoot hunting gear in his Land Rover. I was wondering if you have any idea who'd kill him."

"No, but he was a rather obnoxious fellow. I did allow him to borrow my Gougou fur that I commandeered as a lad. I would like that back. It's very valuable."

Bernie nodded, "Thank you, Mr. Willingham. I'd better be going."

"Very well, Sheriff Block."

Bernie knew the old man hadn't the strength to take down the large and powerful Blackfoot Joe. He opened the squad door and was just about to get in when Harold hollered out, "Sheriff, I gave Blackfoot Joe an advance of two thousand dollars!"

Bernie nodded and waved. He decided to go back to downtown Lumberjack Hollow. He looked at the book sitting on his seat and figured he'd stop in to see the Ostrander clan before getting back to the jail.

He parked in front of the police station and walked past dozens of Bigfoot tourists and townspeople strolling in the hot afternoon sun. The smell of the tall pines filled his nostrils as he entered the Ostranders' store. He maneuvered around the racks of T-shirts and gifts until he got to the back counter where all the Gougou evidence sat. Moll Ostrander came over to greet him.

"Help you, Sheriff?"

"You sell a Bigfoot book to that hunter?"

"Was he killed by Gougou?"

"I don't have everything yet. Was he in here?"

"Oh, yes, I sold him *Monsters of the Northwoods*. I'm a big fan. It's a shame what happened to him. I thought he'd get the best evidence ever."

"He was a rotten person," said Jed. "Probably got what he deserved."

Just then Oz came in carrying a large box, wearing thick gloves that Bernie thought must've made the young man's hands sweat. "Jackass was makin' fun of our museum," he said. "I heard someone stabbed that horse's ass."

"Watch your language," said Moll.

"Thanks for your time," said Bernie as he walked out.

He went out back and lit a smoke. He always thought better in silence, puffing on his bad habit. He was waiting for a *Eureka!* moment that just didn't come. He put the cigarette out and went back to the station. Barnsy was sleeping on the cot, his hands still cuffed behind his back.

"How's things, Whitey?"

"Good. I took a message for you. It's on your desk. I have to get back to my bar, but I do have to tell you something." He walked over to the door. "I was at the bar until 3:30. On my way home, I saw a Sheriff's car in the parking lot next to that Land Rover of the dead fella."

"Angela?"

"I couldn't see. I guess if it wasn't you, it had to be Angela. I also saw someone walking away from the scene in a hurry."

"Who?"

"I don't know. Whoever it was had on a sweatshirt with the hood pulled up. My eyes don't work so well at night."

"Thanks for watchin' him, Whitey," said Bernie as he walked over to the desk. He ignored Barnsy grumbling as he read the note. It was from the NYS Police. They'd be in later to meet with him regarding the murder. He went over to the cell and unlocked it.

"You lettin' me go?" asked Barnsy, smiling, smelling like a baked bar towel. He stood up.

"You got anything in your pockets?"

Barnsy shook his head. Bernie kept the suspect cuffed as he patted the front pocket. He felt a bulge. He reached in and pulled out a large wad of money. It had to be the missing cash from Harold T. Willingham III.

"Holy shit! That ain't mine."

Bernie set Barnsy back down, shut the cell, and went over to his desk and threw the money in the drawer. He called Angela, Harold T. Willingham III, the Ostrander clan, and his counterparts at the NYS Police, asking all to come to the station right away. He had a hunch, but if it proved false, Barnsy burned at the stake—and the money made him think his idea was wrong.

He took off his police hat and threw it on the desk, then violated the law by taking a flask of Old Smuggler out of a drawer. He spun the cap off and took a swig, then lit a cigarette and kicked back, ignoring Barnsy pleading for him to share. He scratched his head while taking a deep drag. He exhaled and thought, and drank some more. He closed his eyes and waited.

One by one, they walked into the police station. Angela arrived first, her hair and uniform back in order, her stone face set back in place. She ignored Barnsy, who heckled her until Bernie told him to zip his mouth. Moll, Jed, and Oz Ostrander came next and sat in the row of chairs Bernie had set up. Harold T. Willingham III came in as fast as his old legs would take him. Bernie and Angela helped him sit in Bernie's cushioned chair, the one with the duct tape keeping the orange chunk foam from spilling out. Bernie began, even though the State Police investigator hadn't arrived.

Bernie paced back and forth. "I'm sure you know why I've called this meeting."

"To book Barnsy for murder," said Harold.

"Bullshit!" yelled Barnsy.

"Quiet everyone." Bernie walked over to his deputy and said quietly, "Hand me your Glock, Angela."

She took a step back. "Why? You think I killed him?"

"Please give me your gun." He held his hand out. Nodding her head, her eyes seemingly glued to the floor, Angela gritted her teeth and set her jaw. She took out the gun and handed it to him.

Barnsy snickered as he stood up. "I told you I didn't do it. Angela set me up."

"Why are we here, Sheriff?" asked Ostrander.

"I'll get to that." Bernie put the gun in the drawer and took out the plastic evidence bags containing the money and Blackfoot Joe's large bowie knife.

"Mr. Willingham gave Blackfoot Joe a cash advance to find proof of Gougou. This cash and the murder weapon were found on and under Barnsy. But he didn't do it. He was set up. He publicly threatened the man's life in Lacky's. Everyone in Lumberjack Hollow knew that. Everyone knows Barnsy has a weakness for booze and a foul temper, so he was an easy mark.

The real killer stabbed Blackfoot Joe to death, took this money and the knife, and then planted it on Barnsy while he was passed out drunk." Barnsy smiled while everyone else started to grumble.

Bernie continued, "Angela, Whitey saw one of our patrol cars parked next to Blackfoot Joe's Land Rover. He didn't see who it was, but it was you. I was home nursing my sick daughter."

Barnsy piped in, "I knew it was Angela."

Bernie waved at him to be quiet.

Angela sat in a chair, head down, hugging her waist, shoulders slumped towards her knees. Bernie went over and got on one knee in front of her. "Pick your chin up, Deputy. What happened?"

"I didn't kill him, Sheriff." Tears carried her mascara down her flushed cheeks. "I had an affair."

"Whore!"

Bernie stood up and glared at Barnsy, who shut up and looked at the floor. Angela put her hands over her face and sobbed.

"Angela didn't murder Bigfoot Joe, did she, Oz?"

"What you talkin' about?" asked Jed. "My son isn't a murderer."

"I have a bloody knife and money that I found on Barnsy. I bet when we run forensics, we'll find Blackfoot Joe's and Oz's fingerprints, but not Barnsy's or Angela's."

Oz kept looking at his fingernails as he chewed. "I didn't do shit."

"Harold here gave Blackfoot Joe the money and the tuft of fur, the

Gougou fur that Harold had plucked off the animal when he was a boy."

"Sheriff," replied Moll. "My son didn't kill anybody. We saw that fur when Blackfoot Joe came in our store, but we didn't do anything."

"You always wear that gray hooded sweatshirt, Oz? You own a lab? I noticed some dog hair on your black pants. I bet Angela's dog jumped all over you when you went in that house. Also, how did you know that Blackfoot Joe was stabbed? I bet if I search you right now, I'll find that fur. Oz killed the Bigfoot hunter, took the fur for the museum, and framed Barnsy. He waited and pounced on Blackfoot Joe after Angela's rendezvous, then went to the house and snuck in while Angela and Barnsy were asleep."

"The bastard deserved it," said Oz. "He made fun of our museum, our town." Oz bolted for the door and had almost made it when Angela awakened from her slump and grabbed his hood, making him fall backwards. She rolled him over and cuffed him while Bernie and everyone stood and gaped. The mild, meticulous, flower of a deputy had bloomed. She stood Oz up, reached in his front pocket, and pulled out a tuft of fur.

It was late at night, and Bernie was glad the Bigfoot Festival was finally over. Barbie was fast asleep, slumped to the side in her booster seat. They'd spent all day at Grandpa and Grandma's house and everyone was tired. Julia was in and out of sleep, trying to keep her eyes open. Bernie was driving carefully; the narrow, windy road back to Lumberjack Hollow was lined with tall pines, keeping all but the most stubborn moonbeams at bay. The trees leaned in, leaving a mere sliver of sky above.

"Do you believe?" asked Julia.

"In Santa Claus? Yes. The Easter bunny? No."

"You're silly." She tapped his thigh, closed her eyes, and leaned her head against the cushion.

Bernie felt relief that he'd solved his first murder case. He was sad for the Ostrander family. They were decent people like everyone else in Lumberjack Hollow. He worried about Angela and Barnsy's marriage. He had a great new deputy and he didn't want to lose her. If only

Blackfoot Joe hadn't come looking for something that didn't exist.

Bernie was shaking his head at the Bigfoot foolishness when something darted out of the woods, causing him to slam on the brakes. A large Gougou stood in the road and glared at him, eyes made red by the headlights. The creature had to be eight feet tall. Bernie ignored Barbie's soft whining and Julia's grumbling. He was in shock. Suddenly, the Gougou hissed and a child Gougou came out of the woods, took her hand, and the pair darted back into the darkness.

"What happened, honey?" asked Julia, wiping sleep from her eyes. "Did we hit something?"

"It was nothing. Sorry to wake you."

Sheriff Bernie Block swore to never be skeptical again. He needed a smoke.

Author Biographies

S.W. Hubbard

S.W. Hubbard has spent many happy hours hiking and canoeing in the High Peaks area of the Adirondack Mountains, the setting for her mystery series starring police chief Frank Bennett. *Take the Bait*, which earned an Agatha Award nomination for best first mystery, was published by Pocket Books in April 2003, and its sequels, *Swallow the Hook* and *Blood Knot*, followed in 2004 and 2005. A Frank Bennett short story, "Chainsaw Nativity," appeared in *Alfred Hitchcock's Mystery Magazine*, and her work will soon be featured in the Mystery Writers of America 2010 anthology. She is currently at work on a new project. Susan lives in Morristown, New Jersey with her family.

John H. Briant

John H. Briant is the author of the *Adirondack Detective* series and *One Cop's Story: A Life Remembered*. He's contributed to twelve anthologies at the Old Forge Library. He is a member of the Adirondack Writers Group at Paul Smith's College and the Police/Public Writer's Association based in Bellingham, WA. He can be reached at www.capital.net/com/jbrnt or by e-mail jbrnt@capital.net.

David J. Pitkin

David J. Pitkin is best known for his researched ghost stories from the northeastern United States. He is a storyteller and frequent talk show guest, and is currently gathering ghost stories from around the world.

Tico Brown

Tico Brown was born and raised in Upstate New York and enjoys vacationing in the Adirondacks. "The Sword and the Stone" is his first published short story. He can be contacted at tico.brown@gmail.com.

W.K. Pomeroy

W.K. Pomeroy has been writing for publication since he was twelve years old, producing television reviews for Ecumedia News. Over the years, he has published more than fifty short stories, articles, and poems. His works have appeared in *Plot Magazine*, *Scavengers Newsletter*, *Dark Regions*, *Random Realities*, *Ladies of Winter*, *The College Crier*, an instructional anthology for the Long Ridge Writers Group, and many more. Mr. Pomeroy has been a six-time president of the Utica Writers Club, and he is currently making a living as an instructional designer while continuing to pursue his writing career.

Paul Nandzik

Paul Nandzik graduated from SUNY Fredonia with his B.A. in English. Soon after, he published his first book, *Twombly McGreen vs. The Mean Steam Machine*. Paul continues to write for various personal and professional projects. Visit him on the web at www.Nandzik.com to learn more.

Gigi Vernon

Born and bred in the South, Gigi Vernon prefers the seasons of Upstate New York, including its beautiful winters. Her mystery short stories, set in various historical time periods and seasons, have appeared in *Alfred Hitchcock's Mystery Magazine* and elsewhere. She is currently working on more stories and a mystery novel set in snowy medieval Russia.

Cheryl Ann Costa

Cheryl Ann Costa is a native of Upstate New York. She has served overseas in both the United States Air Force and the United States Navy. Vocationally, she is both a mystery writer and an internationally-produced playwright. Professionally, she is a security engineer and investigator for a top Fortune 500 company.

Angela Zeman

Angela Zeman, author of *The Witch and the Borscht Pearl* and noted short story writer, contributes regularly to magazines and anthologies. Her recent stories include "Rue Morgue Noir," in Stuart M. Kaminsky's anthology, *On a Raven's Wing*; "Bang," in Linda Fairstein's anthology *The Prosecution Rests*; and "Lah Tee Dah," which is pre-bundled in the Sony Reader. Visit her website, www.AngelaZeman.com.

Dennis Webster

Dennis Webster is the author of *Daisy Daring and the Quest for the Loomis Gang Gold*. He's a member of the Mystery Writers of America, The Mystery Writers of America-New York, and the Utica Writers Club. His family roots are planted in the heart of the Mohawk Valley in Central New York. You can contact him via his website, www.denniswebster.com, or by e-mail at dennis66@adelphia.net.